Acclaim for the authors of
A WESTERN WINTER WONDERLAND

CHERYL ST.JOHN

"Ms. St.John knows what the readers want and keeps on giving it."
—*Rendezvous*

"Ms. St.John holds a spot in my top five list of must-read Harlequin Historical authors. She is an amazingly gifted author."
—*Writers Unlimited*

"*Prairie Wife* is a very special book, courageously executed by the author and her publisher. Her considerable skill brings the common theme of the romance novel—love conquers all— to the level of genuine catharsis."
—*Romantic Times BOOKreviews* [4½ stars]

JENNA KERNAN

"Kernan's engaging characters [and] a colorful backdrop… make this classic western romance something special."
—*Romantic Times BOOKreviews* on *The Trapper*

"Makes for tip-top reading."
—*Romantic Times BOOKreviews* on *Turner's Woman*

"*Winter Woman* is an exciting, no-holds-barred story with unforgettable characters. Ms. Kernan's first novel is a winner!"
—*Rendezvous*

PAM CROOKS

"With its nonstop action and a hold-your-breath climax, Crooks' story is unforgettable. She speaks to every woman's heart with a powerful tale that reflects the depth of a woman's love for her child and her man. The power that comes from the pages of this book enthralls."
—*Romantic Times BOOKreviews* on *The Mercenary's Kiss*

"*Wanted!* was a superior historical western. Fast paced, realistic characters and a very well put together story put this at the top of the genre. Pam Crooks has been a longtime favorite and *Wanted!* was no exception."
—*The Best Reviews*

CHERYL ST.JOHN

Cheryl says that knowing her stories bring hope and pleasure to readers is one of the best parts of being a writer. The other wonderful part is being able to set her own schedule and work around her family and church. Working in her jammies ain't half bad either! Cheryl loves to hear from readers. Write her at P.O. Box #24732, Omaha, NE 68124, or e-mail CherylStJohn@aol.com. Visit her Web site, www.tlt.com/authors/cstjohn.htm.

JENNA KERNAN

Multipublished author Jenna Kernan is every bit as adventurous as her heroines. Her hobbies include recreational gold prospecting, scuba diving and rock climbing. Indoor pursuits encompass jewelry making, writing, photography and quilting. Jenna lives in New York State with her husband and two gregarious little parrots. Visit Jenna at www.jennakernan.com for excerpts of her latest release, giveaways and monthly contests.

PAM CROOKS

Pam read her very first romance novel while living in the ranch country of western Nebraska, where the spirit of the Old West is still alive. Growing up around all those cowboys, well, it wasn't long before she wanted to write about them.

She still resides in Nebraska with her husband (who is not a cowboy) and their growing family—four daughters, two sons-in-law, two grandchildren and Spencer, a good-natured golden Lab mix.

Pam loves to hear from her readers and responds to each and every one. Contact her via e-mail from her Web site, www.pamcrooks.com, or via snail mail at P.O. Box 540122, Omaha, NE, 68154.

A Western Winter Wonderland

CHERYL ST.JOHN
JENNA KERNAN
PAM CROOKS

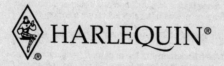

HARLEQUIN®

TORONTO • NEW YORK • LONDON
AMSTERDAM • PARIS • SYDNEY • HAMBURG
STOCKHOLM • ATHENS • TOKYO • MILAN • MADRID
PRAGUE • WARSAW • BUDAPEST • AUCKLAND

ISBN-13: 978-0-373-29467-1
ISBN-10:   0-373-29467-0

A WESTERN WINTER WONDERLAND
Copyright © 2007 by Harlequin Books S.A.

The publisher acknowledges the copyright holders
of the individual works as follows:

CHRISTMAS DAY FAMILY
Copyright © 2007 by Cheryl Ludwigs

FALLEN ANGEL
Copyright © 2007 by Jeannette H. Monaco

ONE MAGIC EVE
Copyright © 2007 by Pam Crooks

www.eHarlequin.com

Printed in U.S.A.

CONTENTS

CHRISTMAS DAY FAMILY

Cheryl St.John

Dear Reader,

Christmas greetings!

A favorite in our family is Grandma Violet's Cookies, named after my husband's grandmother, who always had a batch to pull from the freezer when we stopped by. On my yellowed index card, in Grandma Violet's distinctive handwriting, she called them Aunt Myra's Cookies. Whatever they're called, they don't last long! I always bake a double batch.

Hope you enjoy!

Cheryl

GRANDMA'S SPICE COOKIES

Ingredients:

1 cup sugar
1 cup lard or butter
1 cup molasses
2 egg yolks (save the whites for frosting)
1 tsp salt
1 tsp cinnamon
1 tsp ginger
1 tsp cloves
1 tsp baking soda dissolved in
2/3 cup boiling water

Mix the ingredients, then add enough flour for a stiff batter—about 5 cups.

Mix and chill dough for a few hours.

Roll out thin and cut into shapes with a cookie cutter. (Grandma Violet always used a rectangle-shaped meat can so she didn't have to reroll as much dough.)

Bake in 375°F oven for about 10 minutes. Watch closely, because they will burn easily. Frost when cool.

Frosting

Boil 1½ cups sugar in ⅓ cup water until the liquid reaches soft ball stage. (You will know when a drop in a glass of cold water forms a soft ball.)
Pour slowly over beaten egg whites and beat until stiff.
Add a pinch of baking soda and 1 tsp of vanilla.
Add 4 large marshmallows and stir until dissolved.
Spread quickly over cookies, making even edges.
Will harden as it cools.

Once cooled, layer frosted cookies between sheets of waxed paper in an air-tight container. These freeze well and will appear and taste freshly baked when thawed.

Chapter One

Carson Bend, Colorado, 1886

Marvel Anne Henley had made a decision. Why it had taken her three months to come to it, she wasn't quite sure—except perhaps for the fact that the entire rest of her life hung in the balance. She'd had to choose between spending the rest of her years married to a man for whom she felt only friendship—or living her remaining days as a spinster. Not exactly options to fulfill her long-tucked-away dreams, but in the end the verdict hadn't been that difficult.

"Your friendship is important to me," she told Henry Morrison. Now came the tough part. "But I can't marry you."

He still held his black felt hat. Snow had melted on the shoulders of his black winter coat and the drops glistened in the light streaming through the long beveled glass windows on each side of the front door. Marvel glanced at his handsome graying hair and thinly-trimmed mustache. She'd greeted him in the foyer and hadn't had time to take his wrap before he'd pressed her for an answer.

Henry had been a friend of her father's for as many years as she could remember, so his presence was familiar and reassuring. He and his wife had been to dinner more times than could be counted. Nora had been older than Henry, and a sudden illness had left her weak and housebound. Henry had cared for her until her death in July.

He'd proposed to Marvel in October.

Her heart hadn't fluttered, nor had she caught herself daydreaming of a union. But she'd been tempted—for the first time since she'd been very young, before her mother had died and her father had taken ill—tempted to want more.

Henry held his expression in check, though she knew she hadn't given him the answer he'd hoped for. "I respect your decision, Marvel. But may I ask how you came by it?"

Theirs had always been an easy relationship, one comprised of a fondness resembling that of an uncle and niece, but since his declaration of intent, their exchanges had become increasingly stilted.

"I understand a good many marriages are based on friendship," she began. "Or suitability or even necessity. It seemed sensible whenever I thought of it. You may call me foolish, but being sensible just wasn't enough incentive to make me turn my whole life upside down." She gestured with a wave of one hand. "I realize I'm turning down what is most likely my last hope for marriage. And it's not that there's anything wrong with you or that I wouldn't have enjoyed sharing your grandchildren one day…"

Henry had a grown son. She turned and surveyed the wide doorway that opened into a spacious drawing room where she'd played and later spent countless evenings with her father. There hadn't been another child in these rooms since. "I'm satisfied here. I love this house—my father built it when I was only eight, you know."

"I know."

Of course he did. He'd been around then. She couldn't imagine selling her legacy, her independence, and moving to Henry's home. For one consideration, she had boarders who depended on her for their lodging and their meals. For another…well, she just didn't want to let go.

She loved the house and guarded her independence. She didn't love Henry. Passion was for the young, anyway. "This home and my work here will be enough for me. I've decided I'm content with my life."

Seeming more puzzled than upset, he frowned. "You're choosing a *house* over a husband?"

He couldn't understand, of course. She hadn't expected him to. "I'm choosing to be content where I am."

His dark gaze bored into hers for a long moment. "I hope you don't regret your decision later."

"I don't think I will." In fact, she was sure.

He turned his hat by the brim. "That's it, then."

"Will we remain friends, do you think?" she asked.

"I don't know. We can try."

"We'll see each other at church." She deliberately kept her tone bright. "And around town."

"I'm not angry, Marvel. A little bruised perhaps."

"Good. I mean, that you're not mad." She placed her hand on the damp sleeve of his coat and was ready to lean in and kiss him on the cheek as she always did when she noticed he was holding his expression taut and had cast his gaze downward. Everything had changed. In that moment she knew she'd lost a dear friend. "I'm sorry, Henry."

He met her eyes then. "Be happy, Marvel."

He turned and walked out into a swirling snowfall. Marvel closed the door behind him and hurried to the window where she pulled aside the lace curtain and watched him climb into his black buggy and slap the reins over the horse's back.

The setting sun glistened on the snow that had fallen in the yard, and her breath made a circle of moisture on the window glass. From the foyer came the persistent tick, tick, tick, of her mother's grandfather clock as the minutes and hours marched forward. Sometimes in the silence of the night she could hear the passing of weeks and months and years as her life slipped by. But she didn't believe in magic or miracles or even happily-ever-afters.

She believed in inner strength and pushing past regrets to bring all she could to this day and this hour. She had made the right decision. And now she had the rest of her life to live with it.

The following morning Marvel rose at sunrise and dressed in her forest-green merino wool skirt and puffed muslin chemisette, the worn cuffs of which she'd recently replaced. Opening the fabric-covered box in her top drawer, she selected a delicately painted antique brooch that had belonged to her grandmother and pinned it at her throat. She swept her thick dark hair up into a knot and secured it with half a dozen tortoiseshell pins that had been her mother's.

Leaning into her reflection in the mirror on her tidy bureau, she turned her head this way and that, daubed glycerin at the corners of her eyes with the pad of her longest finger, then swept a trail beneath each eye and a path across her upper lip.

She had no cracks or crevices yet, and she wasn't confident this regimen would prevent them, but she was bound and determined that if she could prevent looking remotely like her ninety-year-old boarder anytime in the near future, she would do so. Marvel was thirty-three, for heaven's sakes, admittedly long past her youth, but there was no call to let herself wither on the vine without a stouthearted attempt at preservation.

She raised her chin and admired the still-firm and smooth

column of her throat. Maturity had a lot going for it if one was prudent enough to take stock. Her features had developed some character actually. Her face had thinned out and her body remained slim and strong.

Buttoning her shoes and checking her reflection one last time, Marvel made her bed, smoothing the quilt evenly over the mattress of the four-poster bed that had belonged to her parents. She made her way down to the kitchen, where she built a fire, boiled water and started tea steeping.

Sometime today the new town doctor would be arriving, and she had agreed to board the man until the current doctor had vacated his house and offices. The doctor's presence wouldn't upset the balance of the household by much. He would be working and visiting patients and whatever doctors did with their days and nights. She had biscuits baked and the dining room table set for three before she heard Liberty's cane tap-tapping along the hallway.

"Good morning, Mrs. Pargellis!"

"Good morning, Marvel Anne."

"We're having biscuits and jam this morning. Does that sound good?"

"Quite good indeed. I shall have time for only one before Ansel Simon arrives for his piano lesson."

"All right. Be seated and I'll pour your tea." Liberty hadn't given a piano lesson in twenty-five years, but Marvel was accustomed to her frequent forays back in time. "Did you happen to cross paths with Leo upstairs?"

"Who?"

"Leo." Marvel poured them each a cup of tea and passed Liberty the milk. "Mr. Brauman? Has lived upstairs across the hall from you for the past four years?"

"Leo," Miss Liberty said thoughtfully. "No, I don't remember him. Did he come on Tuesdays?"

Marvel ignored her question, gathered her skirts and hurried up the stairs, stopping outside the older gentleman's room. "Leo?" She rapped the door with her knuckles. "Are you awake?"

"I'm awake."

"Breakfast is ready."

"Can you bring it up?"

"No. If you want to eat, you can come down and eat with me and Mrs. Pargellis."

"She's as nutty as a fruitcake, and I'm not very hungry."

"Suit yourself." She walked away. He'd been spending more and more time in his room, making her wonder what the problem was. He'd never been what she would call sociable, but recently she'd felt as though he'd been avoiding them.

She and Liberty had each buttered a second biscuit when the door chimes rang.

"That's my eight o'clock," Liberty announced.

"I'll go see." Marvel excused herself and smoothed her immaculate apron. Reaching the front door, she pulled it open.

On her wide front porch, a tall dark-haired young man held a child bundled in a red coat on one arm. A small boy stood at his side. The darkly handsome father removed a black felt hat, and the first thing to strike Marvel were eyes as blue and clear as the winter sky beyond his broad silhouette. "Miss Henley?"

"Yes."

"The name's Paxton, Miss. Seth Paxton."

Tearing her gaze from his eyes, she surveyed the trio of early-morning callers in puzzlement.

"I'm the new doctor," he added.

"Oh!" She opened the door wider, then stepped back to afford them space to enter. The direct way he looked her straight in the eye as he moved past made her stomach flutter.

She closed the door and they stood in the foyer, the scent of wool and crisp winter air strong. Marvel glanced from the red-cheeked boy to the blue-eyed toddler on the man's arm. The honey-colored tress of hair escaping her knitted hat indicated her femininity. The child blinked in curiosity and looked from Marvel to her father.

"I understood that the city council made arrangements for us to stay here."

Marvel glanced at the children again. "Well. The councilmen didn't say anything about a whole *family*."

"Just the three of us," he corrected. "I'm a widower."

"I'm sorry." She hadn't meant to blunder or be rude, but she'd been caught off guard. She wasn't prepared to house children. "I have elderly boarders who require attention and adequate privacy. I'm concerned about upsetting the equilibrium of the household, Dr. Paxton."

"Is it Ansel?" Liberty asked, shuffling into the foyer.

"No, it's the doctor I told you was coming," Marvel replied.

Liberty beamed at Seth Paxton. "Well, aren't you a fine young man, now. And these are your little ones? What are their names?"

"This is Nate and this is Tessa," he answered.

"Well, take off your wraps so you can have biscuits and tea with us."

Nate glanced up at his father with hope in his round blue eyes.

"Marvel Anne makes the best strawberry jam in the county," Liberty added.

The invitation had been extended, and it would be rude to take it back, but Marvel was supremely flustered. She covered her discomfort by saying, "Let me take your coats. We'll talk over breakfast. I'm afraid it's nothing substantial."

"We've been on a train for days, so anything that doesn't rock or spill will suit us," Seth declared with an engaging smile. He placed Tessa on the floor and crouched down to unbutton her wrap and remove her hat. The toddler had long tawny hair that had been tied haphazardly away from her face with a green ribbon, then mussed by the hat.

Marvel hung the children's coats on the hall tree and turned. Seth wore a wide leather holster that held a huge dangerous-looking gun. Carson Bend was s small town and few men besides the sheriff wore weapons. Her surprise must have shown.

"I always wear it while traveling," he explained. "Would you like me to remove it?"

"Perhaps the atmosphere at the table would be more relaxed if you did."

He nodded and unbuckled the holster, wrapped it around the gun and glanced for a place to stow it. Marvel spotted the top of the grandfather clock at the same time he did and their eyes met for a moment before he stashed the weapon.

She led the way to the dining room.

Liberty had settled herself back on her chair and Marvel showed the Paxtons to seats. "This is Mrs. Pargellis," she said.

"Have you been practicing your scales?" the old woman asked Nate with a quizzical lift of one white eyebrow.

The puzzled child glanced from the old woman to his father.

"Mrs. Pargellis taught piano lessons for many years," Marvel explained, placing plates in front of their guests. She handed Seth the basket of biscuits, then moved the butter and cut-glass bowl of jam closer. She turned to the hutch and set out three more cups and saucers.

He prepared a biscuit for each of his children and one for himself while Marvel poured tea and went to refill the china pot.

"Just half, please," Seth requested as she prepared to pour tea into Tessa's cup. She did the same for Nate. Seth sweetened the liquid and filled the rest of their cups with milk.

"You're from Denver?" she asked, seating herself across from the little family.

Seth nodded. "Yes."

"But you're taking over a practice in our little town."

"We needed a change," he told her. "I want to raise my children away from the big city."

Well, that was understandable. "Perhaps you can find lodging at the hotel," she suggested.

"I was hoping I wouldn't have to do that," he said, again meeting her gaze in that forthright manner she found so unsettling. "I like the idea of someplace more comfortable. Less populated. But of course if you're refusing us lodging—"

"It's just that I wasn't prepared," she interrupted.

Again, those eyes. "So you *are* refusing to board us?"

Chapter Two

Nate was studying Marvel as though waiting for good news.

Tessa placed tiny hands on either side of the teacup and raised it to her mouth. She took a big sip and sputtered, sending milky tea across the pristine white tablecloth. "Ack!" she said with a shudder that racked her diminutive body.

Seth quickly grabbed a white napkin and dabbed her dripping chin and the tablecloth. "Sorry," he said, his gaze lifting to Marvel's. "She's not used to tea."

Unperturbed, Tessa picked up her jam-laden biscuit and took a huge bite. Strawberry jam dripped from the corner of her mouth. Seth applied the already-stained napkin again.

"No, it's my fault," Marvel said. "I don't know what I was thinking. I'll get them each a glass of milk." She hurried into the kitchen and returned with two half-filled glasses.

"Thank you," Nate said, and promptly took a long drink.

"I can pay you in advance," Seth told her. "For your inconvenience, I'll pay two dollars more a week than the hotel charges. It shouldn't be more than a week or two until the doctor is moved and the house is ready."

"What will you do with them during the day while you're working?"

"Nate will be in school. I made arrangements with a woman to care for Tessa." He met Marvel's eyes with an appeal in the depths of his. It was obvious that not taking his children to a hotel was important.

Her resolve was like spun sugar under the force of that melting gaze. "I have a room that overlooks the side yard," she told him against her better judgment. "There's only one bed, but I'll set up a cot."

"Nate and I can share a bed and Tessa can sleep on the cot," Seth answered quickly, his relief plain.

"Perhaps you should see the room before you agree."

"I'm sure it will be adequate."

"I'd feel more comfortable if you looked at it before you decided."

He nodded his consent.

After they'd finished eating and Liberty tottered off to the drawing room, Marvel led the Paxtons up the stairs. She opened the door to the unoccupied room and stepped in and to the side for them to pass.

Heaven help her, she caught the man's scent as he passed. Fresh air. Leather. Lye soap. Something inside her chest responded by dipping and sliding crazily. He moved farther into the room and she composed herself with effort.

The space seemed to shrink in his presence. She glanced about the spotlessly clean environment, glad she'd aired the rugs and washed the windows in preparation, wondering why it mattered what he thought of her home.

"The bathing chamber is beyond the kitchen. There will be hot water on the stove morning and evening. Laundry is picked up on Tuesdays and Fridays. You will have to set up your own account if you wish to use their service."

"It's perfect, Miss Henley." He took a leather purse from inside his jacket. He handed her several coins, his fingertips grazing her palm. The sensation made her heart flutter. "That should cover two weeks."

The boy tugged on his father's sleeve and said in a loud whisper, "What about Fearless, Papa?"

"He'll have to stay on the doctor's property until we can join him there," he replied.

The boy frowned at his father's reply, but moved to inspect the room.

"Who's Fearless?" Marvel asked warily.

"Nate's dog." Seth set down Tessa and stepped close to Marvel, so he could speak without the children hearing. "I tried to leave him behind, but it would've broken the boy's heart. The dog traveled in a crate by train and then rode with us in the buggy to get here."

His disturbing blue gaze moved over her hair. Self-consciously, she reached a hand to her already perfect coiffure, but caught herself and swiftly drew it back. "Where's the dog now?"

The boy had gone to sit on the padded window seat and peer through the panes of glass at the yard below. Seth glanced at him before saying, "Tied outdoors."

Tessa was trying to climb onto the quilt-covered bed. Seth picked her up. "No shoes on the bed, little lady."

Marvel had plenty of experience with elderly people who needed special attention and strict adherence to diet and dispensing of medicine, but she'd never been around children.

"Absolutely no dogs allowed," she said, drawing the line.

A warm smile curved Seth's generous lips. "It's a deal," he replied.

A wholly unexpected dip careened in Marvel's belly. Unconsciously she placed a palm over her stomach to steady the queer feeling. Warmth flooded her cheeks and she had to look away. "Breakfast is served at seven, lunch at eleven-thirty—if you're here—and dinner at six."

"You cook all those meals?"

"Mrs. Pargellis helps. She's an excellent cook, although she sometimes forgets what year she's living in. Mr. Leo Brauman occupies the room on the southeast corner. Mrs. Pargellis is on the south, and I'm over here." She moved into the doorway and pointed to her room across the hall.

He didn't say anything and again discomfort warmed her cheeks. Why had she pointed out to this man where she slept? She covered her embarrassment with a brisk "Let me know if there's anything you need."

"We have all we need."

She nodded.

"I'll bring in our belongings. Nate." He strode to the boy and knelt so he was eye level. "I'm going to carry in our things. I want you to look after Tessa. I'll bring her toys first, that way she'll have something to do."

Nate nodded easily.

Seth wrapped his arms around his son and hugged him close. The action pulled his white shirt tight over his back and shoulders, displaying interesting contours. Marvel felt as though she was observing something intensely personal.

Standing, he found Tessa examining the ornate pendant handles on the bureau. "You be good for your brother. I'll be right back with your doll and your blocks."

He strode from the room. Marvel experienced an odd sense of loss and shook herself. She was old enough to be…well to know better.

"Fearless is gonna be a'scared without no one to look out for 'im," Nate announced.

"I'm sure he'll be just fine."

"Do you have a boy?"

"No. I'm, um, not married."

"Oh. Prob'ly there'll be boys at school."

"I'm certain there are."

"Where does St. Nicolas put your Christmas tree?"

Marvel had decorated a tabletop feather tree in the parlor for the past few years, but there hadn't been a real Christmas tree in the house for as long as she could remember. "I'm not sure."

"How many days is it?"

"How many days is what?"

"Till Christmas."

"Well." She thought a moment. "This is the last day of November, so twenty-five days are left."

"Is that a lot?"

"Not so many."

"Pee-pee!" Tessa whimpered with a worried frown. "Pee-pee!"

Marvel turned her attention to the agitated child.

"She gots to go right now," Nate told Marvel.

Marvel hadn't the foggiest notion what to do. She glanced at the doorway as though Seth Paxton would suddenly appear and solve the dilemma. She prayed he would.

"Pee-pee!" Tessa declared more forcefully.

The outhouse was out back and it would take too much time to gather the little girl, descend the stairs, find her coat and hurry out across the snowy yard.

"You got a Jordan?" Nate asked.

"A what? A—oh!" She hurried forward and grabbed the chamber pot from under the bed, removed the lid and held it toward the whining child.

"She don't do it alone," Nate offered in a tone that said she clearly should have known that.

Marvel glanced from Nate to the child, whose face was now red and scrunched in discomfort. Tessa started bouncing up and down.

"Okay, well." Marvel set down the pot and approached the

child, snatching her hands back a couple of times before finally realizing her silly embarrassment was causing additional needless torture. There was nothing to be done but figure it out. It only took seconds to untie Tessa's tiny bloomers and situate her on the chamber pot.

Tessa's look of supreme relief rewarded her.

Marvel was feeling pretty pleased with herself when Seth's boots sounded along the hallway. He set down a trunk outside the door, then maneuvered it into the room and moved it against a wall. He straightened and turned to observe them.

"Pee-pee!" Tessa called with a bright smile.

"That's a good girl," he answered, then to Marvel, "I apologize. I should have taken her out after breakfast." He came close and crouched beside them. "I'll take care of—everything."

Up close, his disturbingly appealing scent was even more pronounced. He had long lashes and black hair that waved becomingly over his forehead. The arresting shape of his mouth held perpetual amusement, even when his eyes didn't confirm it.

Feeling the room close in, Marvel rose to her feet. "Will you be here for meals today?"

"Count on us for supper at six."

She nodded and swept from the room. She had a tablecloth and napkins to treat and soak.

Seth's biggest concern was set to rest when he met Missouri Porter, a middle-aged widow with three of her own children and four others she cared for during the day. Missouri was just over five feet tall and stout, with an infectious laugh and a head of riotous short-cropped red-orange hair.

"Call me Mo," she told him and offered him a strong cup of coffee and immediately settled Nate and Tessa at the trestle table in her warm kitchen and supplied them with hot cocoa and bread slathered with apple butter.

Her house was as warm and inviting as she. Evidence of children was everywhere, in chains of cut-out paper dolls strung from cupboard to cupboard and a stack of worn wooden blocks beside the stove. "My oldest two are in school, and this is Willard. He's nearly three. I have a two-year-old girl four days a week, though, so Tessa will have a playmate those days. My parlor doesn't have a stick of furniture that would seat an adult," she laughed. "It's all child-size and there are dolls and cradles. Wait till you see, Tessa."

"I can't believe my good fortune," Seth told her. "Calvin Peterson recommended I contact you, but I never thought it would be this easy to find someone to care for Tessa while I worked. What about emergencies, Mrs. Porter? I may be called away overnight, and my son would need care, too."

"It's Mo, and I'm always here except on Sunday mornings. Even if it's night, you can bring them. You're a doctor. I'd expect those kinds of calls."

Seth was so relieved he could hardly believe things were working out so well. The pretty boarding house lady had been a little hesitant to accept them, but this woman was more welcoming than he'd hoped for. He was weary of the difficulties involved with raising two children alone, and all his hopes were set on Carson Bend ending his worries.

His work in Denver had been overly demanding, callers at all hours of the day and night, many of them gunshot victims and unsavory characters hurt in brawls and bar fights. He'd had enough of those people being carried into his home.

The incident that had pushed his decision had been when a disorderly patient had been brought to him for treatment. Two men out to settle a score had followed the man to Seth's home and barged their way in. Seth would no longer risk his children's safety. He hadn't signed on for doctoring with a gun strapped on for protection, but it had boiled down to that.

"Why don't you leave the little ones now and let them get settled in?" Mo asked. "You must have errands to do."

He needed to visit the doctor, take stock of supplies, introduce himself to the schoolteacher and get together with the banker. He could at least get a start on those errands. "That would be a blessing." He finished his coffee and kissed Nate and Tessa. "I'll be back in a couple of hours. Play here until I return. And mind your manners."

Tessa stuck a finger in her mouth and pouted. Tears welled in her eyes.

"Papa will be back for you in just a little while, darlin'. I promise."

She gave him a wet kiss, and he headed out into the crisp winter air without his kids at his side for the first time in weeks. It felt odd, but he intended to make the most of these hours.

The office of the retiring doctor was a chaotic jumble of files and instruments and personal items. Dismayed, Seth looked over the rooms, realizing he would need to order more equipment than he'd anticipated. The entire place needed a complete cleaning and fresh paint. The floors could use a good sanding and several coats of varnish, as well.

The living quarters weren't much better. Seth's heart sank. He'd hoped to get the children settled into their new home and keep the disruption to their lives as minimal as possible. Now it looked as though that level of security might take longer than he'd hoped.

Dr. Babe Solomon wore gold-rimmed spectacles on the end of his nose, and his wiry gray hair stood up in tufts above his ears and at the peak of his forehead. The rest of his head was shiny bald.

His clothing appeared clean, though not particularly stylish or pressed, but he was fastidious about washing his hands and his instruments.

"Where are you heading from here?" Seth asked as he followed with a crate of dusty books from the office side of the house to the living side.

"My daughter and her family are in San Antonio. I'm going to test the warmer climate. Play with my grandkids."

"That's quite a change."

"This is my last Colorado winter and I'm not gonna miss a single flake of snow or drop of frozen drizzle when I'm gone."

Seth set down the crate and took stock of the small parlor.

"You can have the furniture if you want," Babe offered.

"I have my own furnishings coming," he said, though he didn't know where he was going to fit everything. And with all the work to be done, he would have to make arrangements for temporary storage.

He was going to need a few extra hands getting the place clean and making it livable. "There's a newspaper?" he asked.

"The *Sentinel*. Comes out once a week."

"Where would I post notice to find some help before then?"

"Post office inside the train station most likely. What kind of help you lookin' for?"

"Odd jobs. Housekeeper. Maybe an assistant."

"You plannin' on makin' enough at doctorin' to pay for all that?"

"Eventually. I sold a lucrative practice in Denver, so after buying you out I still have a grubstake."

"Guess I shoulda asked more, huh?"

"Probably not," Seth answered, not unkindly. The man was fortunate Seth hadn't seen the place first.

Babe took the crate of books from him and set it on top of another.

"I need to ask a favor of you," Seth remembered.

"What's that?"

"I was hoping you'd let me tie our dog out back until we're ready to move here. I didn't have the heart to leave him behind."

"Guess it can't hurt, long as you feed and water 'im."

"Of course. Thank you. Over the next few days I'd like you to fill me in on your regular patients. I'm sure there's a lot you know about them that isn't noted in the files. Things that will help me treat them."

The elder doctor squinted at him. "You aren't what I was expectin'. I thought we'd get some know-it-all young fella right outta university."

"I respect experience, Dr. Solomon. Observation, intuition. Technology is important, but there's more than education and the latest equipment to being a good doctor."

"I'm gonna like you, son. Call me Babe."

Chapter Three

Seth knelt and scooped his children into an earnest hug, inhaling Nate's familiar little-boy scent and touching Tessa's silky hair. They were his world and he had to do his best by them.

"We had a fine afternoon," Missouri told Seth.

"Mrs. Porter let us shape piecrusts into little pans and bake 'em," Nate told his dad, inching away. "I saved one for you."

Seth sat on a kitchen chair and peeled away the edges of a napkin to discover a misshapen piecrust liberally sprinkled with cinnamon and sugar. "I remember my mother making these. It looks delicious."

"While Tessa napped, Nate used the slates and chalk to practice his letters," Mo told him. "He's quite good."

Seth glanced from his children to Mo Porter. Her red-orange hair and round cheeks glowed in the firelight. "I can't thank you enough."

"It's going to work out well for all of us," she told him. "I'll be able to do Christmas for my own children now."

"Let's agree on an hourly wage," he told her. "I feel that's the only fair system for you. Will you keep a tally and I'll pay you by the week?"

"That suits me just fine, Doc."

Seth took coins from his pocket and placed them on the table. "You'll need extra for their meals, and I don't expect you to pay for that ahead. I don't wish my children to be a hardship."

"They're not going to be a hardship, you can be sure."

"Let's get your coats, then," he said.

It was dark when he approached the boarding house carrying Tessa, a weary Nate at his side. The long windows cast welcoming spills of yellow light across the side yard, and glowing rectangles patterned the porch floor. He glanced at the closed screen hesitantly, gave a light tap and opened the door. The tantalizing aroma of beef that met him made his mouth water.

He set Tessa down on the bottom stair. "You two go up to our room while I get water so we can wash for supper."

She reached for the shiny banister and trudged upward, Nate at her heels. Seth approached the kitchen, which was warm and filled with enticing smells. Marvel was bustling between the stove and a sideboard, her hands full.

"Supper smells good," he said.

She turned in surprise. Wisps of hair had escaped her coiffure and curled charmingly at her neck and pink cheeks. She was an exceptionally lovely woman. "Good evening, Dr. Paxton. Dinner is nearly ready."

"I came for water," he said. "May I take the kettle?"

"Help yourself."

"I'll bring it right back." He dipped hot water into the kettle and hurried upstairs.

He hadn't unpacked or hung their clothing yet, so he dressed the children in clean, slightly wrinkled outfits, donned a fresh shirt and brushed the wrinkles from his black serge suit. He left his .44 in its holster on the top shelf of the armoire.

After returning the kettle, he led his children to the dining room where the others waited with expectant faces. Miss Henley welcomed them with a warm smile. "Please take your seats."

Once he'd assisted Nate and Tessa onto chairs, Seth stood at Marvel's side until she was ready to sit. He held her chair first, then lowered his long frame onto the floral embroidered seat of his own.

As she passed a bowl of steaming mashed potatoes and a platter of sliced beef, Marvel introduced Leo Brauman. Seth's attention wavered between the silver-haired, spectacled man and Miss Liberty Pargellis, who had come to dinner wearing an enormous faded red paper rose loosely anchored in the gray curls above her forehead. Each time she leaned forward to take a bite, the rose dipped over her nose.

Neither Miss Henley nor Mr. Brauman seemed to take note, and Seth gave his son and daughter warning looks. They had noticed, but were more interested in the food, thank goodness. The meal was tastier than anything Seth had eaten for months, so he ignored the old lady's bizarre frippery and tasted the rich dark gravy he'd drizzled on his helping of potatoes.

"We had the most delightful game of croquet this afternoon," Liberty stated with a forward-backward-forward flip of the rose. "My George brought me this paper rose."

"It's a lovely rose," Marvel answered. "Mrs. Pargellis made the gravy. She has a knack."

"Croquet in the *snow?*" Nate asked with wide-eyed amazement.

Seth touched Nate's leg to silence him and managed a smile. The old woman was a few inches shy of plumb, but Marvel Henley seemed to take that into respectful consideration at the same time she made her feel useful.

The obviously agitated Mr. Brauman ate his supper while glancing from his pocket watch to the others, nervously eyeing Seth and the children.

"Do you have an appointment, Leo?" Marvel asked after he again checked the time.

"No. No," he replied. "It's just— I should be getting back...to my room."

"Whatever for? You've been in your room all week. We're enjoying your company. Aren't we, Dr. Paxton?"

"Would I be being too familiar if I asked you to call me Seth?"

"Of course not. We're like family here. And you must call me Marvel." Her eyes weren't really brown; more of a warm umber, with golden flecks around the pupils.

The sound of agitated barking came from outdoors. "Your dog has been doing that most of the afternoon. You will do something about it soon, I trust."

"I'll take care of it right after supper," he assured her.

Tessa took only a few bites of roast and nibbled a browned carrot before her eyelids drooped. Her head sagged forward before Seth could reach her, and her face landed in her mashed potatoes and gravy.

Marvel laid down her fork. "Oh, my."

Leo stared.

"She's exhausted," Seth explained, getting up. "Her schedule has been disrupted with packing and traveling."

"I'll get something to wash her with." Marvel left and returned with a length of wet toweling.

Seth raised Tessa's head and wiped creamy potatoes and brown gravy from her cheek, eyelid, and with a clean corner did his best to pluck food from the hair above her forehead and at her temple.

Marvel reached to take the cloth from him, and he scooped up Tessa. "I'll just take her to bed. Excuse me. Nate, be on your best behavior until I return."

"Yes, sir."

Marvel took Tessa's plate and the towel to the kitchen an returned. Nate and Leo were having a staring match.

"Did you practice your scales today?" Liberty asked Na Her paper flower flopped to cover her right eye, but she took bite of carrot and chewed unconcernedly.

"I practiced sums and letters," he replied. "Mrs. Porter said got them mostly right." The boy didn't say a word about Liberty odd appearance or her reference to winter croquet, but he d keep an eye on her. Marvel had to give him credit for goo manners.

The dog barked, and she wondered how it could keep barki without wearing out.

"Fearless prob'ly wants t' see me," Nate told her. "He ai used to bein' all alone for so long. Prob'ly he's lonesome. home he used to come in and lay by the fire of an evenin'. A he slept on some blankets in the pantry when it was cold outside

"I'm afraid I can't accommodate your dog in the manner he accustomed," Marvel told him.

"What's commodate mean?"

"Accommodate. It means I can't put him up inside."

"I guess you already gots lots of people stayin' here."

She nodded.

"Prob'ly you might have a spot in your pantry, though."

"I'm afraid not."

With a disappointed expression, Nate looked at the last carr on his plate.

Seth returned to his seat. "She's sound asleep for the nigh

"Miss Henley don't have no room for Fearless in her pantry Nate said to his dad.

"Doesn't have room," he corrected. "I told you if we broug Fearless, he would have to get by on his own until we got settle

Nate looked up with beseeching wide eyes. "He could sle in our room and he wouldn't be no trouble."

"*Any* trouble, and a dog is not part of our agreement. No more talk about Fearless, Nathaniel. I told you how it would be. We'll take him to the doc's when we're finished eating."

"What about Tessa? You gettin' her up to go?"

Seth's blue-eyed gaze moved thoughtfully from his son to Marvel. He was clearly stumped for a solution. "I...well, I hadn't planned on her going to bed so early."

The child was sound asleep in bed for heaven's sake. What trouble could she be there? "You may leave her sleeping and I will check on her periodically," Marvel offered.

"That's very kind of you," Seth said in a relieved tone.

"You won't be gone long, I trust."

"Not long at all." He returned to his meal, which was probably cold by this time, but finished it appreciatively. When she offered him seconds, he accepted.

"How long did you live in Denver?" she asked to make conversation.

"About five years," he replied.

"And you had a medical practice there?"

"My office and examining rooms were in the front of our house, and we lived in the back."

"My mama is in heaven," Nate supplied.

Marvel didn't know what to say. She merely nodded.

"My grandma and grandpa are there, too."

"I think heaven must be full of nice people," she commented finally.

Seth laid down his napkin. "Thank you for the superb meal."

"Just simple fare," she replied.

"You're an excellent cook and a thoughtful hostess."

Marvel felt her cheeks growing hot under his blue-eyed gaze and the praise. She'd enjoyed having someone to talk with at supper.

"You're welcome to join us in the drawing room of an evening," she told him. "I serve tea at nine."

"Thank you. Nate and I will take care of our errand and be back within the hour. Excuse me now."

Leo removed himself to his room, and Liberty tottered off to play the piano. She still carried a respectable tune, and Marvel often enjoyed her recitals. Marvel looked forward to evenings when she had a couple of free hours to invest in her own interests.

After she had the dining room cleared and set in order and the dishes stacked, she carried a lantern upstairs. Tessa slept soundly on the narrow cot, her long lashes curled against her cheeks. Mystified by the peaceful innocence of the sleeping child, Marvel gently folded the sheet and soft quilt around her shoulders. It seemed peculiar to have such a diminutive person under her roof. She'd never seen anyone fall asleep face-first in their dinner plate before, but Seth took everything in stride.

It was probably much easier to be comfortable with a child when one acquired them as an infant and learned all their quirks as they developed. Marvel searched for her earliest memories and found them associated with the scent of her mother's perfume. She'd had a safe comfortable childhood in this very house. She realized then how difficult it must be for Seth's children to leave their familiar surroundings and start over in a new place.

Like Marvel had been, they were fortunate to have a father who cared for them. But she'd never stopped missing her mother, and could empathize. Tessa was so small she might not even have memories of her mother. Marvel thought of Seth's inquisitive, yet polite son, and compassion moved her.

She returned to the kitchen where she washed and dried the dishes. She had no idea what to do with children, but she was going to keep an open mind and do the best she could during their brief stay. She was a capable intelligent woman. She would figure it out.

* * *

Seth had purchased several bales of hay that afternoon and had them delivered to Dr. Solomon's place. Now he and Nate worked to shape the bales into a dwelling for Fearless. They built the hay structure beside the shed for protection from the wind. Seth used a base of planks to keep the animal off the ground, then added layers of blankets he'd purchased at the mercantile.

"This'll keep the wind and snow off him," he told Nate.

"He'll still get cold, Papa." Nate knelt beside the long-haired floppy-eared yellow dog, and Fearless licked his cheek. Nate scrunched his face and turned to the side, but accepted another gesture of affection.

"Nate, he's a dog. He has fur to protect him."

The child dug mittened hands into Fearless's fur. "I wish I could stay here with him."

"You can't do that. It's not warm enough for a boy."

"I don't think it's warm enough for Fearless, either."

"He's going to be fine." Seth had driven a cast iron hitching post into the ground with a sledgehammer, and now he took a length of rope and tied the dog in place with enough room to get in and out of the house of hay. So far the dog's accommodations had cost as much as theirs.

Nate gave the dog a hug and told him to stay. Fearless whined and thumped his tail.

"Come on," Seth urged. "Let's go."

"He's real sad."

The whining was proof of that.

Seth led Nate to the horse he'd purchased and helped him up, then seated himself behind. The dog barked as Seth used his heels to urge the mount forward.

"He's going to be fine," Seth assured his son.

Nate sobbed as they rode away. Seth was doing everything he could to make a good life for his kids. Why did the details have to be so difficult? The boy was exhausted by the time they arrived at the boarding house. He waited silently while Seth put up his horse, then accompanied him into the house.

Seth helped him undress and tucked him into the big bed. Within minutes the boy was sound asleep.

Downstairs Seth found their landlady in a room tastefully furnished with a plush divan and overstuffed chairs. Several thriving plants on oak stands lent a homey air. A fire crackled in the brick fireplace.

Marvel sat pinning lace to the sleeves of an unfinished bright-blue dress on a stiff dress form. "Make yourself at home," she offered. "There's a selection of books along the wall. I'll make tea in a little while."

Seth perused the walls of leather-bound books, scanning titles.

"This is where I work in the evenings," she said. "Mrs. Pargellis goes up to her room early and Leo doesn't come down much anymore. If you'd rather be alone, you're welcome to use the parlor."

He appreciated her obvious desire to make him feel comfortable. At his silence, her gaze rose to his. A flush tinted her cheeks a becoming shade.

"I'll just rest near the fire if you don't mind."

"Not at all."

He took a seat in a comfortable wing chair and extended his legs. It had been a while since he'd had the opportunity to simply relax.

"You may smoke if you desire."

"I don't smoke."

She moved around the dress mannequin, making a few tucks and adjustments. Seth couldn't help noticing her slender waist, the way she held herself straight and moved gracefully. She wasn't a small woman, but neither was she ungainly. Her soft-looking dark hair, her modest clothing, her fluid mannerisms and the gentle but firm way she spoke exhibited disquieting femininity. Her speech and actions revealed competence as well as confidence.

The fire warmed and relaxed his body and his mind. Why was such a lovely and capable woman without a husband? Certainly her home was well appointed and she lived quite comfortably, but how had it happened that she'd never had a family? She was obviously at an age when most women were raising children. There was certainly nothing wrong with her that he could see.

With a jolt of surprise at his musings, Seth arrested the direction of his thoughts. He refused to taint his relationship with his landlady by having unsuitable observations.

Overly warm now, he leaned forward to remove his jacket, then settled comfortably once again. He couldn't help but be curious about a beautiful unmarried woman so obviously content with her life. He couldn't help being a man, either. With his eyes closed, he still saw the shapely curves of her hips and the dark hair that fell in a wave over her shoulder.

"Are you ready for tea?"

Her smooth low-keyed voice brought him out of his reverie. Straightening in the chair, he glanced up. Marvel was setting a laden tray on a low table before the fire.

"Yes, thank you."

She seated herself across from him and poured tea into rose-patterned china. Seth accepted a cup and saucer.

She added sugar and milk to hers, sipped it, then set down the cup and reached into a basket beside the chair. She pulled out pieces of white fabric with a threaded needle pinning them together. Slipping a silver thimble on the end of her longest finger, she deftly threaded the needle in and out of the fabric.

"For the blue dress?" he asked conversationally.

She nodded.

The dress didn't look suited to her, but he wasn't an expert on women's fashions. Now that he studied it, it looked too big. Marvel had a slender waist, and the dress form appeared larger.

"The dress doesn't look suited to you," he said.

Her expression showed her surprise. "It's for Mrs. Jefferson. She wants it for the holidays, so I'm trying to finish it up."

"You're a seamstress as well as a landlady?"

She nodded. "Not full-time of course, but I sew for several of the women in Carson Bend."

He had assumed the boarding house was adequate income, but thinking it over, he realized she had only two permanent boarders. How much she took in, he could only guess. Just because she owned a well-furnished home and took in boarders didn't mean she didn't need to earn additional money. It must be difficult for a woman alone to support herself.

"Do you garden?"

She didn't look up. "I have flower beds along two sides of the house."

"Vegetables, I meant. Do you put up vegetables for winter?"

"No." She worked the needle through the white cloth and pulled the thread taut before working it back in again. "I buy eggs and vegetables from the farmers and the mercantile."

Seth got caught up in watching her efficient handiwork.

"Did your wife garden?"

Marvel's question caught him by surprise and he met her inquisitive gold-flecked gaze.

Chapter Four

"Yes, my wife gardened. She was raised on a farm."

Seth's wife had been a warm, kind woman. His parents had adored her. His entire family had adored her. He had loved her, too. He'd loved her as a sister-in-law when she'd been married to his brother. But then his brother had died and Seth had honored the promise his brother had requested of him. He'd taken his brother's widow as his own wife. And he'd worked diligently to be the best husband he'd known how. But he'd always known it hadn't been enough.

"What was her name?"

"Sarah." He hadn't spoken her name in a long time.

"I guess this time of year is difficult."

"She loved Christmas. Even the snow." He took a sip of his tea and collected his thoughts. "But I have my children. They make everything worthwhile."

She studied him, her eyes dark with sympathy…and interest.

"Tell me about yourself," he said. "How did you come to be living here and taking in boarders?"

"I've lived here my entire life," she replied. "This was my parents' home. My mother believed she was barren, and she and my father were in their forties when I was born. Thus my name."

"Marvel," he said with a smile.

She nodded. "She died when I was young. It was just my father and me for many years. When he became feeble, I took care of him. His illness lasted years. Doctors and medicines ate away his savings, so, since I was already taking care of the house and my father, I started taking in boarders for income."

"Clever of you."

"I never thought of it as clever. It was simply practical."

"Do you see yourself as a very practical woman?"

She paused in her stitches. "Most of the time."

"But not all the time?"

She sat forward. "Are you ready for a refill?"

A few more minutes in her company would certainly be a pleasure. "Thank you."

She filled his cup and he sweetened his tea.

"So you've never traveled?" he asked.

"I have not. And you?"

"I was born in Ohio, and my father moved us from place to place, so I've seen a good part of the country. I went to university in the east and took a position in Pittsburg. My brother took sick, so I moved to Denver to help my mother and sister-in-law. When he died I stayed on."

"I don't have any siblings, so I can't imagine your loss. I'm sorry for it all the same."

"Thank you."

She laid her sewing aside and opened a drawer in an ornate side table. "I have scenes of eastern states for the stereoscope," she said, taking out a slim cloth bag and locating the slides. She set them on the viewer, pointed it toward the fire to make sure the picture was straight, then handed it to Seth. "Have you been here?"

He took the stereoscope from her and studied the picture of a busy city street. It looked like many he'd seen. "It looks like most big cities. Where was it taken?"

"Philadelphia."

"Perhaps I've seen this street, then." He moved the viewer away from his eyes. "I met a photographer who traveled with the railroads. Many of his photographs were made into slides like these. Most people purchase slides of scenery, but you've chosen the cities."

"They belonged to one of my elderly boarders who has since passed on," she told him. "She gave them to me."

"I see." He stifled a yawn and set his cup on the tray. "If you'll excuse me, it's been a long day."

It might have been a flicker of disappointment that Seth recognized before she gave him an understanding nod. "Good night then."

"Thank you for your hospitality. I didn't realize you weren't expecting all of us."

"We'll make the best of the situation, Dr. Paxton."

"Good night." Seth got water from the kitchen, climbed the stairs to his room where he hung his clothing and washed. Out of habit he tucked the .44 under the mattress. He slid between the fresh-smelling crisp sheets beside his son. This change had been a long time coming.

He stacked his hands beneath his head and stared at the shadowy ceiling. Change was never easy, but he knew this move was right. This was a better environment for his children. Maybe here he could stop feeling guilty about his wife. About wanting to move on with his life. Maybe here he could find a future for himself.

Seth dreamed discordant images of rooms under construction and hoards of patients arriving by train. He didn't have enough rooms in which to place them or supplies with which to treat them. He sent Nate to order disinfectant and bandages, knowing they would never arrive on time, and Nate returned with a goat on a leash. Scenes shifted and Marvel Henley was indignant because the goat had eaten her flowerbed. She pounded on Seth's office door.

Seth had no idea how long he'd been asleep when he realized that insistent rap was real and at his door. Trouble in the middle of the night wasn't a good sign that he'd gotten his kids far enough away. His senses went on immediate alert.

"Dr. Paxton?"

Beside him, Nate sat and blinked. "Stay put," Seth ordered. He jumped up and stuffed his legs into his trousers, grabbed the gun and stumbled to the door.

Marvel stood in the hall holding an oil lamp. Seth's gaze traveled from her face to the thick braid that hung across her cotton wrapper down to her bare toes.

"Do you hear that?" she asked.

It took a minute for the sound of barking to penetrate his sleep-fogged brain.

"That's been going on for nearly half an hour," she said in a loud whisper. "Leo has been down to see what the problem is and says there's a big dog in the yard."

"Fearless?" Nate asked, padding to the doorway in his long johns. "How'd he get here?"

Seth tucked the .44 into the waistband of his trousers and leaned wearily on the door frame as he gathered his wits. "Nate, climb back in bed."

The boy moved away, and Seth met Marvel's eyes for a fleeting moment before she averted her gaze.

"Let me get my boots on." Seth pushed away from the door and sat on the edge of the bed to pull on his stockings and boots.

From her place on the cot, Tessa began to cry. He stumbled across the dark room. "What's the matter?"

She wailed louder. He picked her up and placed her on the bed beside Nate and tugged covers around her. "You're perfectly fine, Tess. Your brother will lie with you and hold your hand. Don't cry now."

"I have to make the nine o'clock train," came another voice from the hallway.

Marvel answered with, "It's only two in the morning, Liberty. Go back to bed until breakfast time."

Seth told Nate to stay there with his sister and closed the door as he stepped into the hall. Tessa's whimper could still be heard.

Marvel was escorting Mrs. Pargellis back toward her room, and Seth couldn't help noticing the shapely outline of Marvel's hips and legs under the fabric of her nightdress. He turned and took the stairs two at a time, grabbed his coat and fumbled with the lock on the front door.

Steps padded behind him and Marvel reached around him to turn the lock. He glanced down. Her breasts were full and loose beneath the flimsy wrapper, and under it the prim white lace of her nightgown covered her all the way to her neck. He had the insane urge to turn and enfold her in his arms, hold her close…comfort her…. Why that last thought had come to him he couldn't figure.

"I'm sorry," he said, his throaty voice not sounding like his own. "About the dog. I'll see to it."

She took a step away. "See that you do, Dr. Paxton. My boarders can't have their nights disrupted."

As soon as Seth reached the porch, Fearless leaped on him with an excited yelp. The dog then sniffed at the front door and sat expectantly, tail wagging. A length of frayed rope hung from his collar.

Seth rubbed a hand down his face. It was a jaunt back to Dr. Solomon's, and he didn't have a piece of rope handy to tie the dog. He could probably saddle his horse and carry the beast that way. But it was barely three in the morning.

Fearless followed him around the side of the house. Seth studied the carriage house where his horse was stabled. There were empty stalls where he could keep the dog until morning. There was no guarantee that the animal wouldn't continue to bark, however.

It was his best shot. Tess might be upstairs right now, afraid of the strange surroundings, keeping the household awake. He should get back to her.

"Come on." He grabbed the stub of rope and led the dog away. "You had a perfectly good place to stay, you ungrateful mutt. I doubt half the population of this town has Hudson Bay blankets as new and nice as yours."

In the carriage house, he led Fearless into a stall and closed the gate. The dog poked his nose through the wooden slats and whined.

"Lie down," he ordered.

The dog sat and stared at him.

He checked the sides of the stall, certain they were high enough to prevent an escape, then gave a tug on each board to satisfy himself that Fearless was secure.

The house was silent when he reentered it. A lamp with a brass reflector had been lit in the upstairs hall so he could see his way to his room. The door stood ajar. Concerned, he entered the room. In the dim light from the hall, he made out Marvel's pale form at the side of the bed.

"I think she's asleep now," she whispered. "They both are."

She had comforted his daughter, and for that he was grateful. "I'm sorry for the inconvenience."

She stood and moved away from the bed.

"I put the dog in the carriage house for the night. I'll take him away first thing in the morning."

She padded toward the door. "I guess if he barks in there, it will at least be quieter than from the front porch."

"I am so sorry," he emphasized.

"All right," she said. "Let's all get some sleep now."

As she passed through the open doorway, the light from the hall illuminated her silhouette. Seth stood mesmerized and she was gone the next moment. The noteworthy impression stayed in his head. Marvel Henley was a fine-looking woman. Fine.

Tired as he was, he could think of little else as he turned and observed both children sound asleep in the bed. He undressed for a second time and wedged his body onto the narrow cot. He could still salvage a few good hours sleep if he applied himself.

The image of Marvel's slender form had been burned into his memory. A muffled bark reached his ears. Seth pulled the pillow over his head and groaned.

"I apologize for the sleep you lost last night," Seth said at the breakfast table the following morning. "I'll make sure it doesn't happen again."

Leo hadn't come down to join them, and Mrs. Pargellis replied with an airy, "Don't apologize. I could dance all night, my dear."

Seth cast her a sidelong glance and noted that Nate was doing the same. This morning Mrs. Pargellis was wearing an embroidered handkerchief pinned to the front of her dress with a cameo. She had rouged her wrinkled cheeks and lips.

Tessa was stirring her oatmeal the way she'd seen her brother do. Seth poured molasses and cream on top for her, and she stirred again.

"I'll make it up to you," he offered, interpreting Marvel's quiet as displeasure. "I'd love to have you join me for dinner in town Friday evening. Mrs. Pargellis and Mr. Brauman, too, of course. I noticed a couple of restaurants on Main Street. Perhaps you can recommend one."

"That's not necessary," Marvel began.

"Dinner would be lovely!" The old woman beamed with pleasure. "I don't recall the last time a handsome man invited me to dinner. I doubt you can either, Marvel. We would be delighted to join you."

Marvel blushed and concerned herself with buttering the toast.

Seth reached for Tessa's spoon and fed her a few bites before she could spill oatmeal on the tablecloth. "I'll pay the laundry bill for the linens," he told Marvel, hoping to redeem himself in her good graces.

"I launder them myself," she replied.

"Papa, what are tears made of?" Nate asked.

"Water from our bodies," he replied.

"Is it sweat?"

"Not exactly because it comes from different glands, but it's similar."

Nate got a wrinkle between his eyebrows when he asked, "Do dogs cry when they're sad?"

"No."

"Do they sweat?"

"Not like you and me because they have fur, but they pant when they're overheated," Seth answered.

"And drool, huh?"

"Let's save this conversation for another time, son. Eat your oatmeal."

Marvel couldn't resist a smile. She was tired and irritated that the dog had kept her boarders awake last night, but her amusement at the doctor's chagrin and his son's constant questions won out.

Tessa pointed to the windows. "Snow! See?"

Sure enough a heavy snow was falling this morning. "Make sure you bundle up well when you go out," Marvel said.

"If you don't mind, I'll go saddle my horse now and come

back in a few minutes for the children. Once I have them settled in for the day, I'll be back for the dog."

"Do they have scarves and mittens?" she asked, then immediately regretted her question. He'd been taking care of them sufficiently for some time, he certainly didn't need her help.

"We do, thank you," Seth answered apparently undisturbed by her lack of confidence in him. "I've left the pile in the front foyer."

"What about Fearless, Pa?" Nate asked with a frown of concern.

Seth stood. "He broke the rope tying him and came here during the night. I have to take him back."

"I'll get the children ready before you return with your horse," Marvel offered. She led Nate and Tessa to the foyer and helped them into their coats, tugging on their hats and mittens.

"Me pway at Miss Mo's today?" Tessa asked.

"Yes, you're going to Mrs. Porter's," Marvel assured her.

"Want my Nancy baby," she said as Marvel secured her red scarf around her face and tied it behind her neck.

"Nancy baby?" she asked.

"She means her baby doll," Nate told her.

Tessa nodded, her eyes round and blue above the scarf that covered the lower potion of her face. "Nancy."

"Your doll, huh?" Marvel glanced out the window beside the front door and didn't see Seth yet. "Stay put. I'll go find her."

She ran up the stairs and opened the door to the Paxtons' room. The bed had been neatly made and their clothing and items were in order. A rag doll in a green dress lay on the cot.

She returned with the doll to find Seth ushering Nate out the door and Tessa wailing over his shoulder. "Nancy! Papa, wait! Nancy!"

She stopped wailing and her eyes lit up at Marvel's approach.

"Here you go." Marvel handed the child the doll, and Tessa hugged it to her wool-wrapped cheek.

Seth turned. "Have a pleasant day, Miss Henley."

"You, too." She closed the door behind them, shutting out the chill wind. Through the side window, she watched him place the children one at a time on the back of the horse and then climb up behind. Shame they'd had to go out in such inclement weather. They would be well taken care of at Mrs. Porter's. She knew what to do with children. The horse and riders disappeared through the blowing snow.

The grandfather clock chimed the half hour, and Marvel turned back to the silent foyer with a disturbing sense of loss. She shook off the feeling. It was time to get on with her day.

The day passed quite uneventfully. Liberty played the piano while Marvel ironed linens. Half-formed thoughts and snippets of images from the night before shocked her as she worked. Try as she might, she couldn't erase memories of Seth with sleepy eyes and a dark growth of beard along his jaw. He'd met her in the doorway of his room bare-chested, the butt of a revolver protruding from the waistband of his trousers and pressed against the taut skin of his belly. *Oh, dear...* He had a dusting of dark hair across his chest. *Oh, my...*

Marvel glanced down, realizing she'd been standing motionless. She jerked the iron upward, revealing a wedge-shaped burn on her mother's ivory damask table cloth. Served her right for her indecent thoughts!

Marvel had taken care of her father's personal needs for years, so a man's body should not have been unfamiliar or shocking...but Seth...well quite honestly there was no comparison. The young doctor was fit and fine looking, and she was an old maid who shouldn't be letting her imagination or her thoughts drift in the direction they'd run all day. She folded the ruined tablecloth and carried it to lie on top of her sewing basket in the parlor. She would have to cut it in half and make two smaller cloths now.

That afternoon Marvel forgot to add sugar to the rice pudding she set in the oven and barely remembered her omission before the mixture had set and browned.

As the remainder of the week passed, she found herself looking forward to the evenings after Dr. Paxton had put his children to bed and came down to the drawing room to read or take tea with her.

On Friday Leo would not be persuaded from his room to accompany them to dinner. Marvel made him a sandwich and warmed a bowl of soup and assured him she and Liberty would be back within a couple of hours.

She had suggested they dine at the restaurant that Everett and Agnes Harrison ran on First Street. Since she was solely responsible for providing meals for her boarders, Marvel rarely ate out. This evening was a much-anticipated treat.

"Nate and Tessa are staying with Mrs. Porter for a few more hours this evening," Seth told them as he assisted Liberty into a rented buggy. "She invited them to share their supper."

"I love the opera house," Mrs. Pargellis said in a cheerful voice. "I can't wait to see the gowns and hear the orchestra."

Seth glanced beside him at Marvel, and they shared a look. He'd grown accustomed to the woman's detachment from the present. It was obvious she suffered from some type of dementia brought on by her advanced years. He admired Marvel's patient understanding and the way she always managed to say the right thing and not make the old woman appear foolish or get even more confused or frustrated.

There was much to be admired about Marvel, and he discovered new aspects with each day that passed.

Seth took their coats and hung them on hooks inside the front door of the restaurant. Agnes Harrison brought glasses of water and recited the supper menu.

"I'd love the crab patties," Liberty announced. She was

wearing rhinestone combs in her hair and had tied a fringed curtain sash from the parlor around her neck.

Agnes turned a questioning glance at Marvel.

"I'll take the meat loaf, too," Marvel said with a smile.

"Make that three meat loaf dinners," Seth decided.

"Coffee?" Agnes asked.

"None for me, thank you," Marvel replied.

"Sherry for me," Liberty suggested.

Seth simply nodded. "With sugar, please."

Agnes brought Seth's coffee.

"The house and office are going to take longer than I'd anticipated," he told Marvel. "I've hired a carpenter and a painter, and only today realized the roof is in need of repair. There was snow drifting onto a bureau in the back bedroom."

"It seems these were things the city counsel should have taken in hand before your arrival," she said with a frown.

"I agree, but there's nothing left now but to do the best I can."

She folded her hands in her lap. "Are you saying your stay may be longer than we'd initially agreed?"

"If you're willing to extend your generosity, Marvel. I could move Nate and Tessa into the house next week when Babe leaves, but I'd be moving them into chaos and construction. I'd rather wait until the work is complete. Keep things as normal and comfortable for them as I can."

"I'm not unsympathetic to your dilemma," she replied.

"Of course you're not."

"The last two days have gone more smoothly than the first two," she noted.

"I've been working at it," he assured her.

"How much of a delay are you anticipating?" she asked.

"I'd like to have us in our house by Christmas."

Carrying a plate in each hand and one on the crook of her arm, Agnes brought their meals. "Enjoy your supper."

Liberty picked up her fork and tasted her meat loaf.

"Christmas is three weeks away," Marvel said.

Seth nodded and spread his napkin on his lap. "We can be out next week if you prefer."

Marvel recognized Seth's flat tone, knew he didn't want to move his children until the house was clean and ready. He was paying her well, and she earned her livelihood housing boarders, so what was she so concerned about? There was really no good reason they couldn't stay another three weeks.

"I want you to stay," she said.

Liberty gave her a smile and nodded approvingly.

Seth studied her.

Marvel picked up her fork and dipped it into her mashed potatoes and steaming dark gravy.

"Thank you," Seth said.

"It's the right thing," she answered.

The meat loaf was delicious, spiced with bay leaf and oregano, and the gravy was smooth and rich. Marvel thoroughly enjoyed her meal. "You don't know what a treat this is," she said, laying down her fork. "I can't remember the last time I ate food someone else prepared."

"I'm pleased you enjoyed it," Seth told her.

Everett came from the kitchen with a tray bearing huge slices of apple pie with cheese melted on top. "Dessert is on the house," he told Seth. "I'm gonna be coming for advice on treatin' my lumbago, and I want to be on your best side."

Agnes showed up and refilled Seth's cup. He sweetened his coffee and drank it with his dessert.

"Will you be giving Everett's lumbago special concern, then?" Marvel asked with a grin.

"There are new therapies we can try," he answered. "If it helps him to think he's getting special treatment, I'll humor him."

"You're the doctor?" Liberty asked with surprise.

"As of Monday I am Carson Bend's new doctor," he replied.

"How is it you don't have a wife, Doctor?" she asked.

Chapter Five

"My wife passed away two years ago."

"My, my," she said with a sad shake of her head. "And she must have been so young."

Seth nodded. "Too young."

"How did she die?"

"Mrs. Pargellis," Marvel cautioned gently.

"Sarah died in childbirth," he replied without offense.

So Tessa had never known her mother. And Nate could only have been four years old. Marvel's heart went out to the man and his children.

"You'll make a good father," Liberty predicted.

"I do my best."

"You *are* a good father," Marvel concurred quietly.

Seth raised those disturbing blue eyes and she felt the heat of his gaze melt through to her insides.

Liberty got up from the table at that moment and started stacking their plates one on top of the other.

Marvel stopped her with a hand on her arm. "The Harrisons will do that."

"Let's get on with it, then," Liberty replied. "I'm tired."

Marvel gave Seth an apologetic glance, but he smiled and retrieved their coats. After helping both ladies with their sleeves, he paid for their meal and walked them out to the buggy.

"I'll stop for Nate and Tessa on the way home if you don't mind," he said.

"Of course not," she answered, hearing the way he used the term "home" for the boarding house, and appreciating her part in making it so for him.

Much later, after the children were bustled home and to their beds and Liberty had gone to her room, Seth took the buggy back to the livery and returned.

Beside the usual pot of tea she brewed each evening sat a stoneware coffee server and a mug. She poured steaming coffee into the mug and handed it to Seth.

"Thank you," he said appreciatively and settled on the sofa near the fire.

"You drank tea every night without saying a word," she observed.

"I enjoyed the tea," he replied.

"But you prefer coffee."

With a nod he said, "I do. But the tea was a nice change."

"I apologize for my ungraciousness, which obviously made you too uncomfortable to mention your preference. I pride myself in making my guests feel at home, and I obviously failed with you."

His bright gaze moved over her in surprise. "No apology is necessary, Miss Henley."

"Yes. It is. Please accept it."

"Very well. I accept your apology."

His smile made his eyes crinkle at the corners. Noticing caused her cheeks to warm uncomfortably. That smile was enough to turn any woman's head, but still she felt foolish for the disturbing effect he had on her. She was an appalling number of years older than he and heartily ashamed at her scandalous reactions.

She reached beside the chair and picked up her sewing. "I appreciate the invitation to dinner."

"It was the least I could do."

"Well, the meal and the—" she hesitated over the word, but dinner with a handsome young man needed to be addressed "—and the *company* were a luxury I appreciated."

He studied her. "You work hard. From what you said you took care of your father for years. Now you take care of the boarders. And sew for the ladies in town. Do you take time to do anything that's just for you?"

She considered his words and they swept her back to a time when she'd had dreams and ambitions. The absence of those dreams left a growling cavity like an empty stomach. "Not anymore."

"Tell me about it?"

She looked up. "What?"

"Whatever it is that gave you that yearning look you covered up so quickly."

She couldn't hide her surprise. How was it he could read her so well?

"You want to be a writer. Or design ball gowns. Travel the rails and see the cities you've seen on your stereoscope, is that it?"

She shook her head.

The fire crackled in the grate; a log rolled and sparks flew up the chimney.

"I saw a lady arm wrestler once," he said with a glimmer in those vivid eyes. "Could it be you want a blue ribbon for arm wrestling?"

She couldn't help laughing. He was like no other person she'd ever known, and his good humor was infectious. She shook her head. "No, silly."

"Very well. You obviously have a very dark, very deep secret, and no amount of badgering on my part is going to draw it out of you."

Truth rang in those words and brought a sinking sensation to her chest. Some things were dark and deep and secret, but what he was asking wasn't really. "All right," she said. "I'll tell you."

He set down his cup. "You will?"

"When I was young I used to paint."

"Houses?" he asked mischievously. "Porches?"

She raised an eyebrow. "Pictures. On canvas."

"Really," he said, his voice thoughtful as if he was absorbing her admission.

She'd never told anyone. She hadn't thought about it for years. Not since her father had become ill and she'd devoted herself to his care.

"Do you still have your paintings?" he asked.

She nodded.

"Will you show them to me?"

She almost opened her mouth to refuse, to tell him they weren't good enough, but something kept her from speaking. She studied him in the dancing firelight, this man so sensitive to the needs and emotions of his children, this man who devoted his life to healing. Intuitively she knew he was someone she could be herself with, someone she could trust. She set aside the fabric, the needle she hadn't touched still piercing the last stitch. "Come with me."

She picked up a lantern and led him through the house, up to the second story and past their bedrooms to a small oak door that opened onto a narrow set of stairs. She led him up into the dark recesses of the low-ceilinged third floor. Striking a match, she lit another oil lamp, arranging both for the most advantageous light. The lamps cast long flickering shadows across the exposed beams above their heads.

"Wait right there," she told him.

She went to a cloth-draped stack of canvases and removed the cover. One by one she took the paintings and propped them against trunks and old dressers until all were displayed. She had forgotten half of them until now.

"All right," she urged him. "Come look."

Seth wasn't surprised at how clean and organized the attic was, considering Marvel's penchant for order. The space was understandably chilly considering the thickness of snow lying atop the roof above.

He took several steps forward and picked up one of the lamps, then moved from canvas to canvas, kneeling here and there to better see her artwork. A few still-lifes portrayed realistic-looking fruit and delicate flowers and china. Here and there a landscape revealed her eye for light and color. But the paintings of houses and barns, porches and stores were the scenes that touched a corresponding chord within him.

Against the doorway of the general store leaned a broom. A pile of dust and dry crumbs lay near the straw bristles as though the owner had only just stepped away and would be right back.

A rocking chair sat on a wide, painted porch, half a bowl of apples on its seat and a pile of peelings on the worn floor. A toy train and a few marbles showed that a little boy had been at play in the dirt at the foot of the stairs. A fat cat slept in the sun on the banister nearby. The missing woman who'd been peeling apples and her child were as real as if they'd been included. The observer expected them to return at any moment.

Seth was amazed by Marvel's ability to paint life and energy into places where people lived. From a crouching position, he looked up at her. "These are amazing."

She caught her lower lip between her teeth.

"No one has ever seen any of these?"

She shook her head. "My father saw some of the first

attempts. I never intended to show people. Painting used to free something inside me. I...I can't explain it."

"You don't have to."

"I just put them away and didn't think about it anymore."

"What about after your father died? Why didn't you start again?"

She shrugged and he read vulnerability in her eyes.

Why had she chosen to share her work now? With him—a near stranger? "Why did you show me?" he asked before he thought hard enough to stop himself.

Her brows lowered in a frown while she considered his question. "I'm not sure," she answered finally. "Somehow I knew you'd understand."

She was quite unlike anyone he'd ever met before, open and honest, yet shyly hesitant in an altogether disturbing combination. And she'd shared something private with him. He helped her stack and cover the paintings. She swept her skirts aside and headed for the stairs.

He followed her down and along the second-floor hall, where he peeked in on the children before continuing down the stairs.

"Why don't you paint anymore, Marvel?" he asked.

She paused at the bottom of the stairs with her hand on the banister and looked up at him. "It was something I did when I was young. I'm an adult now, with responsibilities."

"Artists of all ages paint. I don't see what age has to do with it."

She continued on through the foyer. "I just mean I'm not a carefree child any longer."

"Neither was Van Gogh or da Vinci."

"You cannot compare what I do to a master. That was merely a passion of my youth."

He followed her toward the sitting room. "There's certainly nothing wrong with passion at any age."

By the time they reached their destination, her cheeks were bright with color. She busied herself placing their cups and saucers on the tray.

Seth reached out and gently took her wrist in his grasp, halting her movements. She froze, looked at his hand, then slowly raised her gaze to his.

"It's a shame you've forsaken something that you do so well, especially if it gives you pleasure."

"Life isn't all about pleasure, Dr. Paxton."

"Seth."

"Seth," she repeated, cheeks blazing.

"I believe life should be filled with as many pleasures as we can absorb," he disagreed.

"You don't know me and you don't know about my life."

"I know something about self-denial and sacrifice," he told her.

She could only look at him. Wonder what he spoke of. Wonder why he cared what she did with her life. He didn't know anything about her or the things that had shaped her into the woman that stood before him. His touch on her wrist radiated warmth along her arm and sparked an awakening fire that humiliated her.

This time the look in his eyes was not amusement or curiosity. He was looking at her with sensual awareness, with restless heat and keen longing that ripped the air from her lungs as though she'd been struck.

She lost track of any coherent words she might have thought to say. Her attention focused on his lips, parted now and shaped with a fascinating bow in the upper and tempting fullness in the lower. Her heart chugged like a freight train climbing the Rockies, and her breath caught.

In the seconds that followed, she wasn't quite sure how she came to be standing in the circle of his arms or when he'd released her wrist and wrapped that arm around her shoulder to draw her close against him, but the next thing she knew they were locked in an embrace and she was kissing him back with all the longing and passion she'd buried for a lifetime.

The kiss wasn't wise, but it was real. This feeling that exploded and took over her senses didn't listen to caution, but blazed ahead and turned her bones to jelly.

He was beautiful, this man. Strong arms and hard chest, lips that delighted and aroused, and at that instant she would have given everything to cast the rest of the world aside and know only this man and this moment and never let go.

Everything that had been asleep in her woke up at his bidding and pushed aside the tears she'd cried and the promises she'd made herself. She'd made all the mistakes she was going to. Wisdom was her ruling trait now.

Seth kissed her as though he couldn't get enough of her, as though he didn't need air as much as he needed to taste her. At the velvety touch of his tongue against hers, she sighed and collapsed against him, but he easily absorbed her weight and held her fast.

He threaded his fingers into her hair and she reached to grasp his jaw. His rough chin and cheek were an exotic texture she explored until her palm tingled.

From the outer room the grandfather clock chimed the hour in deep resonating tones, and the sound filtered into Marvel's senses, awakening her to reality. Time wasn't her friend.

She drew her hand from Seth's face to grasp his forearm. He loosened his fingers from her hair, and their lips parted. He touched his forehead to hers, his breathing labored. Marvel drew her hand away and brought it to her tingling lips.

She took a step back. Their eyes met.

She couldn't possibly sort out what had just happened yet, but one thing was certain: she was embarrassed by her actions.

She dropped both hands to her sides and backed away.

"I'll help you clean up," he offered.

"No." The single word stopped him from heading toward the tray. "I'll do it."

He nodded. She didn't meet his eyes again. "Good night, then, Marvel."

The sound of her name from his lips was so intimate it hurt. "Good night," she could only whisper.

When he was gone the room was larger. Colder.

Normal.

Marvel got down from the buggy and waited while Chip Wilkins helped Liberty down. Marvel rented it for church on Sundays and for errands on Mondays and had invited Seth and his little family to share the ride. It would have been senseless to rent two, and she couldn't have allowed him to take the children to church on horseback, although he had transported them to Mrs. Porter's that way each weekday morning.

"I'll be waitin' for you after service, Miss Henley," Chip told her with a gap-toothed smile. He made extra money to help his parents by using his father's horses and buggy.

She thanked him and gathered the hem of her blue merino wool dress away from the snow that lined the brick pathway.

Upon entering the building, conversation hushed and attention focused on the newcomers accompanying her.

"You're welcome to sit with us or claim a pew for yourselves," she offered.

"Can we sit with Miss Marvel, Papa?" Nate asked.

"If you don't mind," Seth answered.

"Not at all." A fellow worshipper had already helped Liberty remove her coat and taken it to the coat room. Marvel shrugged out of hers, and as she did so noticed the shawl Liberty wore. A wedge-shaped brown burn on ivory damask identified the tablecloth Marvel had burned.

The reason she'd burned the linen rose up in her mind and her heart thudded in embarrassment. She'd hidden her mistake in her pile of mending, but Liberty had worn it to church!

"I'll take your coat." Beside her Seth extended a hand.

"Oh, of course. Thank you." She shrugged out of the wrap and he carried it with theirs into the coat room.

Liberty had tottered off down the center aisle, so Marvel scurried to catch up. "Wait!"

She plucked the tablecloth from Liberty's shoulders, swiftly refolded it so that the burn was hidden, then tucked it back around her. "There you go."

Liberty stood waiting for Marvel and the Paxtons to slide into the pew ahead of her. "She likes to sit on the end," Marvel explained softly.

"Hell-bent on a quick getaway?" he asked under his breath as they took their places.

"In here that would be *heaven*-bent." A teasing smile accompanied her whispered reply.

The choir filed in and led the congregation in an opening hymn. Reverend Newton took his place behind the pulpit and welcomed the newcomers. Mothers with eligible daughters snapped to attention, and young ladies craned their necks for a better view. Seth smiled graciously. After a few announcements the singing resumed and the service proceeded as usual.

Marvel's attention wavered from the message to what had happened between her and Seth on Friday evening. She'd thought of little else since, but this saintly atmosphere doubled her confusion. That kiss had been impulsive. Foolish. But every time she remembered the intensity, thought of Seth's strong arms and the scent of his hair and skin, she experienced the same wondrous sensation all over again. Her heart changed its rhythm, a smile touched her lips….

She should have said something afterward. Let him know it

wouldn't be happening again. Why had it happened, anyway? What would cause the man to kiss her like that?

The sooner he was out of her home, the better. She vowed to be strong and wise and weather his presence without repeating that night's shameful actions.

The service concluded and Marvel joined the people milling about. Sylvia Ellis approached her. "Would you have time to make one or two shepherd costumes for this year's program? Most of the outfits have seen so many Christmas pageants that they're falling apart. I think when Clark was a boy, he wore the same one our son wore last year." Clark was her husband. "New ones are long overdue."

"I'd be glad to make a few. I'll take an old one home to use for a pattern."

"You're a peach." Sylvia accompanied Marvel to the back room where they dug through several cartons until Marvel found what she needed. Back in the emptying sanctuary, Sylvia nodded toward the rear of the building. "Your new boarder doesn't stand a chance, does he?"

Marvel followed Sylvia's gaze. Seth stood in the center of a ring of women of all ages, most smiling and vying for his attention. Jane Richards, the mayor's daughter, had worked her way to Seth's side and was speaking to him, her delicate white glove on his black sleeve. Blond-haired and blue-eyed, she was the loveliest of all the young women gathered near. A peach-colored dress emphasized her pale, youthful skin to its best advantage.

Marvel couldn't help but notice the striking contrast between Seth's near-black hair and Jane's pale tresses. Jane had joined the ladies' quilting society this year and was a sweet person besides being incredibly beautiful.

An infinitesimal twinge, barely recognizable as jealousy, rose to the surface, and Marvel stifled it without conscious thought. She was Seth Paxton's landlady and nothing more.

The jumble of people shifted. Sylvia made a comment and joined her husband. Marvel recognized a familiar tall form in a black suit. Henry Morrison was making his way through the crowd toward the doors at the same time Marvel reached the small vestibule. They drew up face-to-face. Henry gave her a polite nod. "Marvel."

"Hello, Henry."

He glanced away, then let his gaze trail back to hers. "You're looking well."

"As are you." Everything had changed. A week ago he would have asked about her boarders or mentioned hearing from his son. She might have invited him to the house for dinner. Now they faced each other awkwardly like two strangers.

Several families exited at the same time. Cold air swirled inside and chilled Marvel as the crowd grew considerably thinner.

"Good morning, Marvel," Reverend Newton said, his stiff black robes swishing.

She offered her hand.

He smiled. "Your new boarder seems to be making himself at home in Carson Bend."

"It seems he's getting established," she replied. "I know he's looking forward to having his children settled in their home soon."

At that moment she sensed a presence behind her and turned to discover Seth, his arm laden with coats. Hers was on top, and he held it open with the satin lining exposed. "We'd better not let Mrs. Pargellis get a head start."

She chuckled. "Thank you."

"Seth Paxton," he said to Henry and extended a hand.

Henry's raised brows revealed his surprise at the familiar exchange between Marvel and the new doctor. "Henry Morrison," he said without expression in his voice. "Doctor, you're younger than I expected."

Henry's statement rang inside Marvel's head.

Seth tilted his mouth in that I-dare-you grin she found amusing and attractive. "If it's any assurance," he said. "I get older every day."

Henry appeared flustered.

Seth chuckled. "My credentials are in order and I practiced in Denver before coming here."

Henry looked sheepish then. "It wasn't my intent to question your abilities, Doctor. Forgive my rude observation."

Seth didn't appear perturbed. "Nothing to forgive, I assure you."

"If you'll excuse me now." Henry entered the coat room and returned wearing his familiar hat and ankle-length coat. He headed straight for the door.

"Had his cap set for Marvel Anne, he did." Liberty had come up beside Seth. "His nose got out of joint when she turned 'im down."

Acutely mortified, Marvel shot Liberty a quelling look and deliberately avoided Seth's eyes.

He hunkered down and busied himself with preparing Nate and Tessa to go out in the cold.

Marvel tried to catch Liberty's eye with a stealthy reprimand, but the woman waited nearby unconcernedly.

All the way home Marvel rehashed the scene in the vestibule, feeling Henry's disapproval and reliving Liberty's intimate disclosure. She hadn't even been aware that Liberty knew the details of Henry's proposal or of Marvel's reply.

She glanced at Seth as the buggy bumped in and out of frozen ruts. At least she had been offered marriage once. Unfortunately Henry's age didn't paint her in the most appealing light. What did she care what Seth thought?

The subject wasn't mentioned again at dinner or throughout the rest of the day and for once Marvel was grateful that Liberty forgot things nearly as soon as she'd said or done them.

Chapter Six

The following day Chip again brought the buggy. Monday was errand day, and Marvel assisted Liberty from the vehicle to the boardwalk on Main Street.

"Same time as usual, Miss Marvel?" Chip asked.

"At the mercantile as always," she agreed.

She settled Liberty for a visit with Mr. Hodgins in the barber shop before she ventured across the slushy street to the bank and the post office. She returned for Liberty and they made their way to the mercantile. The frosted display window held a sled and a doll, boxes of glass Christmas ornaments and a miniature feather tree. Inside, she gave August Evans her list of supplies.

While Liberty sat with a box of thread on her lap, Marvel perused the fabrics and catalogs and wrote down her order. She stopped in front of the oak display case holding toilet preparations. A glance proved that Liberty was entertained and August was occupied with another customer. Marvel read the advertising signs with interest. Bring Back the Color of Youth and Remove the Telltale Marks of Time, one boasted. Interest piqued, she read more.

Orange flower massage cream is a luxury no woman
should deny herself. A regular course of facial massage removes horizontal lines, takes out laugh wrinkles and erases
crows feet.

Glancing into an oval pedestal mirror, which stood right there
on the scratched glass counter, Marvel studied her face for lines,
wrinkles and crows feet. She'd earned a few freckles in her
flower garden last summer and they hadn't completely faded yet.
She picked up a bottle to examine the benefits of the potion:

Removes wrinkles from under the eyes and restores plump
cheeks. Brings fresh bloom to faded faces and smoothes
away age lines and age marks. With continued use, skin
will be healthy and rosy.

What a confusing menagerie of remedies and ointments!
However, with the purchase of orange flower face wash, benzoin
and almond lotion, massage cream, freckle ointment, skin food
and complexion powder came a free booklet with diagrams and
simple instructions explaining the methods ladies of refinement
and fashion used to stay young looking. Marvel held up the com-
plimentary hand-painted cobalt-glass puff box that came with the
set.

She looked into the mirror again and Jane Richards's peachy
complexion and sparkling blue eyes hovered tauntingly over her
own image. Just then August's wife Cordelia pushed aside the
curtain draping the doorway that separated the back room from
the store.

"Good morning, Marvel! Are you laying stock of your baking
supplies for Christmas goodies?"

"I am," she replied. "I'll take one of these orange flower
beauty sets," she added. "Will you wrap it up, please?"

Cordelia's expression revealed more pleasure than surprise. The entire array cost a pretty penny, and it was probably rare to sell a whole set. "I'll throw in some of these Dutch sandalwood sachets for you," she told Marvel. "They'll make your bureau drawers smell real nice."

Marvel thanked her and met August who had finished with his last customer and was making a stack of her supplies on the front counter. "Got a new supply of molasses 'cause I knew you'd be asking. I'll have your order delivered after lunch, Miss Henley."

"Throw in a can of coffee, will you, please?"

"Coffee?" He stopped making check marks on her list to peer over the tops of his spectacles. "Don't recall you ever buying coffee before."

"The young doctor likes coffee," Liberty piped up from her chair near the woodstove.

"I'll remember that when the city counsel sends him a welcome package," August answered.

With a tight smile, Marvel nodded. She turned to the front window and checked, seeing that Chip had come for them. "Let's be on our way, Mrs. Pargellis."

The woman joined her, and Marvel guided her out into the winter air before she could reveal anything else.

That night Seth put the children to bed and joined Marvel and Mrs. Pargellis in the drawing room. He picked up the book he'd been reading the evening before and thumbed through to the page where he'd left off. He dealt with the same trouble concentrating that he had for the past four nights. His thoughts had been enraptured since the night he'd kissed Marvel. She'd been so alive and vibrant in his arms. Kissing her was a heady soul-regenerating experience he wanted to repeat.

He'd never known the sense of belonging and purpose that

he had in those fleeting moments. Watching her serve meals and sew and do ordinary things had become a fascination.

It was growing more and more difficult to keep his eyes from wandering to the soft curves of her breasts and hips beneath her dress, to halt his thoughts from straying to imaginations and day-dreams of holding her, having intimate conversations. He wanted to ask her things he shouldn't. He wanted to know more about her…all about her.

He held an interest in her childhood and her dreams and all the things that had made her who she was today. He was fasci-nated. Captivated. In over his head.

The gentleman in black, Henry, had offered for her hand, and she'd turned him down. How long ago? Why? What had their relationship been? She didn't owe Seth explanations of her private life, but that didn't stop him from wondering.

"You know I have a recital tomorrow." Mrs. Pargellis got up stiffly and walked into the parlor. Moments later, the notes of an Austrian waltz drifted to them.

"She's really very good," he commented.

"One thing she remembers is the music," Marvel replied. "It's a blessing. Have you seen others with the same condition?"

"A few. Even to those in the medical profession it's still very much a mystery how the mind works. You do an excellent job of keeping her from becoming agitated. Life is often very frus-trating for someone in her situation because she probably knows she can't remember. You're always calm and rational, respect-ful of her feelings."

She spread her sewing on her lap and smoothed the material.

"Marvel," he said.

She raised her brows as if answering.

"Did your father suffer from dementia?"

"No," she answered. "His mind was alert well after his body had given out. His situation was every bit as frustrating as what

Liberty goes through, though. He thought and reasoned just like we do, but his body stopped cooperating."

Seth nodded his understanding. She had obviously taken very good care of her parent. Again questions rose in his mind. "Henry seems like a nice fellow."

She looked at the fabric on her knees, then back at him. "He is."

"You know him well?"

"He and my father were friends for many years. I've known him since I was a child. He's always been like an uncle to me. More so since my father's been gone. Until recently." She got a little frown between her brows.

"When he asked for your hand?"

She gave a slow nod. "Now it's all changed. I don't think it can be fixed."

"Because you declined his offer."

"Because I declined his offer."

"Why?" The question popped out before he'd thought.

She looked up, her expression unreadable.

He had no right to press her for answers just because he was insanely curious. "That was an impertinent question. You don't have to answer."

"I regard him as an uncle. A friend. For some women that may be enough, but…" She paused and shook her head. Apparently she didn't mind discussing her relationship with Henry Morrison. "It wasn't enough for me. So I made my choice. I love my home and I have a good life. It's enough."

Seth had kissed her. Held her in his arms and experienced her passion and vitality. He couldn't believe she was truly satisfied settling for a loveless life when she had so much to give. Marvel seemed to bury passions and desires, and he didn't understand why. "Perhaps you've told yourself it's enough, just like you've forsaken the life and energy that you once put into your painting.

I don't think you're really satisfied. How could you be when there's so much more burning inside you?"

A shadow passed behind her eyes. "You don't know me. How do you know what I want or need?"

"I sense it in everything you do. In your paintings. In your kiss."

She laid down her needlework. "It's quite ungentlemanly of you to mention that."

"Are you sorry?"

She wouldn't meet his eyes.

"I'm not," he added. "You fill a place inside me that's been empty for a long time," he told her. "I just figured out that what I've had in the past isn't enough for me."

She stood and adjusted her skirts. "I'll make your coffee now."

He noticed her innocence and her pain and that she was far too brave about things. Noticing didn't take a genius. "I'll help you."

She raised a palm. "No."

He stood and gently wrapped his fingers around her wrist. "Why not? Are you afraid to let yourself get too close to me? Afraid you'll want to kiss me again and I'll have the same notion?"

"You're far too bold, Dr. Paxton."

Beneath his fingers her pulse hammered. "Dr. Paxton again, is it? If that's your tactic to hold me at arm's length, I don't think it's going to work."

She looked up then, a combination of fear and longing in her gold-flecked eyes. Her gaze flickered from his eyes to his lips. Revealing color infused her cheeks. She was delectable, and she didn't even know it. He wanted to hold her close and chase away the shadows with each yearning beat of his heart. He wanted to kiss her until she forgot her resistance and admitted she wanted him as much as he wanted her.

He wanted to discover the silken textures of her hair and skin, to learn her mouth and neck and hidden curves with his lips. Everything about her drew him like a thirsty man craving water in the desert. She had no idea how desirable and lovely she was…and that vulnerability charmed him.

"I think you liked kissing me," he said, her wrist still held loosely in the circle of his fingers. Her dark liquid eyes held his gaze, and she raised her chin. Defiance? Desire? "I think you're afraid of liking it *too much.*"

Chapter Seven

He raised the backs of his fingers to her cheek and caressed her satin-smooth skin. Her lips parted and she moistened the lower one with her tongue.

Seth lowered his head and touched his mouth to her damp lips, testing her softness, petitioning her acceptance. His entire being focused on gentle, undemanding contact. He sensed the instant she set aside her uncertainties and let herself feel. Her breath rushed out against his lips and she melted into him with a sweet sigh.

Kissing her felt so right. Holding her indulged his every sense and whispering nerve ending. He released her hand so she could reach for his shoulder and he folded her into an embrace. She was everything he'd ever wanted or needed and he couldn't get enough of her. His desire for her took him by surprise. He'd never been so alive.

Their lips parted and she rested her cheek against his chest. Seth gave himself over to another impulse and threaded his fingers into her hair.

Marvel grasped the fabric of his shirt with both hands. "This is wrong." Her voice held a sorrowful edge. "I can't let this happen."

"It's not wrong," he argued, not understanding. "It feels right. My feelings for you are true and honest. Real for the first time ever. This is it for me. You are the woman I've missed and longed for."

She leaned back to look up at him. "You mustn't say those things. We barely know each other."

"I know what I need to know. Marvel, I know how you make me feel, and I want us to discover everything together. This connection is something I've never had."

Her brows drew together in concern. She loosened her grip on his shirt and took a step back. "What about your wife? What are you saying?"

"Don't think less of me for being honest," he told her. "I cared for her, of course, but I never loved her."

Marvel's expression showed her puzzlement. She pulled away, her eyes locked on his. "You married her. You had children together."

"Why are you so surprised? You said yourself when you were talking about Henry that for some people friendship or compatibility is enough foundation for a marriage. There are plenty of reasons people marry, and I'd wager a guess that a very small percent of those are based on love."

"But you," she said, her eyes showing true concern. "Your love and devotion for your children is obvious. You're kind and…" She turned in a half circle and then back. "*How* did you come to marry a woman you didn't love?"

The notes from the piano in the other room ceased, and Marvel noted the creak of the stairs as Liberty took herself off to bed.

Seth glanced behind him. "Come sit beside me on the divan." She did so, arranging her skirts with her focus on him. He took her hand and raised it to his lips for a gentle kiss. "Laura was first married to my brother, Andrew," he said, folding her hand between both of his. "I had graduated from the university and taken a position in Pennsylvania when he took ill. I resigned that job and went to help my family. Andrew became bedridden. Laura and my mother needed me. Before he died, Andrew begged me to take care of Laura. He adored her, and he asked for my promise. I gave him my word."

Seth locked his gaze with hers as though he could make her understand. "After his death, I married her."

Marvel absorbed the resignation behind Seth's words. He'd told her only a day or so ago that he knew something about sacrifice and self-denial. At the time she'd had no idea what that meant, but now…now that she knew, she was forced to comprehend the enormity of what he'd done. His selflessness said everything about his strength of character, about the quality of man he was, about the loyalty he felt toward family.

And yet he'd been lonely in a loveless marriage, yearning for more and knowing more was not his fate…until…

The hope in his eyes was more than she could bear. She shook her head. "You deserve a love like you dream of," she told him earnestly. "You'd make any woman feel cherished."

He squeezed her hand.

"But I'm not that woman, Seth. Surely you've reasoned that fact."

"I believe you are."

She withdrew her hand, gathered her skirts and stood. "I'm not. I'm sorry."

She had headed to tuck the shepherd's headpiece into her sewing basket when he caught her arm and turned her to face him. "Why deny the passion you feel?"

She had her pride. Too much, perhaps, because she couldn't push out words to admit that she was too old for him. All she managed was a shake of her head. "Bank the fire before you go upstairs, will you please?"

"Marvel."

"Good night."

"Marvel, wait."

In the kitchen she dipped water into a stoneware pitcher and carried it to her room, where she undressed and stood before her mirror in her chemise and pantaloons.

Half a dozen jars and bottles were arranged with labels facing outward, her new cobalt-glass puff jar beside her hand mirror. Marvel picked up the orange flower face wash and read the directions. She tied up her hair and splashed her face with water, then worked the cleanser against her skin with tiny circular motions. After rinsing, she used the massage cream and gave her skin and underlying muscles a workout.

That regimen left her nose area and lips burning, but she moved on to the next step, frequently checking the booklet for the correct procedures and following them to the letter. The skin food had her face tingling, but she tolerated the discomfort while counting the required minutes. By the time she washed off that mixture, her face was bright red, except around her eyes. Nothing on the labels or in the booklet mentioned this unpleasant side effect, but beauty and youth were worth the discomfort, weren't they?

She was standing with the jar of benzoin and almond cream in her hand, contemplating the last step, when the front door chimes sounded. Startled, she jumped up and grabbed her wrapper. She didn't need Liberty awake at this hour, nor did she want the Paxton children roused from their beds.

She stuffed her feet into her slippers and hurried down the stairs. She hadn't reached the door before a loud pounding resonated up the stairwell.

"I'm *coming!*" She flung open the door and braced herself against the frigid cold.

"The doc is needed right away!" Chip Wilkins announced, out of breath. Then he squinted and stared at her. "You all right, Miss Henley?"

"What's wrong?" she asked in concern.

"We need the doctor," he repeated.

"I figured it was someone for me," Seth said, coming up behind her still fully clothed and with his gun stuck in his waistband. "What's wrong?"

"I got a wagon," Chip said. "You got your bag?"

"What's happening?" Nate stood at the top of the stairs. Beside him, a sleepy-eyed Tessa in a long flannel gown and bare feet had started to cry.

"I'll get my bag," Seth told Chip. "You'd better stand inside out of the cold for a minute."

Tessa's wail carried down the stairs, growing in volume. "Stay, Papa!"

"Can't Dr. Solomon handle it?" Marvel asked.

Seth looked at her then and his eyes opened wide. "What is wrong with your face?"

"Nothing. Are you going to need that gun?" She turned to Chip. "Is he going to need a gun?"

"The gun is just a habit," he told her.

"Why can't Dr. Solomon help?" she asked Chip.

"It's the doc what's hurt," Chip replied. "Cain't walk. He sent me for ya."

Seth gave Marvel another puzzled look, but he ran up the stairs and picked up Tessa. "Will you see her back to bed, please? She's just disoriented, being awakened like this. She'll go right back to sleep."

Marvel grabbed the hem of her wrapper and climbed the stairs. She took Tessa from his arms. "I'll get her settled. Go."

"Miss Marvel will sit with you, Nate." The boy followed his father into their room. Seth struck a match and lit the lamp on the washstand, then strapped on his holster, settled the gun and picked up his bag. He gave Nate a reassuring pat on the shoulder. "Don't give Miss Marvel any trouble, now."

Another glance at her prompted him to say, "I'll have a look at your face later."

He disappeared through the doorway, and the sound of his boots pounded down the stairs. The front door opened and closed. By the glowing light, Marvel stirred the fire and added a log to the base burner, then settled Tessa and Nate together in the big bed and tucked the covers all around them.

Tessa had stopped crying and stared up at Marvel with round wet eyes. "Owie," she said around the finger in her mouth.

Her wide stare proved it wasn't herself she spoke of, but what she was seeing when she looked at Marvel.

"My face looked like that when the Founder's Day parade was too long and the sun was too hot," Nate told her.

Marvel rolled her eyes and stepped to the mirror over the wash stand. Gracious! Her skin was a more intense red than it had been even several minutes ago. No wonder Seth had gaped at her as though her hair was on fire. What had she been thinking when she'd bought all those potions? Vanity had taken over her common sense. She lowered the wick. "Nothing to be done about it now."

Tessa whimpered.

Marvel returned to the bed, sat beside the little girl and feathered her disheveled hair away from her forehead.

"Sometimes Papa lies with us when we're a'scared," Nate told her. "In the middle 'cause then we kin both feel 'im close."

There had probably been plenty of times when two motherless children had needed the comfort of their father close by. Marvel didn't know anything about children, but she knew about loneliness and loss.

She raised the covers to crawl over Tessa and settle into a spot between brother and sister. The bed was comfortable and warm. Over the sounds of the roof creaking as the house settled and the hiss of the burning logs in the heater, she became aware of soft breathing on either side of her. A foreign sound.

The covers moved as Nate turned to lie on his side facing her, and the warmth of his hand rested on her shoulder. His breathing grew slow and even.

Tessa tossed and made little sounds of distress, but Marvel didn't think she was fully awake. After another whimper, the toddler rose and leaned over Marvel, then snuggled herself into a cuddly position half lying on Marvel's chest and hip. Hesitantly, Marvel wrapped her arm around her. Rubbing her back came quite naturally.

The little girl smelled warm and sweet, like line-dried cotton and talcum powder. The satisfactory weight of her body was a warm and pleasant new experience and Marvel tested her reaction to it with growing awareness.

So trusting. So vulnerable and innocent were Seth's offspring. She couldn't help thinking of the man conceiving them with a woman he didn't love, but she pushed away the thought. He loved *them* and that's all that mattered now. He'd honored his brother with the sacrifice of his own freedom to choose a wife. No greater love had she ever imagined than that.

Was this what having a family was like? Protectiveness and a desire to comfort and provide? It seemed her parents had always been old and ill and that she'd had to grow up to take care of them. What must it feel like for a woman to have her own family? Her own children? Her own husband?

Downstairs the clock chimed the hour, but the resonating chords barely registered. Long ago Marvel had cherished hopes and dreams. Hopes for a husband to love and dreams of children. That fantasy had been dashed by her foolishness and impetuous naiveté. She'd been so hungry for something more, so completely and blindly caught up in a delusion, that she'd thrown away her chance. No man would want her once they knew.

She'd known from the moment she'd seen Seth and his children on her doorstep that she was going to regret their presence in her home. In her life. In her heart.

It was easy to shut out desires when they were only hazy images. It was impossible to deny those same longings when they were personified. In a real man. Real children. Warm. Living. Breathing.

Tessa's sweet weight and Nate's trusting acceptance were more than she could bear, but she was unwilling to end the torture and miss one second of *feeling*. Even hurting, she'd never felt so alive.

Seth's image wavered in the dim glow on the ceiling. He'd spoken words of desire. Unashamedly revealed that he found her alluring. It was wicked and wanton to return feelings for a man so young, a man so vital and incredibly appealing, but she couldn't help herself. It could never be, but *imagining* that it could be had her tied in knots and trembling at his touch.

It was unfair not to draw a line of propriety. But her heart wanted to soar and her head followed in flights of fancy. How could it be that a man such as the likes of him could want her?

Her last thoughts were images of his face…his hands…his lips….

Seth returned in the early hours of dawn. His room still held the heat from the base burner, but the lamp wick had burned out. He approached the bed and his heart lunged in his chest.

Marvel lay with her glorious hair spread across his pillows. The redness he'd noted the night before was gone from her face. Nate lay spread-eagled with the back of a hand across her cheek. Tessa lay curled against Marvel's side. Marvel's wrapper had come open, exposing an ivory silk chemise that left little about the size and shape of her breasts to his imagination.

He couldn't look away. He didn't want to. He was torn between the maternal image of her presence with his children and the erotic vision she made in his bed. His children needed a woman, a mother. He needed a wife—and not just any wife, but the wife of his choice. He needed Marvel.

She spoke to every level of his soul. She didn't need him, not the way the other people in his life had always needed him. She was strong and capable in her own right. But she wanted him. And that *marvel* was what he wasn't about to let get away.

He'd done his best by Laura. He'd treated her with loving respect and tenderness. He'd loved her in his own way. He'd made a marriage with her. A child.

Silently he removed his boots and found a spot beside Nate. He loved this boy more than life. More than most men probably loved their biological sons. It had never mattered a lick to him that Nate was his brother's child. Perhaps the fact that he could hold and keep a part of his brother made the boy even more precious. He was Seth's son in every way that counted. Some day Seth would tell him the truth. But not until Nate was grown and ready to accept the fact.

Andrew had known Laura was pregnant when he'd secured Seth's promise to take care of his wife after his death. "Marry her, please," he'd said. "Be a father to my son or daughter."

Seth had assured Andrew he would fulfill his wishes. And he had. He had no regrets.

Especially not now. His gaze drifted to Marvel. Especially not when his life had taken this unexpected and most welcome turn. He'd found the woman he wanted. The woman who set him on fire and filled every corner of his heart. She wanted him, too, he was convinced.

Nothing was going to stop him from marrying Marvel.

Chapter Eight

That morning Marvel awoke alone in Seth's bed. In the hall she found warm water in a pitcher outside her door. She washed and dressed and hurried downstairs, prepared to find the household waiting for her to start the day.

Instead the kitchen was warm; pans littered the cabinets, and the sound of merriment came from the dining room.

Dressed in a sleeveless lavender tulle gown, a red-and-white-checked apron and a fur hat, Liberty was serving eggs and bacon to Nate and Tessa. Seth stepped from the sideboard with a plate of pancakes and spotted her. "Marvel! Did you sleep well? Come join us. We're having second helpings, and we made plenty."

Even Leo had come down that morning, and he looked pleased to be tucking away a stack of syrup-drenched pancakes.

"Good to see you present for breakfast, Mr. Brauman."

Seth rested the platter on the table, held out her chair and opened a napkin with an exaggerated flourish before laying it on her lap. "Mrs. Pargellis made tea. I'll bring you a cup."

Marvel took the platter of pancakes he handed her and forked two onto her plate in awe. "You did all this?"

"We did it together. Nate set the table."

Nate spoke up immediately. "Not with the good plates. The ever'day ones."

"Everything looks wonderful." She remembered falling asleep with the children, and wondered how they'd come to rise and dress without waking her. Seth had obviously returned sometime during the night or early morning and hustled them from the room in silence. "This has never happened before. No one but me has cooked breakfast in this house since…well since I don't know when."

Seth poured her tea. "You certainly look refreshed and lovely. Did you enjoy your extra hour of sleep?"

Delight shimmered in her heart at his compliment. "I did, thank you."

She'd only taken enough time to assure herself the redness was gone when she'd looked in the mirror, but perhaps the orange flower therapy had been beneficial. She couldn't shake her amazement over this man's interest.

"I'm afraid Babe has injured his foot," he told her, seating himself across from her and speaking of the other doctor. "It will heal, but for now he has to keep it elevated and not put any weight on it."

"I'm sorry to hear that."

"It means I'm going to be supervising the work on the house at the same time I'm taking over Dr. Solomon's patients. My hours will be monopolized, I'm afraid."

"How can I help?" she asked immediately.

Liberty placed two eggs and a few slices of crispy bacon on Marvel's plate and Marvel thanked her.

"The roof is repaired the best it can be until spring and it looks solid enough. It was only one small spot where a limb had done some damage. The rest is sound.

"Most of the heavy work is coming to completion, so I would

appreciate your input on the kitchen. And paint for all the rooms. Perhaps you could select rugs and wall coverings."

"Goodness! You don't want to do all that yourself?"

"Is it too much?"

"No, it's just, well I might not select the same carpet you would. You said you have furnishings in storage. What if I pick something that clashes?"

Seth's gratitude was obvious. "I'm sure you'll do fine. You can run anything by me for my opinion if it makes you more comfortable. Your help will relieve a huge burden."

"All right," she agreed with a flick of her hand, then dug into her food.

"Are we gettin' a buggy today, Papa?" Nate asked sometime later.

Marvel glanced at Nate, then in the direction of his concern. Outside the dining room windows a heavy snow was falling.

"I'd have to ride to the livery and bring back a buggy, Nate. Then I either have to keep it all day or go get it again before I pick you up. It's easier if you and Tessa ride with me."

Nate didn't say anything.

Marvel didn't like the thought of the children going out in another snowstorm. "Why don't you let them stay here today? I'm not going anywhere, and it seems a shame for them to go out in this weather."

"Nate has school," Seth reminded her.

"Oh. Of course," she replied.

"Although if the children from the outlying farms don't come in, the teacher may have only a few students and send them home." Seth glanced from Nate to Marvel. "I can send word to both Mrs. Porter and the schoolteacher not to expect Tessa or Nate today."

Nate grinned and turned to his sister. "We getta stay with Miss Marvel!"

Seth's gaze touched on Marvel's pleasure in the children's re-actions. He remembered her lying in his bed in the hours before daylight, and he could picture seeing her that way every morning for the rest of his life.

She met his eyes over the tabletop, and the conversation melted away. He wanted nothing less than to make this woman his wife.

As could be expected of December in Colorado, snow con-tinued to fall throughout the week. Seth assured Marvel that once it had stopped and the streets had been cleared there would be plenty of time for her to run errands for his house. Meanwhile he filled his position as town doctor ahead of schedule, moved Babe Solomon to a rented room where he could tend the man's injured foot away from the last of the heavy cleaning and work on the house.

That left Marvel to discover the intricacies of full-time care-giving for young children. Their honest observations and blunt comments made her laugh. Their sweet natures and painfully naive attitudes made her cry.

In the short time since the Paxton family had arrived on her doorstep, she'd grown accustomed to Nate's ceaseless chatter and fond of Tessa's cherubic smiles. Their presence added a di-mension that had long been missing in her home. Children brought new life and contagious vitality to the big old house. Their presence turned her thoughts from passing years and lost dreams and focused them on the here and now.

On Saturday while Seth was occupied with a delivery at the train station, she gathered the children and the necessary ingre-dients in the kitchen and stoked the steel oven.

The room was so warm, they worked with their sleeves turned back. Marvel had fashioned Tessa's hair in a topknot like her own and given them both an apron.

"My mother used to make these cookies when I was a little girl, and I've made them every Christmas since. It's a lot of fun, because we get to roll out the dough and cut it into shapes."

Nate studied a bottle of dark heavy liquid. "What's that stuff?"

"It's molasses."

"Ain't that for animals?"

"Sometimes ranchers put it in grain, and I heard Hazel Keaton say she fed it to her goat, but its flavor is what makes these cookies so special."

"Me gonna help make cookies, too!" Tessa said emphatically.

"Yes, you are. I need your help for this."

Marvel measured ingredients for a double batch and instructed the youngsters when to add the cups and spoonfuls of ingredients as she stirred. The dough got thick and dark, and the ginger and clove made the mixture smell just the way she remembered from her childhood.

"Okay, it's time to roll it out and cut shapes," she told them.

She showed Nate how to use the heavy rolling pin, then took over and smoothed the dough.

"A star!" Tessa said, holding up a cutter with a red-painted wood handle.

"Where'd you get these fancy cutters?" Nate asked.

"I ordered them from a catalog a long time ago."

Each of the youngsters took a metal cutter and pressed shapes, which she helped arrange on baking sheets. "Now they go into the oven. After they're cooled, we'll make icing and frost them."

"Acky!" Tessa had bitten one of the unbaked stars and spit a mouthful of gooey brown dough onto the tabletop.

Marvel didn't blink an eye before grabbing a rag and wiping up the table and the child. She poured her a cup of milk. "They're better baked and frosted, baby."

Tessa took a long drink, then grinned at her with a white mustache. "Nancy wants to help, too."

Marvel washed her hands and helped her down. "Run along and find Nancy."

She switched baking sheets, and Nate doggedly cut shapes until all the dough had been shaped and baked into cookies. "Stay right where you are while I go find your sister," she told him. "Don't touch the baking pans or the stove because they're hot."

"Yes, ma'am."

She found Tessa in the parlor, sleeping on the floor with her doll while Liberty played the piano. "She has an appreciation for music," Liberty told her.

Marvel picked up Tessa and carried her up to her cot, where she tucked her in for a nap. Brushing hair from her forehead, she pressed a kiss to her hairline. She didn't know how wise it had been to offer to keep the children with her all week. Holding them at arm's length had been much better for her heart. She tucked the doll into Tessa's loose embrace.

She'd been selfish, really. Mo Porter was a kind and caring woman who took care of them well. The night Marvel had comforted them after their father's hasty departure had changed her. She'd had more than a glimpse of what she'd missed out on. Now it seemed she wanted more than was safe to want. More than she deserved.

Leaving the door open, she returned to the kitchen, where Nate waited obediently.

"She's sleeping, so it's you and me icing these cookies," she told him.

"Papa says t' give every job your best," he replied.

"Let's give it our best, then." She hugged him and he returned the embrace so naturally it brought tears to her eyes.

Using the hem of her apron to blot the moisture, she silently chastised herself. What was she doing falling in love with the doctor's children?

An odd scratching sounded at the door behind them startled

her. She turned and approached to cautiously look out onto the back porch. She couldn't see anyone, but soon a whine joined the persistent clawing.

Nate's eyes got as wide as saucers and he jumped down from the chair where he'd been perched to join her. They exchanged a glance, and Marvel slowly opened the door.

A yellow dog with snow caked in its dirty fur leaped into the room and pounced on Nate. Chunks of snow landed on the floor.

"Fearless!" The boy chuckled and sputtered, and the dog licked his chin and cheek in a joyful reunion.

Marvel watched with chagrin and a measure of awe. That animal had found its way back again! Strange town and all. The smell of wet dog mingled with the once-appealing aroma of their baking. The dog lowered itself to all fours, sniffed the air and shook. Ice chunks flew in all directions.

Nate looked up at her as though she was the master of a guillotine and the mutt was a convict ready to walk the stairs. At that moment more ice was melting in her heart than on her varnished and waxed floor. Now she knew why Seth had corralled the animal in a cage and traveled with it all those miles from Denver so as not to cause the boy distress.

Denying the freckled imp was impossible.

"I think the frosting is going to have to wait a little while," she told him. "Fearless is in need of a bath."

Nate's grin lit the winter day and warmed her heart even more. What was she doing?

"Papa!" Tessa shrieked, and ran toward the foyer. "We made goat cookies!"

Marvel and Nate glanced at each other, then followed at a more sedate pace. Dog bathing, brushing and drying, kitchen cleaning and then bathing themselves so they could finish the cookies had been exhausting.

"Goat cookies?" Seth hung his coat and hat, rolled his holster and placed his .44 on top of the clock, then bent to pick her up. "Meaning they're made from goats or made to feed to goats?"

Tessa blinked at him with a finger in her mouth.

A questioning look at Nate and Marvel didn't encourage an answer, either. "Well, let's have a look at these cookies."

He followed the entourage to the kitchen and came to a complete and stunned stop when he saw the clean yellow dog with the shiny coat lying beside the range chewing on a soup bone.

"Look, Papa! Fearless found us again."

Seth's gaze rose to Marvel's and she avoided it.

"We gave 'im a bath and made 'im smell all better so he didn't stink up Miss Marvel's house."

Marvel poured glasses of milk and arranged spice cookies with shiny white frosting on a blue transferware plate. Seth placed Tessa on a chair and took a seat, bowled over by Marvel's change of heart.

The taste of the cookies was like nothing he'd ever tried before. They were soft and spicy with hardened icing, and the cold milk was a perfect companion. "Have I ever mentioned what a good cook you are?" he asked.

Her smile reached her eyes. "I don't recall."

"Add that to the list of things I appreciate about you, then."

"What's 'preciate, Papa?" Nate asked with a little furrow between his brows.

"Well. When we appreciate someone it means we're thankful and admiring of the way they do a certain thing or the way they look or what they've said. I think Miss Marvel cooks delicious meals and keeps a warm, inviting home. I also think she's beautiful and generous and quite smart."

"Me'n Miss Marvel is bof pretty," Tessa added.

"That's right," he answered.

"I 'preciate you, too, Miss Marvel." Nate's blue eyes showed his sincerity, and the ring of cookie around his lower lip made her grin.

"Thank you both." She stood and picked up the pitcher of milk. "You're going to teach him to be a smooth talker if you're not careful."

Being able to come home to this woman would be the best turn he could imagine his life taking.

"Let's go into the drawing room and give Miss Marvel some time alone before supper," he suggested. He didn't want to wear thin the level of acceptance she'd shown them recently.

Later, after preparations for the meal were well underway and Liberty hadn't shown up to help as she usually did, Marvel found everyone in the drawing room. A wooden box half-full of stereoscope slides was on the low serving table, and Leo and Liberty each held a viewer. Seth and the children were sorting slides into piles.

"Where did all of those come from?" Marvel asked.

"Babe was going to toss them out—the other viewer, too, so I rescued them. There are hundreds here, Marvel. Leo especially likes the Taj Mahal."

"I saw it back in '34," he said, turning to Marvel.

"You've been to *India?*" She stepped into their midst. "You never told us."

"I was in my twenties," he said.

Leo had been drawn from his room more and more since Seth's arrival. Intrigued as much as the others, she listened to his story and took a turn with the viewer until she remembered her boiling potatoes and dashed for the kitchen.

Supper was a lively chatty event, and after the dishes were washed and put away and the boarders had settled into their rooms for the night, Seth put the children to bed, then found Marvel ironing costumes in the kitchen. Fearless lay contentedly nearby, napping.

"If you wouldn't mind," he said hesitantly. "Tessa's asking for a good-night kiss."

She blinked at him before comprehension dawned. "From me?"

"Do you mind? I can put her off, but she's pretty determined."

"I don't mind." She hung the shepherd garment beside the last one she'd pressed and hurried upstairs.

"Good night," she told Tessa.

The little girl opened her arms for a hug, and Marvel embraced her and kissed her cheek.

Nate studied her from his place in the big bed and she paused beside him. "Good night, Nate."

"Night, Miss Marvel. "I 'preciate the very good potatoes an' gravy. I 'preciate you bein' nice to Fearless, too, and lettin' 'im come in outta the cold. An' I 'preciate you got hugs for Tessa. She's still a baby an' babies need lotsa hugs."

"Everyone needs hugs, Nate. Not just babies. I didn't even know I needed hugs until I met you and your sister."

"An' my dad. He gots strong hugs."

She leaned over the bed. "I think I need one of your hugs tonight. Would that be all right with you?"

He sat up and wrapped his arms around her neck. Tears prickled at her eyes, and her nose got tingly from holding them back. She cupped the back of his head and held him close for a moment, feeling the rapid thud of his little heart against her shoulder.

"Thank you, Nate. I appreciated that hug."

He settled back on the pillow, adjusted his head to one side and closed his eyes. Marvel tiptoed out of the room, closing the door softly.

Seth was waiting for her in the kitchen. He'd taken the dog out, then brewed a pot of tea and set the pot along with two cups and the sugar bowl on a tray. "Shall we sit by the fire for a while?"

She followed him into the drawing room and pulled two chairs closer to the fireplace. Nails clicking on the floor, Fearless followed and settled himself neat as you please on the hearth.

"He will sleep in the kitchen," she told him firmly.

Seth nodded, then sweetened her tea and handed her a cup.

"I'm still not used to anyone doing things for me," she said. "Especially…"

"Especially?"

"Especially a man."

He grinned.

"A handsome *young* man."

He looked up in surprise.

Marvel took a sip, remembering he'd called her beautiful and uncertain of her feelings about that.

Seth didn't take the chair, but instead moved a velvet tufted ottoman so he could sit near Marvel. He didn't pick up his cup.

Sensing the anticipation he exuded, she forgot to take a drink. "What is it?"

"Marvel."

She widened her eyes in reply.

"I know we haven't known each other long. I looked at the calendar today, actually, and was amazed because it seems I've had these feelings for a lifetime."

When he spoke of his feelings, her heartbeat zigzagged in disbelief. "No, it hasn't been long," she agreed.

"I don't want to wait. I've missed enough and maybe you have, too, so that's why I'm going to say this. Ask this."

"What?" she asked, searching his blue, blue eyes.

He took the cup from her and set it aside, then reached for her hand and placed it against his shirtfront where his heart beat in a solid steady rhythm. "You have my heart. I told you I'd never felt this way about anyone before and it's true. Please don't get the wrong impression, that I need someone to take care of my children or make them a home, because I've done that already. I'd be asking this if I didn't have them."

"Wait," she said, sensing with foreboding dread what was coming.

"I can't wait. I can't let you slip away."

"Seth, don't do this."

"Marry me."

Chapter Nine

Her heart stopped.

The fire crackled.

His heart chugged beneath her fingers.

Heat climbed her limbs and infused her body. The heat of shame and regret and helplessness. "I...I can't."

Had she spoken it or had it been only a keening cry of disappointment from her soul?

"Are your feelings for me merely—" he swallowed "—physical? Don't you think you could love me?" His forehead wrinkled in concern.

Marvel wanted to weep. Everything inside her ached. She didn't want him to think he wasn't the best thing that had ever happened to her. "It's not that. Not at all. You're—" she poured her feelings into searching his gaze "—you're more than enough. You're perfect."

"Then what?" he asked.

"It's me," she told him, the words an ache in her throat. "I can't marry you. I can't marry anyone. Oh, I—" she pulled her hand away and balled it into a fist on her knee "—can't make you understand."

"I'll try to understand," he assured her. "Just tell me."

Marvel stood, the impact of what he was forcing her to say stirring annoyance to life. She stepped away from the heat of the fire and pulled back the curtain to look out at the darkened yard. Snow glistened in the moonlight. "You're not unintelligent, Seth. You're not blind. All you have to do is look at me."

"I look at you all the time." His voice indicated he was still across the room, and she exhaled with relief. Her resistance was weak. "You're beautiful," he told her.

"I'm too old for you." There she'd said it. He'd made her say it. "I've been on the shelf for quite some time, and the years aren't going to turn backward. It's a simple fact of life." She released the curtain and composed herself to face him.

He'd stood but hadn't moved closer. "How old you are doesn't make one bit of difference to me."

"How can it not?"

"Have I ever behaved as though I even noticed or cared? What do a few years mean? Nothing if two people love each other."

He meant those words. She knew he did. He just had no idea what he was considering. "My parents were older when I was born. My mother died and I grew up without her."

"You're not as old as your mother was when you were born, are you?"

"Not yet, but you want a wife who can give you more children, don't you?"

"Well. Yes." He looked puzzled. "How old *are* you, Marvel?"

She walked toward him. "I'm thirty-three. How old are you?"

"Twenty-six. That's only seven years difference. Plenty of women have children well past your age."

"Not their first children and not with men who are so much younger than themselves," she argued.

"I never realized you had these feelings," he said.

"Henry's wife was many years older than him," she told him. "He spent the last ten years taking care of her, and now he's looking for a new wife. I don't want to be a sick old woman you have to take care of."

"Marvel," he said kindly, coming closer. "You're not that many years older. When I'm fifty, you'll be fifty-seven, not ninety. We have a lifetime ahead of us to share."

She shook her head and avoided him to return to the chair. The buoyancy she'd experienced the rest of the week dissipated, leaving her feeling sullen and discouraged. She'd known from the first moment she'd laid eyes on him and his children that the axis her world revolved upon was going to be shaken if she wasn't careful. And once again she hadn't been careful.

"I'll change your mind," he told her.

"You won't. You can't."

"I think I can."

"How? You can't turn back the clock seven or ten years…and if you did you'd be only— Good gracious sixteen years old! You'll never catch up. I'll never go back. We are what we are."

He knelt beside her knees and reached for her hand. Cupped her cheek. "I don't see years when I look at you. I see the woman I want for my wife."

"That will change," she told him. "The more years that pass, the more the difference will show."

"No. It won't. Why are you so stubborn?"

"Why are you so foolish?"

"Because I'm in love."

The words drove a deeper pain into her chest.

"That won't change," he told her. "And if you'd let go of your vanity for five minutes you'd see that I'm a person worth loving, too."

"I never said you weren't."

"Then love me, Marvel. Let me love you."

Vanity, was it? Vanity to not want to saddle a vital young man with a woman who would eventually become a burden? Vanity to believe he had better options? "I'm tired."

He released her and backed away. "You should get some sleep, then. We can talk when we're both rested."

Standing to her feet, she picked up the tray. "Sleep won't change anything."

Leaving him to take care of the fire and the lamps, she swept from the room. She left the pot and cups for morning and hurried up to her room ahead of him.

The array of potions and miracle cures littering her bureau accused her of the same vanity he had mentioned. Of course she was concerned with aging. What unmarried woman wasn't? What woman who'd ever received the attention of a younger man hadn't been? What rational thinking person didn't consider and prepare for the future?

Marvel couldn't turn back time.

If she could, she would turn the years back to a lonely time when she'd been caring for her bedridden father. When a young man with flattering words and captivating smiles had offered her a few hours relief from the drudgery and promised blue skies and undying devotion. If she could undo that mistake, perhaps she could consider Seth's insistence that the years between them didn't make a difference.

But she couldn't do that. So, looming between them was not only a chasm of years, but the shadow of her shame. She didn't believe in magic or miracles or even happily-ever-afters. Not anymore. Hope was for the young. Passion was a self-delusion that led to trouble. It wasn't real or lasting, and it certainly wasn't meant for her.

It was midnight before a lonesome howl carried up the stairs. Half an hour later, Marvel loosed Fearless from the kitchen, followed him up the stairs and watched him sniff the bottom of the door that led to the Paxtons' room.

She opened it enough to let the dog slip through and returned to her bed. They'd all be gone soon, anyway. What difference did a few nights make?

Tick. Tick. Tick. The middle week of December moved past with agonizing slowness. Marvel's eyes had been fully opened to all she'd missed out on by the turns her life had taken—by the choices and mistakes she'd made. Each day she witnessed a slice of life the way it unfolded for other people.

By the following Tuesday the sun had melted snow and turned the roads to muddy ruts, but she had promised to help Seth with his home. The sooner she did it and the dwelling was finished, the sooner he would move and her life could go back to normal.

He wasn't letting her off the hook easily, however. He sat with her on the evenings he wasn't working, kissed her senseless whenever her guard was down and continued to prove in countless ways how empty her life had been before his arrival.

It was Saturday, one week before Christmas, and he had taken Nate and Tessa to Mrs. Porter's before riding out to call on a woman whose baby he had delivered a few days earlier. Marvel stood in his newly repaired and painted house inspecting the wallpaper that had been pasted that week and the floors that had been sanded and varnished to a dark sheen.

At the first of next week the rugs would be delivered. She would hang drapes and Seth could have his furniture brought from storage.

There was a knock at the door, and she laid down the clock she was holding to answer. Babe Solomon stood in the doorway, his winter coat bundled around him and a cane supporting his weight. "Come in, Dr. Solomon," she said quickly.

"Just wanted to have a look around before I head out. My train leaves this afternoon." He limped from the parlor down the hall to the kitchen, and she followed. "Doesn't look like the same place."

"No, it's all new," she answered.

He sized up the office section of the building. Seth had ordered partitions constructed so that two patients would have privacy while others waited in a narrow room with a rack for books and newspapers. Seth's equipment had been delivered and set up. Glistening glass-front cabinets held the latest utensils. Easy-to-read labels identified containers and vials and bottles of medicine.

"He wasn't what I was expectin'," the doc said.

"Me, neither." She'd imagined someone older. Someone... not like Seth.

"Thought he'd be a young pup fresh outta school who thought he knew it all and had a point to make." He chuckled. "He ain't like that a'tall. He's a helluva doctor. And a fine man to boot."

She could only nod.

"Don't 'spect he'll be single long," he said.

She shot her gaze to his face.

He grinned. "Got any thoughts on that?"

Was her desperation obvious? "Why would you ask me that?"

He wandered back through the door that divided the offices from the living quarters and paused before reaching the door. "Just somethin' I picked up on when I was around 'im. He talks about you."

"Oh?" She pretended interest in a speck of paint on the woodwork and scratched it with her thumb. "What does he say?"

"Just what a fine woman you are." He reached for the doorknob. "Your father would've liked 'im."

She absorbed those words slowly. Dr. Solomon had spent a lot of time with her father during his illness. Sometimes he'd come by just for a chat, and she'd appreciated the effort he'd made to break up her father's week with a visit. "You were good to my father, Doc. Thanks for everything you did for him. And for me."

"You spent a lot of your life doing the right thing, Marvel Anne. Makin' selfless choices. Do somethin' for yourself now before you regret that you don't."

He limped out onto the porch. She closed the door behind him and leaned back against it. Letting Seth anywhere near her house had been a huge mistake. No longer could she deny that she wanted more. How could she go back to life the way it had been before he'd melted her resolve and made her feel again?

Chapter Ten

A<small>s</small> the community bustled with activities in the week preceding Christmas, Marvel made a decision. Each night after the boarders and the Paxton family went to bed, she crept down the stairs and pulled on a paint-spattered apron, opened her valise of oil paints and meticulously clean brushes. The invigorating glow of anticipation caught her anew each time.

As always the sight of the paints cast a challenge. Individually, the colors were plain, garish even, but in combinations and variations, the exquisite possibilities were limitless. She loved it when she found just the right eye-pleasing shades and shapes to transform the canvas into a creation of beauty.

This midweek night she worked on the pillars across the porch of her fabricated house, using white softly blended into shades of red, yellow and black to produce a pleasing illusion of light and shadows.

Humming softly, she lost herself in the freedom of expressing romance and beauty. She was penciling in a trellis when the sound of footsteps startled her. Placing a hand over her racing heart, she spun to face Seth, who stood just inside the doorway. "Oh!"

He studied her in the glow of half a dozen oil lamps, strands of her shiny hair fallen loose around her face and a braid trailing down her back. She made a lovely picture in a silk wrapper and paint-mottled apron that emphasized her narrow waist and the curves of her breasts.

She glanced over her shoulder at the half-finished painting, then back.

"You started painting again," he said.

She nodded.

He stepped closer, and she moved aside. Studying the half-finished rendering of a small house and blooming garden imbued with shades of rose and gold, he recognized the same energy that was in the paintings she'd shown him. The same acute awareness of that missing factor was coming to life even in this unfinished state.

"The family's just out of sight," he said. "Inside, perhaps, or at the far edge of the garden."

He turned and found her warm gold-flecked gaze on his face. Her attention wavered from his eyes to his lips and back. Seth couldn't resist the temptation of kissing her. Her lips were warm and soft and the same reassuring sense of completion settled over him as it did each time he held her. She pulled away first.

"Why do you do that?" he asked, turning again to the canvas.

"Do what?"

"Make the people just out of reach? They're so real that the onlooker can feel them, but they're elusive. Faceless."

"I don't know," she answered. "I never thought about it like that. I just paint what I feel."

"And you feel…in the shadows? On the edge of life? Just out of reach of having what other people have. Is that it?"

A pained expression drew her brows together. "Maybe that's it."

Without hesitation he pulled her close and held her, not caring if paint touched his clothing. If only he could make her see how much she had to offer, how much he wanted to give her, how good a life together would be if she would let it happen. She relaxed and they stood that way, holding each other, feeling each other's heartbeat.

"We'll be moving soon," he told her. "I don't intend to let that separation in our living arrangement dissuade me from convincing you to marry me."

He leaned away to touch her cheek with the backs of his fingers and gaze into her eyes. "That missing 'something' is right here for the taking."

"What makes you so sure you're what's missing for me?" she asked.

He shrugged and took a step away. "Neither of us will know unless you give us a chance. I'm counting that you will."

He turned and left the room.

Marvel tore her gaze back to the painting. Could she live the rest of her life with what-could-have-beens? What-should-have-beens? Could she pretend that nothing had happened and that she was satisfied with this big old house? It was likely her current boarders wouldn't be around in another ten years, and then what? Take in a few more elderly renters to give her purpose? Nothing wrong with that—if all she wanted was more of the same lackluster life she'd been leading.

She could still feel the imprint of his fingers on her cheek, as she would always feel the impact of his love on her heart. This life would ever be enough again.

"What about a tree?" Nate asked at breakfast Friday morning.

"It's Christmas Eve," Seth mentioned to Marvel.

"If you and your father want to bring home a tree, it's all right with me," she said to Nate.

The boy let loose with a shout of excitement, then got up from his chair to hug his dad and Marvel in turn. "This is gonna be the bestest Christmas ever!"

That day she carried cartons of ornaments down from the attic and moved a chair and ottoman in the drawing room to make space for the tree.

Seth had carefully trimmed it and shaken loose needles before he brought it in that afternoon.

"Papa rented a wagon and we found the most beautifulest tree in the world," Nate declared. He'd removed his boots and stood in his wool socks and damp trousers, his shirt charmingly untucked.

"Pretty tree!" Tessa said, pointing.

"I think hot cocoa is the first thing all of you need," Marvel said after regarding their reddened cheeks.

She prepared it and carried a heavy pitcher along with stoneware mugs to the hearth where Seth had stoked the fire.

Mr. Brauman had heard the ruckus and come to see what was going on. Liberty had dressed in a brown skirt and ruffled white blouse that day and fashioned her silver hair into a chignon, nary a paper flower or a drapery tassel in sight. Now she sat in a chair near the fire and watched the children's delighted faces.

Marvel showed Seth the boxes of delicately painted German ornaments she'd carried down.

"I think you'd better hang those," he told her.

"We need popcorn," Nate said with concern furrowing his brow.

"We do?" Marvel asked.

"To string on the tree," he explained.

"Of course. I'll go pop a big pan full."

Fearless ate as much popcorn as eventually got to the tree, because every time a kernel fell while the children were stringing kernels on thread, he snapped it up and sat watching for more.

Seth had thought to order and bring home a basket of cranberries. Liberty enjoyed threading the berries into chains.

The tree was soon lush with both elegant ornaments and handmade touches.

Seth held Tessa above his head to place a glittery papier-mâché star on the topmost branch. He and Nate got a dustpan and hand broom and cleaned up the rug and the floor along the wallboards.

"I haven't seen a tree like this since my Alfred brought one home the year our son was born and decorated it for him. I strung the cranberries."

Marvel was sitting on the hearth near Liberty's chair. She looked into the old woman's lucid brown eyes. "I didn't know you had a son, Liberty."

"His name was Roy. He was a frail little thing. Never looked healthy like these children. He was sickly, and the doctors said his heart hadn't developed quite right. I had a fever whilst I was carryin' him and I always knew that was what caused it."

Marvel had never heard the woman speak so coherently or of anything so personal. This revelation took her by surprise.

"He was only three when he died. It was a relief, to tell the truth, after watching him struggle for every day he stayed on." Marvel could only imagine how many years ago that had been. "Alfred put up a tree every year after that, and we sat together and remembered our boy."

"I'm sorry," was all Marvel could think to say.

"Don't be sorry for me. We never had any more children, but Alfred was a wonderful husband. A good man. I loved him beyond measure. Besides losing Roy, and besides the mistakes we made along the way, we were happy. And we were content. Life is about starting over is what Alfred used to say. We started over every Christmas Eve. I wouldn't have missed a moment of it. Not a moment."

Marvel's eyes burned with unshed tears. She covered Liberty's hand with hers and saw the truth of those words in the old woman's eyes as she gazed at the Christmas tree.

Life was about starting over.

Not remorse. Not looking back. Not what might have been. About today. And tomorrow. With no regrets.

"You're like a daughter to me, Marvel Anne," Liberty said, looking directly at her now. She chuckled and corrected herself with, "Or rather like a granddaughter."

Marvel smiled through a blur of tears.

Liberty patted Marvel's hand on the back of hers. "Thank you for every day."

"Thank *you*."

"Don't hold back."

Not anymore. "I won't."

Darkness blanketed Carson Bend as the household dressed for church and rode in the buggy to arrive early for the pageant. Nate and Tessa had parts in the play, so they had to dress in their costumes and rehearse with the rest of the children while the adults visited with the cheerful citizens and sipped hot apple cider.

Eventually the children took their places in the front of the church. The older ones took turns reading the Christmas story from the book of Luke, and the younger ones acted out the parts. Nate wore one of the new shepherd costumes Marvel had sewn while Tessa was a sleepy lamb who leaned against her brother's leg and nodded off.

Seth made his way down the aisle amidst chuckles to pick her up and carry her back to the pew where she slept on his lap throughout the rest of the program.

Impatience quickened Marvel's movements and compelled her to say her goodbyes and help Liberty and Nate with their coats while Seth carried Tessa to the buggy.

Liberty had been chatting to Missouri Porter about piano lessons and her schedule, so Marvel knew the woman's moment of mental clarity had passed. She took her hand, thankful for those few hours and Liberty's peace of mind.

She was intent on securing some time alone with Seth and finally had an opportunity to speak to him as she helped him removed Tessa's coat. The sleeping child made the process a chore.

"I want to talk to you," she told him, her stomach taking a nosedive now that she'd gotten that far.

"All right."

"Alone," she added.

"As soon as the children are settled I'll be down."

She nodded. "I'll be in the kitchen."

She hurried to the kitchen and rolled out a couple of pie crusts. She had them filled with sliced apples and was making lattice tops when Seth returned.

"You're baking this time of night?"

"Tomorrow's Christmas and I just wanted to have a few things ready ahead of time."

"You seem a little nervous."

She slid the pies into the hot oven and wiped her hands. "Yes. Well. There's something I want to tell you."

He picked up an apple peel from a pile on the table and nibbled it.

"Maybe you should sit," she said.

His eyes widened, but he accommodated her request.

She had trouble looking at him. Maybe this hadn't been the best place. Or the right time. Her chest ached with heaviness. Maybe she should wait for Christmas to be over before she opened up this whole uncomfortable business and changed his opinion of her.

"What is it?" he asked.

"Perhaps this isn't the right time," she said. Her hands were cold now.

He leaned from his chair to snag one of her hands and pulled her closer to where he sat. He raised her fingers to his lips for a kiss that sent her heart skittering like a girl's.

"Are you planning to tell me we've worn out our welcome and you're tossing us out tonight?"

"Of course not."

"You've changed your mind about that smelly dog and he has to go back outside."

She shook her head.

"What then? You've sold a painting to the Louvre and you're an overnight success in the art world. Perhaps you're leaving for Paris and—"

"Stop. It's not silly. It's serious. It's...it's why I said I couldn't marry you. Why I know you won't want me. It's a secret I need to share with you. Even if it changes how you feel about me."

He didn't release her hand. He just looked at her expectantly. "All right."

"My father was ill for a very long time. I've told you that. Eventually during that time money ran out. I had to keep the house going, had to pay for his medicine and doctors, and that's when I first got the idea of taking in boarders. My father was furious about the idea and the intrusion into our lives, but I think that was just his pride. He didn't approve, but I had to do it."

"It was a wise choice," Seth told her.

Her knees were trembly, so she lowered herself to the chair beside his. "We'd been close, my father and I. I didn't have friends or outside interests, and..." She waved her hand. "I'm making excuses. I was lonely."

Seth's blue eyes still shown with acceptance and trust.

"A young man boarded with us for a few months. He was

interesting. Had traveled to all parts of the country and done many different things."

As soon as she'd said those words, Seth's heart ached with the words and the truth of the hurt that he knew was coming next. This was Marvel's burden. The shame she carried and used as a defense against caring and loving anyone who got too close. He didn't want to hear that the conclusion he'd swiftly drawn was true. He didn't want to think of her pain, but she had to say it. He knew she had to say it.

"He told me he was changing his plans to travel and that he wanted to stay put for a while. Later, after time had passed and my situation had changed, he would take me with him and we'd see cities and new places together."

The smell of cinnamon and apple surrounded them as the fruit baked. The heat of the stove warmed their sides.

"I believed it all. He came to my room and…" Her eyes didn't quite meet Seth's any longer.

Because she was the most courageous person he'd ever known, he would expect nothing less than this painfully honest admission. "He took advantage of you."

"I wanted him to. I liked it. That's the most shameful part." Tears escaped beneath her lashes and moistened her cheeks and lips. She raised her free hand to wipe them away.

"Marvel." Seth slid from his chair to kneel in front of her. "It's not your shame. You were young and alone, hungry for a diversion from your life, from the pain of seeing your father dying. He took advantage of that."

"I didn't tell my father, of course, but I think he knew. Somehow he knew. I disappointed him." Her voice broke.

"You were disappointed and feeling hurt and guilty. I'm sure your father didn't know."

"But, Seth, now you can see it's not just years between us, it's what I did. Even when Henry asked me to marry him, somehow I knew I never would, so I never contemplated telling him. But now that you've asked me, now that I have this…this burden of *hope* inside me, I have to face what happened."

"Marvel." He got to his feet and pulled her to stand before him. "I'm sorry for the hurt that stupid boy caused you. I'm angry about the years of guilt and regret you lived with. Whatever happened was a long time ago, and it doesn't make any more difference to the way I feel about you, or the fact that I love you, than those years you think are so all-fire important.

"I love you, Marvel Anne Henley, world-class kisser, painter extraordinaire."

His acceptance touched every cold, lonely place inside her and made them as warm as the heat that radiated from the oven. His smile brought a lump to her throat and new hope to her soul.

"We never have to talk about it again," he told her. "You never have to think it matters one bit to me, because it doesn't."

She leaned into him and their lips met in sweet abandon. For the rest of his life when he smelled apples baking he would think of this moment, the moment that Marvel gave her heart to him.

"I love you," she said against his lips.

He'd never heard sweeter words. "And I you. I have something to share with you, as well, before you agree to be my wife."

"You're not getting out of this now," she warned him.

"I don't want out. Ever." He explained to her then about the circumstances of Nate's birth, about how he'd come to take his brother's place as Nate's father.

She laid her hand along his jaw. "You're the man I want loving me for the rest of my life."

"So you'll marry me?"

"I will. I want us to be a family."

He kissed her until her head swam.

"We have a big day ahead tomorrow," he told her. "Christmas Day and our announcement and all."

"A big day indeed," she agreed.

"We'd better get some sleep."

She smiled and leaned into him. "I don't think there's any chance of that, Doctor."

His laughter rang in the warm cinnamon-scented kitchen.

Upstairs, Tessa stepped over the softly snoring dog to climb into bed beside her brother. "Hear that, Nate?"

"What?" he asked in a sleep-slurred voice.

"St. Nicholas!"

The dog got up and sniffed both of them, then lay across the foot of the mattress.

"You're dreamin', Tessa. Go to sleep."

* * * * *

FALLEN ANGEL

Jenna Kernan

Dear Reader,

I love this holiday. Christmas holds so many special memories for me.

Every December my family would don snow boots and mittens to search our hillside for a Christmas tree. Our scrappy, pliant pines showed many gaps, but I never noticed. To me, they looked perfect. This is why it seemed natural to begin my first Christmas novella with the selection of that all-important tree.

While locating my setting for this story, I searched for a grand old hotel in a snowy spot with surrounding mountains and plenty of pines. The Strater, in Durango, Colorado, fit the bill. When I discovered that a few rooms even had pianos, I knew I had found the place, changing only its name to The Gilford.

Abby and Ford are in for a trying time this holiday, but in the end they will realize that Christmas is not really about the tree, the cookies or the carols—it is about family and it's about love.

I hope you enjoy this slice of Christmas past. Merry Christmas to you and yours.

Jenna

JENNA'S CHRISTMAS BREAKFAST SCONES

Ingredients:

2–3 cups ready-made biscuit/pancake mix
1/2 cup sugar
1/4 cup softened butter
2 eggs
1/2 tsp vanilla
1/2 cup cream
1/2 cup green candied citron
1/2 cup sweetened dried cranberries
1/2 cup golden raisins

Topping

1/4 cup light cream
2 tbsp sugar
Citron/raisins/cranberries to garnish

Preheat oven to 400°F. Mix ready-made biscuit/pancake mix with sugar and cut in butter. Set aside. Mix eggs, vanilla and cream. Add these ingredients to the dry ones and blend thoroughly. Set aside some candied citron and a few cranberries and raisins to use later as a garnish, then stir the remainder into the dough. Add additional flour (up to a cup) and blend by hand until the dough is firm enough to shape. Divide the dough into two equal pieces. On a floured surface press the dough into a circle, approximately one-half inch thick. Brush the surface of the dough with cream and then sprinkle generously with sugar. Cut the dough into eight wedges, as if you are cutting a pizza. Transfer the wedges to a greased cookie sheet. Garnish the scones with the remaining citron, cranberries and raisins.

Bake for 10 minutes only. Scones should be pale, never brown.

Directions for preparing scones ahead: Prepare scones as directed, but stop at the point before you coat the dough with cream. Then freeze the scones on a cookie sheet. Once they are frozen, store them in a freezer bag for up to three weeks. You can take them out Christmas morning, then brush the surface with cream and decorate before baking.

This story is dedicated to all the Christmas angels
out there who know the joy of doing for others
during this season and all year round.

Chapter One

Durango, Colorado, 1887

A Christmas tree did not seem too much to ask. Getting the mule to cooperate in this endeavor turned out to be another matter entirely.

Abby March paused on the hillside, just east of Durango, to wipe the sweat from her brow. Her breath came in small vaporous puffs in the crisp December air.

Her eight-year-old son, Daniel, had done without many things of late and if he wanted a tree, she was bound and determined to get one, even if that meant slogging through snow on the hillside above the main road. She would do anything for her son. The borrowed mule, however, was not like-minded on the topic and turned out to be as stubborn as, well, a mule. He regarded her with big brown eyes from his sitting position as she wondered how to overcome their impasse. She, at least, wished to be home before nightfall.

"Here's one, Mama!" called Daniel, the excitement ringing in his voice.

Abby tugged hopefully on the bridle. The mule only blinked

at her, so she tied him to a tree and waded into the drift that topped her shins. She found Daniel with his hand proprietarily on a small spruce that topped his height by more than two feet. It was a very pretty tree, with wide green branches and a symmetrical shape. Daniel had even managed to place one of his red mittens on top of the evergreen, where the star should be.

As she drew near, she realized two things simultaneously: first, that Daniel was dangerously near the edge of the cliff and second, that they were not alone.

A man huddled in the cover of a wide juniper on the steep rise behind her son. The rifle he shouldered appeared to be pointing directly at Daniel.

Her heart clenched in horror as she dashed through the snowdrift. In those seconds of her waking nightmare, she feared she would lose her son, as well. The undisturbed snow slowed her progress as the man cocked the trigger and closed one eye.

Finding her voice, she shouted, "Daniel, get down!"

Her son's gaze flashed from his mother to the stranger. But instead of doing as she bade, he swiveled to look over the cliff on which he stood.

He cupped his bare hands to his mouth and shouted. "Look out, mister!"

The stranger rose up as Abby dove, her fingers clasping around cold steel as the shot cracked, vibrating through the barrel and scorching her fingers. A second shot sounded from the road below her and a pain, hot as a branding iron, seared across her left shoulder. The shooter shook her off and she fell into the snow. He stepped over her and raised his gun again, pressing his cheek to the stock. She did not see him fire as she turned to find her son. Daniel stood slack-jawed beside his little tree then took a step backward. His arms waved as he tottered and then tumbled over the cliff.

"No!" she shrieked, reaching out for him, but found only one arm responded to her command.

Again, the crack of the rifle came from the road. Beside her, the stranger staggered, dropping his Winchester, before toppling facedown into the snow.

He lay unmoving, but she did not pause to tend him. Instead, she crawled on hands and knees toward the little tree. Her vision swam and her shoulder burned with each breath, but she forced herself onward. She knew she had been shot, but it would not stop her from reaching her son. Abby made it to the place where Daniel had stood moments before, proudly claiming his little tree. Beside the packed snow she found the other red mitten.

She cried out, bringing the damp wool to her mouth and then forging on to the precipice.

Abby held her breath as she peered over the edge. Daniel sat in the snow a mere three feet down, safe on the little shelf that kept him from a fall of more than thirty feet. Relief washed over her as she realized he was unharmed.

On the trail below, someone shouted, but she needed all her concentration to reach her son.

"Mama?" He stared at the blood that flowed from beneath the cuff of her worn coat, painting her hand crimson. "You're shot."

"Come now," she motioned, startled at the breathy quality of her voice.

She reached with her good hand and Daniel stood to clasp it. He was small for his age and for once she was glad. Had he weighed even one more pound, she doubted she would have had the strength to drag him to safety. In a moment he was in her arms.

She tried to hold him, but he wriggled free.

"Hey, mister! Hey, up here! My mother's shot!"

She wanted to ask him who he saw, but she could not seem to form the words. Blood warmed her side and she glanced down, quite glad that her threadbare brown coat was thick enough to hide the sight from her son. She must stay awake to help him. She would not die here on the mountain. That much was certain.

Altogether too many people had abandoned Daniel in his short life, and she would not be added to the list. They needed to cut down that tree and bring it back to town before nightfall. She needed…

Abby slumped to her side and realized she lay beneath Danny's little spruce. His red mitten still topped the tree, shining bright against the gray sky.

"Mama!" Daniel sunk to his knees beside her.

She smiled up at him. "It will make a fine Christmas tree, Danny-boy."

Abby meant only to blink, but when she closed her eyes, she found she could not open them again. The last thing she heard was her son's frantic voice.

"Mama? Mama! Mister come quick, I think she's dying!"

Chapter Two

Ford Statler had just stepped into a nightmare. Images and sights blurred together as he left his horse to scale the cliff face. Above him the boy shouted for help. His muscles strained and his boots slipped as he scrambled up the icy hillside. What in the name of heaven had he done?

He recalled the warning cry and then the man drawing a bead on him. He never would have had his rifle out in time, if not for that boy.

What was a child doing up on the cliff?

The first shot had sparked off the rock to his left. So he had returned fire. Anyone would. He had aimed at the center of the man's brown coat, but as he had squeezed the trigger the image shifted into a man and a woman fighting over the gun.

He had seen her fall and the horror of that moment had paralyzed him until the shooter lifted the rifle again. Ford aimed higher this time for a head shot, and he had not missed.

He grasped an outcropping of rock and heaved himself up to the small ledge near the top.

"Mama?"

The panic in the boy's voice urged him on as he hoisted himself the final feet to reach the pair.

The boy's pinched face glistened with tears as he cradled his mother's head in his lap. A cascade of dark-brown hair spilled out over his narrow legs and onto the snow.

"Mister, she's bleeding bad."

Ford glanced at the motionless shooter still clutching his rifle. He kicked it away and then knelt down beside the woman, staring at her upturned face. Her pallor and beauty combined to give her the countenance of some otherworldly being. She reminded him of an angel fallen to earth.

"My God," he gasped.

"Mister, you gotta do something. You gotta save her."

The boy's words snapped him to action. A cold, stabbing panic ripped through him as he noted her shallow breathing. His gaze traveled south, taking in the torn wool coat where his bullet had rent the fabric. Her blood dripped relentlessly from her motionless fingers, melting the white snow beneath them.

Ford unfastened the buttons of her coat and lifted the flap, pausing too late. The boy had seen the blood. His pallid skin made his wide blue eyes seem huge in his small face. He wore no hat or gloves, and his light-brown hair stood up in all directions, reminding Ford suddenly of a street urchin.

"Is she dead?"

"No, son. She's breathing." Ford lowered the flap. "That man over there, you know him?"

"No, sir."

"Go fetch his rifle and gun belt."

The boy hesitated, though whether from fear of the corpse or the unwillingness to leave his mother, Ford could not tell.

"What if he isn't dead?"

"He is." Ford spoke with a confidence born from seeing his shot hit home.

The instant the boy was on his feet Ford lifted the coat. Blood soaked her bodice as far as her waist. He had to stop the bleeding.

He lifted her to him, surprised by how slight she was. It was why he hadn't seen her immediately. Her height, brown hair and her draping coat had made her nearly invisible against the larger man.

He glanced at her face once more, wondering why a woman of such beauty wasn't dressed in bright colors. If she were his, he'd dress her in red velvet. What had gotten into him? She wasn't his, nor did he want a full-time woman. No, surely he did not want that ever again.

But she sure was his responsibility.

He ground his teeth as he stripped back the woman's coat.

He glanced at the boy, finding him holding the rifle and staring at the corpse. If he could think of another way to distract the child, he would have taken it. Perhaps a stranger's blood was easier on the eye than the blood of a loved one. He'd always found it so.

Quickly Ford tore the woman's blouse, baring her shoulder. What he found relieved him somewhat. The bullet had cut away a strip of flesh and some muscle of her left upper arm, but was not deep. The amount of blood surprised him. It seemed too much for such a shallow wound. The gash was as long as his index finger. He probed the area, but found no shattered bone. A mercy, he thought.

A flesh wound. But to have damaged such perfect flesh made him physically sick. He drew out his handkerchief, fresh and clean from a laundress in town. The scent of bleach and soap greeted him as he pressed it to her shoulder.

She groaned softly, but did not rouse.

Guilt flooded him. "I'll take care of you, angel. And I'll try to make it up to you, I swear."

"Mister?"

The boy stood beside his mother looking wary and uncertain. He'd retrieved his hat and held the rifle in one hand and the gun belt in the other.

"Wound's not deep, son, but long. That's why she's bleeding so. We need to bandage it. Drop those and hold the kerchief."

The child dropped to his knees and pressed the cloth into place, while Ford tied it with his yellow neckerchief.

"Why you up here?" asked Ford.

"We were getting a tree."

Ford's brow wrinkled. "A tree?"

"For Christmas."

He'd nearly forgotten, or hoped to. It was late December. Ford propped the woman up and waited a few moments, relieved to see that the blood did not soak through the cloth.

"You know that feller?" The boy motioned at the body.

"'Fraid so."

"Why'd he try and shoot you?"

"Keep me from shooting him, I expect."

"You a marshal?"

"Bounty hunter. Name's Ford Statler. What's yours, son?"

"Daniel, Daniel March, sir." The boy removed his hat and extended his hand. It appeared his angel was raising a gentleman.

He took the boy's small, cold hand in his and felt a fresh pang of guilt. He released him as quickly as possible.

"Well, Daniel March, I want to thank you for saving my life."

The boy flushed with pride and then seemed to remember his ma.

"Is she going to be all right?"

"I imagine she'll feel poorly for a while. Where's your pa at?"

The boy studied the snow before his feet, and Ford braced for bad news. "He ran off when I was four. Ma doesn't like to talk about him on account of her parents turning her out for marrying beneath her, but he was taller than her by several inches, I swear." He met Ford's gaze with a face that shone with truth and innocence. Ford nearly had to look away. "Anyway, that's what I heard my Aunt Barbara tell Ma. But then *she* stopped coming round, too."

He glanced at the woman taking in the worn coat and shabby black boots. Abandoned first by her family and then by her husband. She had taken a hard fall, indeed. "You have a horse?"

"Mule. It's Mr. Krasnoff's back at the stable." Daniel's eyes rounded as he remembered something. "We got to have him back by dark. Ma promised."

"We best get along, then. You think you can fetch that feller's horse?"

Daniel turned a full circle looking for the animal.

"Just follow his tracks, son. I'm going to carry your ma."

Daniel set off at a run and in a moment had disappeared from sight.

Ford left the woman to check on Donahue. He used the toe of his boot to roll the body to its back. Snow clung to his beard and open eyes. Ford studied the face he had seen only on wanted posters. He was even uglier in person.

Ford narrowed his eyes. "That'll teach you to blow up trains that still got folks riding in 'em."

Donahue had picked the high ground, waiting to murder him as he passed beneath on the road and he would have killed him with that first shot, if not for his guardian angels.

"I found the horse!" shouted the boy.

"Bring it here."

The boy emerged from the brush leading a bay gelding, saddled and ready to ride.

"Think you can lead my horse up here?" asked Ford.

The boy nodded.

"Where's that mule?"

"Over that way." He pointed and then left the reins of Donahue's gelding in Ford's hand.

The horse didn't like the smell of blood, but he managed to

get Donahue's body tied down onto the worn saddle. As he did so, he noted the poor condition of the horse's feet. They were worn down and unshod. The horse stared balefully at him.

He stroked the gelding's thick winter coat. "We'll see if we can find you an owner that gives a damn."

Ford located the mule and tied it to the gelding then returned to the woman, finding her shivering. He sat in the snow and drew her into his arms, unbuttoning his coat to bring her closer to the warmth of his body. He hummed as he rocked her, knowing there was no one to see, no one to mock the bounty hunter who knew a lullaby. This one, "Cockles and Mussels," had been one of Ellie's favorites. He exhaled against the painful memories as he held the woman. Gradually her shaking stopped. He'd feel a damn sight better if she'd open her eyes.

He heard the thump of Dancer's feet before the boy appeared, dwarfed by the blue roan quarter-horse that trailed patiently behind him.

Dancer had always been good with children, back in the life before everything changed.

Ford stood, bringing the woman up with him.

"Come take charge of your ma." He waited until Daniel was seated before lowering her to the boy's lap. He couldn't account for his reluctance to let her go, but it troubled him as he tied Donahue's horse to Dancer's saddle. He returned to lift the woman and waited as Daniel hobbled to his feet.

"Legs gone all pins and needles," he explained, thumping his thigh with a small fist.

"Can you climb onto that mule, Daniel?"

The boy scampered up and Ford mounted Dancer, still holding the woman to his chest. She seemed to fit there somehow.

But that was crazy. Hadn't he spent the past eight years avoiding the fairer sex? Living solo was the only way he knew to avoid suffering that kind of sorrow again.

He gazed back over his shoulder at the boy.

"Ready?"

Daniel gripped the mule's mane and nodded. He clucked his tongue and Dancer was off at a smooth walk that reminded him of a rocking chair.

Ford stared straight ahead trying to ignore the ache that holding a woman brought to him. Her warmth seeped into his skin, making it feel hot and itchy. She smelled of vanilla and nutmeg. He inhaled her fragrance, isolating the earthy scent that was all her own. At last he could ignore her no longer and he gazed down at her angelic face. Her lips were parted and her breath came slow and even, as if she only slept.

He needed a distraction.

"How you holding up, son?"

"Fine, sir."

"You can call me Ford."

He gleaned no response to that, so he studied the road. Only a quarter mile to the center of town. He could see the blacksmith's already.

She snuggled in his arms, her long fingers clenching the front of his sheepskin coat as she buried her face in the lamb's wool.

The simple gesture aroused him, and he found himself gasping at the cold air. Ahead he sighted the railroad depot and warehouses. He had only moments left to hold her. Regret pierced him.

Once she awoke, she'd want no part of the man who put a bullet in her and he could hardly blame her. But deep in a place he didn't allow to do much talking, he heard the voice of hope. He squashed it immediately. This woman—any woman, it did not matter. What was gone was lost to him forever.

He knew full well that the last thing in this wide world he needed was a woman and a child. And that was why he couldn't understand why he longed to brush back the dark strand of hair that fell over one cheek.

"You know the doc?" asked Ford.

"Which one?"

"Any one—a surgeon. He's got a shingle over there." Ford pointed at the house with the evergreen garlands draping the porch. "See it? The brick one."

"Yes, sir."

"Run and tell him about your ma. Bring him to the four-story hotel on Third Avenue."

"We got a room above the milliner's on the north end, Ma says it's just temporary."

Ford did not think he could feel worse, but this news brought him lower.

"*I'm* getting her a room. You fetch the doc."

Daniel's mouth formed a little *O* and then he slid off the mule and dashed off to do Ford's bidding.

The woman's fingers kneaded his coat lapel and then slid into the gap. He inhaled sharply as her hand stroked him. For a moment he wondered just what she did here in town. The most obvious sprang to his mind first, along with a surprising surge of jealousy. But she didn't dress like a whore. His experience with whores was that they spent most of their money on under-garments and opiates. Seeking confirmation, he recovered her seeking hand and studied her fingers. Her nails were chipped, short and free of polish. He turned the palm face up and discovered calluses at the base of each long finger. His angel earned her living on her feet.

When he glanced at her face he found her eyes open and staring up at him. They were large and a startling pale blue like a summer sky. She blinked, sending long dark lashes fanning her pale cheek.

"You've been shot, angel. I'm getting you help."

Her full lips parted and she struggled to speak. Her word came on a breath, just a whisper.

"Danny?"

"He's fine."

Her eyes fluttered closed and she went limp once more. He peeked beneath her coat. The sight of her blood soaking the bandage twisted his gut. He pressed his heels to Dancer's flanks, urging a faster walk.

At last he reached the hitching post outside the Gilford Hotel. He slid down and then dragged her off the horse and ran into the lobby, startling the desk clerk who stood behind the counter.

"What in the world?"

"She's been shot. I need a room."

"I don't think—"

"I'll pay double the rate."

The clerk straightened. "This is the Gilford, sir. We don't do such things."

Ford loomed. "Listen, mister, this woman gets a room or you're going to be sorrier than I can say."

The clerk reached for a key. "Seven is available."

"You got an adjoining room?"

"No, sir, but ten is a suite, sleeping quarters and a sitting room."

"I'll take it."

"It's thirty-five dollars a week."

"Did I ask how much it cost?"

The clerk fidgeted with his bowtie and glanced out of the large leaded glass doors to Ford's string of horses. "Good Lord, is that a body?"

"Yes. The room?"

The man's neck and face turned scarlet as he reached for the other key with trembling fingers and then glanced at his register. "We'll do this later. This way."

The clerk huffed like a small steam engine as they mounted the stairs. At number ten he turned the key and swept inside, holding back the door.

Ford stepped past the sofa and padded chairs and into the adjoining room where he laid her upon the feather bed.

The clerk hovered by the door seeming uncertain if he wanted to approach the bed as he stared at the woman. "What happened?"

"I shot her. Now fetch the sheriff."

The man did not take asking twice.

Daniel arrived a moment later.

"I found the doc downstairs in the restaurant. He's getting his bag."

"Good boy," said Ford.

Daniel ran to the bed and stood motionless beside his mother.

They waited in anxious silence until the doctor crossed the threshold.

The surgeon's skin had an unhealthy gray tint, and wrinkles lined his thin cheeks. His mop of wiry gray hair stuck out beneath his hat like steel wool. The only thing about his appearance that recommended him was his coat and trousers. They were of good quality and clean, showing he knew his trade well enough to prosper in this railroad town.

He took in the room at a glance as he continued toward his patient until he regarded Mrs. March from the foot rails. "The boy says his mother has been shot."

"Caught in crossfire," said Ford. "Bullet grazed her arm."

"Let's have a look." The doctor unbuttoned her coat revealing the drying blood.

The boy's face paled.

"Daniel," said Ford. "Your ma will want some cold water when she wakes. Can you…"

The boy was already charging out the door.

Ford helped the doctor get the woman out of her coat and removed the bandage.

The older man shook his head. "The wound isn't much, but all this blood, must have nicked the artery."

Chapter Three

Abby shifted in her sleep, and the throbbing pain brought her to awareness. She lay in that shadowland between sleep and wakefulness, wishing for a few more minutes of slumber but feeling certain she needed to do something. She always needed to do something. What was it that called to her now?

Her mistress, Mrs. Fenderland?

The memory kicked her hard in the stomach as she recalled that her employer, who had hired Abby as a companion for the journey west, had sacked her nearly the instant they arrived in Durango. The humiliation of that still tore at Abby.

She needed a job. No wait, she had one, as a cook at the Grand Victorian. Her mother would be mortified. Her daughter—a servant? But her mother would not know, since she had turned her back on her oldest girl the instant she learned of her tragic marriage.

Daniel! The image of her son falling backward through space sprang upon her like a wildcat from a cliff. The rifle, the fall.

Dear God.

She startled awake, bursting from her lethargy and coming upright.

"Whoa, there."

Abby turned in surprise toward the male voice and stared in confusion at the stranger who rested a firm hand upon her shoulder.

Where was she and where was her son?

He pressed but she resisted settling back. She knew him, had seen him somewhere. Then she recalled him wiping her brow with a cool cloth. Was that a dream?

"My son?" she whispered.

"Right as rain and frisky as a pup."

"Where is he?"

"Fetching his mama some broth."

Still she did not believe him. She needed to see her boy with her own eyes, to be certain this was not some cruel trick.

"He'll be back in two shakes of a lamb's tail, I'd imagine. Anyways, you're the one we're all fussin' about."

Abby took her gaze from the door, drawn by that velvety voice with its easy reassurance and soothing tone. It brought her to stillness as she turned to regard the man sitting beside her bed as if she were his concern. But no one cared what happened to her, not since Henry discovered there would be no reconciliation with her parents, and so no money forthcoming. Henry had wanted her for one reason only and had left without a backward glance. Small consolation that he hadn't gotten so much as a dime, but then, neither had she. A hard life lesson that, but she had gotten Danny and he was more valuable to her than any fortune.

Her guardian's clean-shaven face made it easy to admire his strong jaw, punctuated by an appealing cleft at the center. High, prominent cheekbones and unruly chestnut-brown hair that brushed his collar added to his good looks. But it was his eyes, which were the gray-green color of dried sage grass that scorched her with their intensity. In them she recognized an air of danger, and so she was not fooled by the gentle smile curving his lips. The man exuded a primal aura that frightened her.

She eased her back onto the pile of pillows, simply to be free of the heat of his disturbing touch.

"Who are you?" she asked.

"Name's Ford."

"Why were you worried about me?"

"You're the one's been shot. Don't you recall?"

Shot? Yes, she remembered now, both the blood and the pain. She shrugged her shoulder and winced.

"That's right." Again he cast her a reassuring smile that never reached his compelling eyes. "I see it's comin' back."

"Who shot me?" But she remembered that, too. It swept over her like a northeastern wind, the ambush, wrestling with the large man for the gun as her son called for help.

"You're the man on the road. You're the man who…"

The warmth left his smile as he finished her sentence. "Who shot you."

She took the news well, he had to admit, inching away only slightly as she glanced toward the door as if for rescue. He was a stranger, and all she knew of him was that he had shot her and that they were alone. If she knew the rest, she'd have real cause for fright. But he'd never killed a man not wanted for hanging and he'd never shot a woman, not until today that is.

He rubbed his cheek thinking how to set her at ease as she inched the covers up closer to her chin. He'd spent so many years stalking and killing that he was at a loss as to how to relieve her mind. He scowled. Maybe it was best for them both that she did shrink away like the others. But it hurt him to see the disquiet in her eyes. He only meant to protect her and see her well. As soon as he set things right, he'd be more than happy to be on his way.

"Did you kill him?" she asked. She held herself still, revealing her fright only by the tremor in her voice and the rapid draw of her breath.

She meant Donahue. Ford nodded and watched her gulp. Her pupils dilated, taking much of the blue from her eyes. Her terror called to him and he eased forward to comfort her. She flinched, reminding him that he was the cause of her fright. Sighing, he eased back.

She had no way of knowing he'd been careful about the men he hunted, choosing only the most savage predators for his prey. He knew two things about such a choice: the world would be better off without the men he killed and one day one of them would kill him. That had nearly happened today—if it hadn't been for her son.

He should be grateful but wasn't. For him, living meant there would be no reprieve from the sorrow, no peace from the ghosts that haunted him still. What was there to live for now except revenge?

She looked around the ornate room and gasped. "*You* brought me here?"

The music of her voice caused him to lock his gaze to hers. His breath caught again. Wrapped in a nightgown and swathed in white sheets, her hair now falling thick and loose upon the pillows, she looked even more like the angel than when he'd first beheld her.

"How's the arm? The doc left you some laudanum."

She lifted her good hand in refusal and stared at the door. "Not until I see Daniel. Could you, I mean, would you be so kind as to locate him, please?"

How she talked made it damned difficult to refuse, but Ford was loath to leave her, even for the time it took to walk to the door and shout. There was something in her eyes that spoke of peace, and peace was something he had not caught hide nor hair of in all of his hunting.

Wordlessly she implored him. How many women had cast their eyes on him begging for, well, one thing or another, and always he had been unmoved. But her distress caused his gut to twist. He gave a nod and rose from the place he had not left since he deposited her in that bed many hours before.

Abby stifled a gasp as he turned from her bed. Only then did she note the true size of him. Her gaze slid over his broad chest and down to the crisscrossing gun belt slung low on his right and left hip. The holsters looked worn but the steel of the handles appeared lovingly tended. The fluid ease of his stride reminded her of a stalking mountain cat. It rekindled her original impression that this man was as wild and dangerous as the predator he so resembled. The speed with which he reached the door brought her uncertainty back in full measure.

Who was he?

He opened the door and bellowed her son's name into the dark hall. If Daniel had a lick of sense, he'd run in the opposite direction. But it was only a moment before she heard the familiar pounding of small feet on the stairs. Her heart leaped with gratitude.

"She's awake, son."

Daniel burst into the room, slipping past the menacing stranger as agilely as an eel cuts through water. He slowed his run as he neared her bed.

Ford was struck by the look of pure joy and relief that shone on her face. She extended her one good arm and her son leaped, like a pup, to her side.

He noted the look of pain that wrinkled her brow as Daniel bounced the bed in an effort to reach her, but not a whimper issued from her pressed lips. As she wrapped her arms about her child, he thought of his little girl. The wave of sorrow nearly buckled his knees. Damn them both for making him remember. He had set Ellie's memory aside most days, not thinking of her, because thoughts of his little girl always ended in images of her death. He believed himself a strong man, but he wasn't strong enough for that. He reached for the door and stepped into the hall.

"Thank you," she said. He glanced back and saw her face, wet with tears.

He paused.

"Thank you for watching over my son."

He nodded, intending to close the door firmly on the scene of tender affection, but found he could not. His gaze fixed on the woman, Abigail, as she brushed the hair back from her son's forehead.

"I fetched the doctor for you," said Daniel proudly.

"You did?" Her gaze flicked to him, still standing in the shadows of the hallway like a thief. Her eyes held a question, as if trying to calculate his part in her coming here.

"Ford, he carried you all the way here."

She cast her troubled expression on him again and then returned it to her son, forcing a smile. "Did he?"

How could the simple upturning of her soft, full lips hit him like a well-placed punch to his gut?

"And where exactly are we?"

"The hotel, Mama, the Gilford."

Abigail paled and tried to sit up. Ford found himself at her bedside before she could remove the coverlet.

"The doc said you're to lie still and let that wound knit."

"Oh, but a hotel. We can't afford it." Her wide eyes seemed to take in the size of the room for the first time and she gasped. "Oh, no. This is a terrible mistake."

"No mistake," said Ford. He didn't want to touch her again and so could not explain why his fingers curled around her un-injured shoulder. She trembled beneath his touch and he wondered if it was fear or desire that caused her disquiet. There was no mistaking his reaction. For the second time today he felt a yearning along with the aching need to protect her. He never thought to care a lick about anyone ever again, and that included him. But it was natural to feel this way, wasn't it? After all, he was the reason she was lying there in the first place. He just felt responsible for her troubles.

Keep telling yourself that, Ford.

He eased her back onto her feathery cushion and stepped quickly away. "I got the room. You're not to worry about it."

"But, Mr. Ford, I can't pay you back. I've hit a rough patch, you see."

His temper flared. "Did I say anything about you payin' me back? Did I?"

She instantly dropped her gaze to the snowy coverlet, and guilt pricked at him again. *It's not enough you shot her, now you're yelling at her.* He wasn't fit company for proper folks. Somewhere over the years he'd lost the capacity to be civilized. Yes, he'd lost that with the rest.

"I'm so sorry for presuming, Mr. Ford."

He rubbed the back of his neck. "It's just Ford. That's my first name. Ford Statler, and I'm asking you to allow me to pay for your room. It's little enough to do after causing you and your boy such trouble."

Trouble—ha! That was one way of saying you bloody well shot her. If she'd been a few inches farther to the right the bullet would have hit her in the spine. That thought sent a shudder down his back.

"Mind if I sit here a spell?" He motioned to the chair he had claimed after the doc finished putting stitches in her shoulder. It was his fault an ugly red scar now marred the perfection of her skin and would do so for the rest of her life, he supposed.

She nodded and he sank into the seat, feeling the springs just beneath the fabric.

Abby eyed the man beside her bed. He looked miserable as

a dog with a face full of porcupine quills. It showed the man had a conscience. That in itself was rare enough. Henry was certainly never bothered by one.

"Can you account for how I came here? I find I don't recall with any clarity."

Her language was sure high-brow, like she was a duchess or some such. He gave his jaw a nervous rub, gathering his thoughts when Daniel jumped in.

"We were going to get my tree, remember? Mrs. Marshall allowed you to have a half a day off and you got Mr. Krasnoff to let you borrow the mule after you promised to wash his laundry for a month."

Abby's breath caught. *The mule! Oh, mercy, had they lost it? How much did a mule cost? More than she had, that much was certain.*

"Danny, what happened to the mule?"

"Ford tied it out front with the other man's horse."

She settled back into the fluffy pillows. She hadn't had such a luxurious bed since before her marriage. She turned to the window, staring hard to keep back the wave of shame. Her parents had been right about everything, including the hard truth that he never loved her.

Tiny crystals of ice tapped against the window, white specks against the velvety black beyond.

Another thought jarred her. "But I need to get the mule back by nightfall."

Ford's broad callused hand was on her shoulder again and there was no rising against it.

He glanced at her son. "She always this much trouble?"

Danny grinned, showing a missing upper front tooth as he nodded vigorously.

"Traitor," she whispered to him.

Her guardian drew a breath as if to gather patience from the air.

"Let's go over this again. You've been shot. The mule and every other damned thing can wait, for so help me, I'll not have you—"

Whatever he meant to say never materialized as he glanced at the boy and seemed to think better of it. But she knew, heard it as clearly as if uttered. He'd not have her dying on him. Had she nearly? The thought of leaving Danny made her sick to her stomach.

"Who was the man on the ridge?"

"Name's John James Donahue. He killed—" he paused and cast another sidelong look at her son "—he's wanted in Montana and Wyoming, dead or alive."

And this man had delivered him dead. Abby studied Ford's haunted expression and rigid posture. He looked as menacing as any outlaw and wore no badge, but she held out hope.

"Are you some kind of lawman?"

The glint in his eyes and his reluctance to answer told her unquestionably that he was not.

"A hired gun?"

"He's a bounty hunter, Mama. The sheriff says he's due a reward." Daniel bubbled with exuberance while Abby recalled the man falling facedown on the ice.

She could not hide her condemnation. He saw it, and his face hardened into an unapologetic mask. For just an instant she witnessed what it must be like to be hunted by this man. All the warmth died and his gray-green eyes turned icy.

Her son scrambled off the bed to reach him. The look of admiration he gave Mr. Statler saddened and worried Abby in equal measures.

This man, this hunter and killer of men, was not the kind she wanted her son to set in high regard.

"The sheriff thanked him, too, and shook his hand," said Daniel, relaying this meeting with due reverence. "Said it'd make the rest of us sleep easier at night."

Abby cocked her head. She'd never thought of it that way. And she had seen the black, merciless stare of John James Donahue as he ignored her innocent child and stepped over her to take aim. She shuddered and glanced at Ford Statler, still reluctant to give him his due.

It wasn't as if he was ridding a kitchen of spiders. They were men, after all. With mothers and wives. And this mercurial stranger before her, who glowed with warmth one moment and froze her to the spot the next, this man was definitely not the type to whom she wished to owe a debt.

He turned his cool stare on her again, and she felt chilled to the bone.

"Something you want to say, Angel?"

She swallowed hard but found her mouth still too dry to speak.

"Good. Now you listen here. You are under *my* protection. You don't have to like it, but you best heal up, 'cause I'm not leaving till then."

Chapter Four

Judging from the woman's expression, she didn't like the situation any better than he did. Ford thought she looked as if she'd just been forced to eat a bug and didn't much like the taste. Well, that made two of them. But he'd be damned if he'd shoot a woman and leave her lying in the woods. Until she was up and about, she was stuck with him.

Lord help him, he hadn't taken charge of a woman since Rebecca. *Don't think about it. Don't.* But even as he struggled to push them down deep in his heart, he saw his daughter's innocent eyes staring up at him and felt the raw anguish that always overtook him.

He glared at the woman. She was bringing it all up again, she and her son. But she hadn't asked for this. It was just a mistake, one he needed to set right. No reason to blame her for that which was not her doing.

She tried to sit up and turned pale, relaxing back into the goose down pillow with her eyes squeezed shut, but rallied a moment later. The woman had guts, he'd give her that. He knew what a bullet wound felt like and she bore it like a seasoned fighter.

Her voice trembled, proving what it cost her to speak. "Mr.

Statler, is it? While I do not wish to appear ungrateful, it isn't proper for me to accept your kindnesses."

He made an effort to keep his jaw from dropping open. "You ruffled about taking charity or about what folks will say?"

She nodded, drawing Danny to the bedside as if to shield him from her dark guardian.

"Angel, you got bigger things at hand. That bullet nicked an artery. You nearly bled to death." He noted how her eyes widened at this. Didn't she know how grave her injuries had been? "You can't see to yourself just now, them stitches have to knit. I asked around. Folks say you're alone, working day and night as a cook. But if you got someone you want me to call, you just say so."

He waited in the silent standoff, as she set her lovely jaw.

"Thought not."

She did not go down easily, he'd give her that. For at his words, her nostrils flared and that stubborn chin lifted once more. Seemed she had nothing left but her pride, and my how fine she wore it. He could only imagine how lovely she'd look if she wasn't half-dead from blood loss.

"We'll manage."

Her snippy tone set him on edge. "That so? How?"

She pointed her icy stare at him, and he smiled at the challenge he read there.

"How you gonna wash pots with one arm? You can't even dress yourself."

She stared down at the white cotton nightgown for the first time, and her eyes widened before flashing an accusation at him.

"The doc," he said, and watched her visibly relax, "helped me."

She flushed scarlet and he smiled, enjoying her discomfort. She was a fine-looking woman, no doubt. When he helped the doc strip her down, he had told himself to divert his eyes, but he wasn't a man to miss a chance to see a woman as God made her. At the time, he saw the blood staining her side and felt sick at what he had done. But now he recalled other things, like the curve of her breasts, her narrow waist and the flare of her hips.

"He said you're to stay in that bed and drink lots of broth. I mean to see you do." He lowered his chin expecting a fight, but she only glanced about as if searching for something to throw at him. Rebecca had heaved a kettle once. But when they had made up she was sweet as sugar.

He tensed, realizing she'd done it to him again.

"I cannot stay here with you." She had not realized how tightly she gripped her son until he wiggled in an effort to escape her grasp.

"Ma?"

Abby released his hand, turning her attention to his troubled expression. No doubt their savior frightened Danny even more than he did her. She cast him a smile she hoped would reassure. "What is it, Danny-boy?"

"Are we going to miss Christmas?"

She blinked at him a moment as she tried to understand. Her smile faded as she began to consider his question. She did not speak the denial that sprang to her lips, for she wouldn't lie to him. In the past she had always managed to make Christmas special. Last year they had made ginger cookies and she had sewn him a fine new coat. But with only three days until Christmas, how could she manage?

"Your tree," she said, running her fingers through his thick brown hair. "You had to leave it."

Danny dropped his gaze to the carpet. "It doesn't matter." But his posture said otherwise.

"And your mittens?" The ones she had knit to go with his coat.

"I forgot them." He met her gaze, remorse evident in his sad eyes. "I'm sorry, Ma."

She placed a hand upon his shoulder. "You had other things to attend to."

He nodded.

"We'll have Christmas here," said Ford.

They both looked at Mr. Statler, looming from the footrail of her bed as if he belonged by her side.

"Oh, that's not necessary."

"You're going to fight me on every damn thing, aren't you?"

She was so shocked by his language she could only gasp. Danny stared at her to see what she would do next.

"By Christmas you should be up and around, barring unforeseen circumstances. If all goes well, we'll celebrate together and then part ways. How's that strike you?"

The parting sounded good, but could she suffer this man's overbearance for three days? More important, did she want her son exposed to such a man?

"Please?" Danny actually clasped his hands together before him as if praying to God Almighty.

Abby stared at her son in astonishment. Here she had been trying to think of a way to get him clear of this killer, but one look at Danny's face told her he did not share her opinion.

In that moment of indecision, Danny slipped from her bedside and scampered to stand beside the bounty hunter.

"Can we have a tree?"

"Why not?" Ford heard himself answering, but could not for the life of him understand why he was insisting. He hated Christmas and had dutifully ignored the day since he had buried his old life with his wife and daughter. Christmas had always been the happiest of days for his young family and he could not bear to relive those fleeting moments of joy. They burned him like acid for they were lost to him forever.

Danny threw himself at Ford, clutching his leg in an exuberant hug that so reminded him of Ellie his heart ached. Without thought, he placed a hand on the boy's back and thumped him like a hound. Danny broke away, grinning his gap-toothed smile.

"This will be the best Christmas ever!"

Ford glance at Abby to find her returning his worried gaze. "First we got to get your Ma well. How about you get her that broth?"

Danny ran out the door and his boots thumped upon the stairs as he made his descent. Ford watched him go and then drew a deep breath before facing the wildcat in the bed. Instead of the hostile captive he expected, he found her dewy-eyed with one hand pressed to her heart.

"That was very kind of you."

He found himself backing up, unsure how to cope with this unpredictable female. He'd just gotten used to bossin' her and quick as lightning she went gooey as heated molasses.

"What was?"

"To offer to get Danny his tree. It's his Christmas wish, that he have one, just like the other boys in his class. It's all he can talk about."

"No trouble, ma'am."

Her smile made his heart ache with its beauty. How could the curving of her full lips make such a difference in her appearance? She was radiant, blinding him as surely as the sun.

"I fear we will be nothing but trouble."

"That's why I sent him out. I wanted to make my intentions plain."

Her smile faded and she clutched the bedcovers to her full breasts, making him think of another kind of proposal.

He lifted a hand in supplication. "No, angel, nothing like that. I got no intentions on your person." *At least none he'd admit to.* He cleared his throat. "I just want to set things right. I never meant to harm you, but what's done is done and that makes you my responsibility. I'll see you through this before I set back out. Least I can do."

"I'll pay you for the room." She looked as if she had no notion as to how, but her determination was clear enough.

"No, you won't, because if I hadn't shot you, you wouldn't need a room. You'd be home with Danny's tree and I'd be lying dead in the road. Your boy saved my life. I hope you know I'm grateful."

Abby stilled as the truth settled over her. She recalled telling Danny to get down, but he hadn't, because he could see what she could not, the target of the cowardly assassin. Her son was a hero.

"He did, didn't he?"

"So are we all square?"

She had little choice. He had correctly determined that she could not work. Regardless of the scandal this arrangement would cause, she would stay in this room for as long as it took to heal. She'd lived through a humiliation far greater than this, though it had changed her, she'd admit. A woman could not suffer a divorce and remain unscathed. She had lost more than her innocence to him, she had lost her youth, for his departure had forced her to grow up. She made her own decisions now, including accepting the bounty hunter's offer.

"Yes, Mr. Statler, and I am grateful for your generosity."

Was he blushing? That couldn't be. Hardened bounty hunters did not flush.

He moved to her bedside. "So, you'll agree to my nursing and I'll agree to be gone by Christmas day—that is, if you're well."

She accepted his offered hand and found it a mistake. The strength and heat of his grasp set of small quaking excitement in her belly. How was it possible to feel this way about a complete stranger? She lifted her attention from their clasped palms to find his hot gaze upon her. She recognized the longing instantly, as it so closely echoed her own, but there was sadness, as well, and for that she could not account. He looked at her as if she broke his heart. But how could that be? He made his living hunting men like animals. Surely his heart was not subject to such frailties.

"You are sure we are not delaying you?"

"I guess I can give those rogues a holiday and just pray they don't kill anyone until I find them." His gaze turned inward, and his expression changed to stormy.

She'd never thought of bounty hunting that way, as if it were some kind of race.

"Is that why you do it?"

He returned his attention to her and, as if just discovering he still retained her hand, released it.

"What?"

"Hunt them."

His gaze lost its vulnerability, taking on a hard glint. "You ever read a bounty poster?"

She shook her head.

He reached inside his black vest and drew out a folded page. He carefully pressed the creases flat before offering it to her.

She accepted the page and read:

$1000 REWARD
John James Donahue
For Train Robbery
Dead or Alive
Notify Authorities
Denver, Colorado

"I do it for the money." He aimed a finger at the page. "A thousand dollars for killing a man who blows up trains that's still got women and children aboard." His finger trailed downward. "Dead or alive. But I only deliver them dead."

Their gazes met, and she wondered how he could sleep at

night? She made no attempt to disguise the horror she felt at his chosen profession. He broke eye contact first.

Carefully she folded the page, feeling suddenly queasy as she returned it to him.

He slid his poster into his trousers.

"I'll just get my things."

She nodded and watched his hasty departure.

Wait. Did he say he was getting his things?

Chapter Five

Independent, that's what Ford would call her. The kind of woman who did for herself or did without. He watched her hold the soup bowl with one hand and tip it so she could drink, as he sat beside her bed with a napkin at the ready. She drained the contents in four long swallows before allowing him to relieve her of the china and accept the cloth. She wiped her pretty rosebud lips and Ford tried to ignore the flip of his stomach. The throbbing in his groin was harder to ignore.

The woman went to his head like hard whiskey, but it was his lower half that worried him the most. He hadn't wanted a woman in so long he'd forgotten the burning desire. He shifted in his seat, painfully aware that these next three days would be pure torture.

Ford cast a glance at Danny, who still knelt on the chair by the window in the adjoining room, watching the comings and goings in the street one story below.

His gaze returned to his angel, roving down the column of her throat. Think of something else, you rascal. His search landed him on the outer edge of the bandage, visible at the opening of her collar. The lust swept from him faster than water swamping a canoe.

"It wasn't your fault," she said.

He lifted his gaze to meet hers. "Ma'am?"

"You didn't see me, isn't that right?"

"That damned brown coat, same color as Donahue's lambskin jacket. And your hair's brown and you only reach chin high." His shoulders sagged. "I never saw you till it was too late. I never meant to hurt you."

Her smile radiated understanding.

"Mr. Statler, it won't surprise you to learn that I have made mistakes, as well. Some just cannot be undone."

"But I'll see you back on your feet. I swear."

She rested a hand upon his. "I know."

It was a gesture meant to comfort, but as soon as Abby's palm touched the back of his broad hand, she regretted her folly. Currents of excitement flashed up her arm, warming her face. Her lips parted and she found him staring at her with undisguised desire flashing in his eyes. What was happening between them?

She slid her hand back, retreating, as if she'd just discovered she touched something dangerous. The tension remained, sizzling between them.

He cleared his throat. "You want something else?"

What she wanted was best pressed down deep inside herself, for all time. Why was she forever falling for the worst sort of man? There must be something wrong with her to have no control of her hidden desires. To let them show on her face, well, it was just not done.

She inwardly groaned as she recalled the last time she'd acted on such emotions. A disastrous marriage was the result. She knew her inner compass could not be trusted, for it had pointed her straight to Henry. Her mother had been right about the fortune hunter, and in disregarding her council, in favor of her own foolish desires, she had lost both him and her family.

Abby had no question about what her mother would think of Ford Statler.

"Angel?"

She took a deep breath. "Yes?"

"The doc left some medicine for the pain."

The pain she had was too deep for laudanum. Besides, she was not leaving her son in the company of a bounty hunter, not when Danny was at such an impressionable age.

"I just need to rest a bit."

She hoped that would cause him to withdraw, but it did not. Instead, he drew a book from his bag. "Would you like me to read to you?"

Why did it shock her so? It wasn't that he could read so much as the book he slid from his leather satchel, Mark Twain's *The Adventures of Huckleberry Finn*. She was about to refuse when she glimpsed Danny, who had left his vigil by the window and now climbed into the chair beside Statler's.

"All right."

He opened the cover and Danny dragged his chair closer to their benefactor. Abby smiled at his eager expression. Her boy loved stories. They had been reading about King Arthur together.

The bounty hunter had a low, melodious voice that mesmerized her son and caused an irritating catch in her breathing. *It's the bullet wound,* she assured herself, but did not succeed in convincing herself. The man's words melted over her like warm honey, giving new meaning to the expression sweet-talker.

She had not meant to nod off, but somehow she had. When she blinked awake, she discovered a quiet room. It took only a moment to orient herself and search for her son. He sat facing Statler across a narrow table. Both he and Danny leaned forward intently.

Poker. She scowled, drawing a breath to object when Statler spoke.

"Check."

Danny drew himself to his knees to stare at the small wooden chessboard. Abby's jaw dropped. First novels and now chess. Her first impression of this man now clashed with what she witnessed with her own eyes.

Statler pointed at a small black piece and then to another. "Castle."

Danny touched a piece and Statler shook his head. Danny retreated, regrouped and chose another, but waited with one finger upon the piece, until he had a nod from his opponent.

Her son did not play chess—until now.

This man had not only kept her active boy quiet, so she could rest, he had kept him occupied with an admirable endeavor. She glanced at the side table beyond them at the stack of dirty dishes. And kept him fed!

Gratitude bubbled within her, and she smiled at the picture they made. She had misjudged him, her Mr. Statler, seeing only the face he presented to the world. But like everyone, he had a private side and, to her astonishment, a tender one.

It seemed so out of character for a man who made his living apprehending dangerous killers to spend his leisure time playing chess. But what did she know of him really—where he came from or what he did?

She tried to sit up to better watch the game, but the movement caused a sharp pain to shoot down her arm, and a small cry escaped her lips.

Instantly he was on his feet. He reached her in two strides.

"You all right, angel?"

"Why do you call me that?"

His dark brows lifted. "When I first saw you lying in the snow, your face all pale and, well, you looked like an angel to me."

She felt her face heat, knowing she was far from an angel,

unless you measured by coming so close to death. He had a right to know who he was caring for, but it did seem hard to tell him.

"Could you help me sit up?"

He did, easing an arm gently about her and adjusting the pillows behind her back. Through the thin veil of her cotton nightgown she felt his muscles tense. He smelled of leather and coffee. Once she was settled, he hesitated as if reluctant to release her.

At last he stepped away. "How's that?"

Danny slithered between the bed and Ford's legs, gaining the position beside her.

"Ma, I'm learning how to play chess!"

"So I see." She beamed at her boy. How well she remembered playing with her brother, Keith. The smile dropped away as she remembered that her younger brother would no longer speak to her.

"Want me to teach you?"

"Oh, I play quite well."

"Do you?" Both males spoke in unison. She enjoyed their shocked expressions. It was understandable for Danny to be unaware. The last few years had left her little time for play. Her job with Mrs. Matthews and now in the kitchen took most of her waking hours. Ford knew nothing of her past and she did not really know what he thought of her, but she owed it to him to tell him, especially when he had taken them in.

She met his startled gaze. "Might we have a word?"

He nodded. "Go back to the board, boy. It's your move."

Danny skipped the few feet into the adjoining room.

"Mr. Statler, Ford. First I want to thank you for looking after Danny."

"Not necessary."

"I also felt I should warn you. I am not what you think I am."

That comment caused one of his dark brows to quirk over an eagle eye, but he made no verbal conjecture.

"You have taken us under your wing, so to speak. I feel that necessitates my telling you something of a personal nature. I would not want you to enter into this arrangement unawares, and I understand if you should feel you cannot continue to look after me."

Ford had to force himself not to lean in to catch her next words. What the devil was her secret? As far as he knew she was a lady's companion whose employer had dumped her here when she caught her husband taking advantage. Likely that was what she was carrying on about, though he couldn't care less.

She hesitated.

"Well?" He waited. "You didn't kill anyone, did you?"

When she didn't immediately refute this, he felt his stomach clench.

"Worse, I'm afraid. I am a divorcee, Mr. Statler."

His jaw dropped. Not from her silly revelation, but from the absolute solemnity with which she spoke. It gave him the distinct impression that she felt he should give a damn.

"My husband abandoned me shortly after our marriage."

Fool. That was his first thought. The man must have been blind or dim-witted to leave such a fine woman.

"I would understand if you felt you could not keep to our bargain." She lowered her head as if awaiting his verdict.

"That it?"

She stammered. "Well…why, yes."

"All righty then."

Now it was her turn to gape. "Don't you have any objections?"

He wanted to say it was the best news he'd heard all day, but he wasn't ready to go that far. Burying a woman, one you set the moon by, takes away your courage. He wasn't strong enough to stand alone over another grave. But she did make him think how fine it would be to step back into the world of the living. She waited for his answer. Was she holding her breath?

"Angel, I don't care what you did with your husband, unless there's a bounty on your head because of it. If you divorced him, I'm certain he gave you cause. Shows guts to do what you done."

She couldn't have been more shocked if he'd shaken her hand in congratulations. The event that had shaped her world had banished her from all social circles—could it be that this mattered to him not at all? Perhaps he did not understand. "But the scandal."

"I don't believe in them."

"I beg your pardon?"

"Scandals. They're for people who give a damn what folks think. I don't. Not anymore. That's why I'll be sleeping on that couch next to your bed."

"You will?" she squeaked.

"Doc says you might have a fever, and you need someone checking on you through the night. That'll be me."

She stared at her unlikely nursemaid. Tall and gruff and hard as wrought iron. He leaned and pressed his hand to her forehead and held it there, beginning his job immediately. Seeming unsatisfied, he leaned closer and pressed his lips to the same place.

"A mite warm," he whispered.

Of course she was. It was one thing for her to kiss Danny's forehead to check for a fever. It was quite another for Ford to do so to her. His nearness caused her entire body to flush with heat.

"Where did you learn to do that?" she gasped.

He gave her a wry smile. "Would it shock you to learn I had a mama?"

She sputtered. "Oh, my, no. I mean, of course you did."

He straightened and stepped back, no longer looming over her. "You hungry, angel?"

"Would you call me Abigail?"

He seemed to consider it for a moment and then shook his head. "I like angel."

She frowned.

He should withdraw, he knew it, but he hovered by her side, unwilling to break the connection that bound them. She could feel it, couldn't she?

There was no use denying it. Though he never expected to feel this way twice in a lifetime, he found himself fascinated with everything about her. That she was divorced only made her more appealing. The woman had gumption. He added that to her list of virtues and began to worry.

You made a deal. You only have her until Christmas day. And even if she did want him, he'd be a cad to accept, with her lying there vulnerable as a new foal. He had nothing to offer but a heart as withered as fruit left too long on the vine.

Loving her would feel like a betrayal to his Rebecca. His wife's death left him with nothing but a black vengeful hole where his heart once beat.

But if that were so, then why did his heart ache when he looked at her beautiful face?

Chapter Six

Abby slept fitfully during the night. Feverish and uncomfortable, she kicked off the covers, only to find the motion set forth a throbbing pulse in her arm that reminded her of a toothache.

Ford appeared at her bedside, a silver shadow in the moonlight. He was barefoot and wearing only a pair of black trousers. The perfection of his form, all muscle and grace, quite took her breath away.

"Can't sleep?" he whispered.

Her gaze swept from his dark eyes down his muscled neck to the girth of his torso, traveling lower to the juncture, where the fine dark hair met the silver buckle of his belt. He did not speak or move, seeming immobilized by her stare. When she returned her attention to his face, she found his gaze burning with heat.

"You shouldn't do that, angel."

"What?" She tried to sound innocent, but failed. Her thoughts were purely carnal and she could not deny the accusation in his gaze.

"Look at me as if I were dessert."

"My apologies." Why couldn't she look away? Now he seemed to hold her hostage. "You are finely made."

She had almost added that it had been a long time since she had seen so much of a man, and never had she seen his like. He looked like Adonis cast in silvery moonlight.

His hand pressed down on her forehead as if he had decided she was out of her mind with fever.

"You feel hot."

No doubt from his touch. He let his hand slide away slowly, trailing down her cheek.

Ford knew he should draw away, but he didn't. Instead he took full advantage of the situation and leaned forward to place a tender kiss on her brow. How he longed to slip alongside her warm body and hold her in his arms.

He drew away, regret twisting him into knots. At the wash basin he wetted a cloth and brought it back to her, placing it on her forehead.

"Would you like some water?"

She hadn't realized how thirsty she was until he asked. She nodded and he poured her a glass.

"Laudanum would help you sleep."

"It only hurts when I move and Daniel might need me."

"I'll see to him."

She gave him a skeptical look.

"I helped raise five brothers after my pa passed. We got them all grown, didn't lose a one."

"But he doesn't know you."

"He does, angel. We spent all day playing chess and reading about Tom and Huck."

Abby didn't know how she felt about that. Her first emotion was dismay, that Daniel could so easily replace her company. Next she worried about the influence this man might have on him. Danny was so impressionable, and Ford painted a romantic figure. She knew Danny longed for a father, but this wandering hunter could not be that for her boy.

More's the pity, she mused. He did have many admirable qualities, if you could overlook the dual gun belts that criss-crossed the armrest of the sofa beside her bed.

When had he moved the sofa next to her?

He caught her staring at his revolvers. "Force of habit."

"Where is Danny?"

"Sleeping on a pallet on your other side." Ford motioned into the darkness. "I got him ready for bed, washed behind the ears and asleep by nine. He's a fine boy, angel. Easy to handle." He'd been about to say easy to love. Where had that come from?

She shifted again.

"Laudanum?" he asked.

"Privy."

He flushed, glad the darkness covered his embarrassment. Anticipating her need for privacy, he had requested a folding screen. This hotel even had a chair with a chamber pot built right in. After he'd adjusted the screen and seat, he returned for her.

He helped her to a seated position. "Want me to carry you?"

"I think I can make it."

Regretfully he slid his arm from around her waist. She rose and walked, slowly but surely, until she disappeared behind the blind.

"I'll be close by. Call if you need me." He moved into the other room and added coal to the stove.

She didn't call, but the sound of the mattress squeak brought him back to her side. She lay on the bed, panting, with eyes pinched closed.

"Perhaps," she said, "I will have some laudanum."

He poured a spoonful and hoisted her as gently as possible. Her groan tore at him, and he noted she was perspiring. She downed the dose without difficulty and he set her back into the pillows.

"Won't take long and you'll be feeling no pain."

"It's warming my stomach already," she whispered. "Will you sit with me a few moments?"

He smiled and lowered himself to the mattress beside her.

"Don't you worry. I'll look after your son and everything else while you're resting." He reached for her hand, clasping it in his.

She didn't pull back, though she thought she should. But here in the darkness there was no one to judge her, no one to gossip.

Not like before.

He lifted the washcloth and bathed her face and neck. Next he moved to her arms, up and down in a slow, rhythmic pattern, soothing away her worries. Ford would watch over her. She had no doubts. For reasons she did not understand, she trusted him.

Then she recalled the last man she had trusted. How wrong she had been. And if she could make such a mistake once...

His outline grew hazy as she opened her mouth to speak. Struggling against the drug did no good.

Danny. No.

She slipped away, drifting on a warm sea, descending down and down until her mind lost touch with her surroundings.

When next she moved, the sunlight fell across her bed. She peered at her hands, neatly folded upon the white sheet.

Her mouth felt dry as cotton and a bitter aftertaste remained there.

Water. She was so thirsty.

Abby reached for the glass on her bedside table and succeeded only in knocking it to the carpet.

"Welcome back, missus." The female voice bore a distinct Irish lilt.

Abby turned to find a young woman wearing the attire of a chambermaid, perched in the chair beside her bed, knitting on the sleeve of a gray wool sweater.

"I'm Bonnie Leary, missus. Mr. Statler asked me to sit with you until he returned."

"My son," Abby croaked.

"He's gone, as well. Off on some secret adventure and no word on where or when. Thick as thieves those two, if you don't mind me saying so." The woman lowered her knitting and retrieved the glass, easily pouring water from the pitcher and offering it.

Abby's thirst vanished in a wave of panic. He had her son and she'd allowed it by taking that vile drug.

She forced herself to a sitting position, disregarding the stabbing pain the movement caused. "When did they leave?"

"Just after breakfast." Bonnie's startled expression showed that she had thought nothing of their disappearance. "He said not to wake you."

Abby threw her legs over the side of the mattress. "Get my clothes, Bonnie. Hurry."

"But he said you're to stay in bed. You've a fever and Mr. Statler said—"

Abby's temper flared. "He has my son! God only knows what has happened." Tears burned in her eyes, but she refused to let them fall.

Bonnie rushed to gather Abby's garments and lay them on the bed. "Your boy seemed more than eager. I never thought— should I call the sheriff?"

"Yes. Hurry and get some help."

The maid ran from the room.

Abby abandoned her bloomers and stockings and slid into her dress, succeeding in slithering through the skirts. She could not get her injured arm into the sleeve but did manage the other.

Where would a grown man be taking a boy, when his mother had her back turned? All sorts of nefarious possibilities bubbled into her frantic brain. She had done it again— trusted a man blindly and without reason. And now he had Danny.

With her dress gaping over her nightgown, barefooted and with her left sleeve dangling from her side, she rushed across the room just as the hotel door burst open.

Chapter Seven

"Mama, look!"

Danny held his red mittens aloft, grinning widely.

She gasped, dragging him to her with more force than necessary. "Danny!"

He stilled as she sank to her knees before him. All the exuberance fled from his features as he realized her fright.

"Mama? You're bleeding again."

She ignored him, gripping his shoulder tight as she scanned him for injuries. "Where have you been?"

"We were just—"

"What have I told you about going off with strangers?"

"But it was Ford. We just—"

"—worried me half to death."

Ford arrived, with an equally jovial grin on his face and a Christmas tree slung effortlessly over his shoulder.

One glance and he dropped the tree, rushing to her. She stared in shock as the pieces of the puzzle fell into place.

"It's my tree, Mama. Ford said I should have it."

Her lip began to quiver as Ford reached her.

"All right now, angel. I got you." He lifted her into his arms, cradled her as if she were a child. He carried her to the bed and laid her gently upon the rumbled coverlet. "Danny," he said, not taking his eyes off Abby, "Go fetch the doc. Tell him what happened."

She was crying now. Relief and shame swirling within her like a tornado. Tears coursed down her cheeks as she tried to catch her breath.

"I thought, I thought—" But she couldn't voice the evil deeds she had marked against him.

"I should have woken you. I should have had your say-so. He's your son, after all, and you don't know me yet, not really. But you were finally resting after tossing half the night." He tucked her legs back beneath the covers. He drew her dress up about her hips and gently lifted it over her head, then cast it aside. "I'm so sorry, Abby. I hadn't the right. He's your son, not mine." But he wished it weren't so. In only two days the boy had wheedled into his heart like a weevil in a cotton boll. "Rest now. You have to lie still."

He wiped the tears from her cheeks. "Come here, angel."

Ford drew her into his arms, holding her tenderly. Her tears burned him, scalding like boiling coffee.

How could he do something so lame-brained? He had been a father. He knew the panic that came from losing sight of your child. Memories of the day by the lake rose in his mind. He and Rebecca running along the shore, scanning the murky water. The horror of that moment filled him anew, and he felt his own eyes mist.

"I'm sorry, angel."

"I just don't want anything to happen to him. He's all I have."

He knew too well what resulted from losing all you have. He was living proof of the scars left by such bereavement.

"I just wanted the boy to have his tree. I swear, I'm dumber than a coal bucket, sometimes." Her weeping tore at his heart.

The heart he thought he no longer had, was alive and aching once more. He'd tried to keep it safe, but she had brought it back to life with her tears. "Quiet, now, or you'll pull out them stitches."

He drew back enough for her to see the unshed tears clouding his eyes.

"Ford? What is it?"

He couldn't tell her about Ellie. He tried to tell himself he did not want to burden her, but that was a lie. He didn't want her to know that he hadn't been able to keep his own child safe. "I'd never hurt your boy."

Abby stared a moment and he nodded.

"My heart knows that. But my mind wouldn't listen." She searched his expression of grief. What had happened to him? She hoped he might tell her, but the seconds ticked by and he only pulled her close, his rough cheek nuzzling her neck. She tried to draw him out.

"You lost your pa when you were a child?"

"He died during the war, in Andersonville. I was sixteen."

Another piece of the puzzle that was Ford Statler slipped into place. Growing up without a father, just like Danny. It was hard on a boy.

He drew back and she lifted a hand to cup his chin, studying his expression. Where she had once seen only the hardened stare of a killer, now she discerned the mask that hid his grief. Why hadn't she seen it before?

Was he trying to drive everyone away, to keep himself from losing another loved one?

"You lie back now and wait for the doc." He eased her to the pillows.

She did, putting her faith in this strange, haunted man. They waited in silence. He never let go of her hand until Danny returned with help.

The doctor discovered she had torn out several of her stitches, and she had to endure the process once more. Ford sent Danny out for that ordeal, and she found herself grateful once more. By evening she felt weak as water but well enough to eat.

After her supper Danny and Ford erected the tree, nailing the base to wooden cross braces and placing it opposite the fireplace, within the adjoining room, giving her a clear view from her bed.

"It looks much bigger inside, doesn't it?" She looped a hand around Danny, who now sat perched beside her on the bed.

"Only two more days and it's Christmas." Danny's voice rang with excitement.

Abby's heart clenched, knowing she had no gifts to hang from his lovely tree.

"Needs some decorations, don't you think?" asked Ford, regarding the tree with arms folded before him.

"Back home, we used to string popcorn," said Danny.

"That's a start." Ford scratched the dark shadow growing on his chin. "Can you mind your ma while I see about a bowl?"

Danny leaped off the bed, bouncing with excitement. "And darning needles and thread."

Ford rested a hand on the boy's shoulder, bringing Danny to stillness. "You can't jostle her, son. Keep still when you're on that bed."

"Yes, sir." Danny crept back to her as if balancing a book on his head. "I take good care of her."

"I know you do." Ford winked at Danny and then disappeared.

When he was gone, Danny took over as chief caregiver.

"Do you need another pillow?" The solicitousness in his tone warmed her heart. This was a side of her son she had not seen. She had spent most days caring for him, and with no younger brothers or sisters, Danny had little opportunity to be in charge.

"I'd like more tea, please." She tried not to smile as Danny carefully poured a cup. She didn't need to tell him that she liked it sweet with one spoon of sugar, for he had taken note of that. He cautiously lifted the cup and saucer, holding it out to her.

She accepted the cup, leaving him with the saucer, and took a sip.

Danny hovered. "Is it too cold?"

It was, but she'd swallow her tongue before she would tell him. "It's perfect."

He grinned, perched on the chair by her side.

"Danny, about Christmas, I don't think we'll be making cookies this year." She watched him nod as if he already knew as much. "And with all that's happened, well, I haven't made you anything. I'm so sorry, I don't want you disappointed."

"That's all right, Ma."

He was taking this news better than she expected.

"Saint Nicholas will bring me something, if you can't."

Her heart sank. She had not the heart to tell her little boy that he wouldn't be coming this year, either.

"What do you want for Christmas, Ma?"

"Oh, I'm just happy we are both safe and together." She tried not to think of the gun she had seen pointed at her boy, but the image would not be put aside.

Danny fidgeted in his chair as she finished her tea. The instant the cup hit the saucer he sprang to his feet.

"Do you want to play chess?" The eager expression on his dear little face chased off the fatigue.

"Only if I can be white."

Danny hurried to retrieve the board.

That was how Ford found them, with their heads bent over his chessboard. Abby's hair falling in wisps about her face. In the lamplight, her hair glowed with red highlights. She moved her castle into jeopardy and he frowned at the foolishness of the move, until she lifted her head and winked at him.

She was letting Danny win!

Danny leaped to his feet, in a hurry to take her poorly played piece. The smile on her face as her son seized her rook left no doubt that she was throwing the match. He disapproved. Danny should have to work to beat her. How else would he get better? How else would he feel true satisfaction at the win?

He cleared his throat. Danny glanced up, still gripping her white castle as he danced across the room to him.

"Mama's playing me in chess!"

"Is that what you call what she's doing?"

His comment sailed over Danny's head, but did gain him a conspiratorial smile from Abby. It warmed him like no fire had ever done.

He stepped into the parlor and laid the large box on the end table. "Getting dark. Best light the other lamps, Danny."

It was a task she never allowed Danny, but he took to it like a fish to water. Perhaps she should have given him more responsibility, instead of treating him like her baby and not a boy nearly out of short pants.

Ford moved in close. "How are you feeling?"

Her arm ached and she felt clammy, but she forced a smile. "Wonderful."

"Well enough to help trim the tree?"

Her heartbeat accelerated at his words, leaving her to wonder if it were the festivities or his proximity that caused her dizzying thrill.

"Oh, yes," she said, sliding her feet off the edge of the bed.

Before she could take the first step he gently lifted her into his arms.

"Oh, Mr. Statler, I can walk, I do assure you."

"You look about done in."

Did she? The thought of looking tired and ill before him robbed her of some of her delight. She felt the bone weariness, lurking just below the surface, but pushed it back. She relaxed in his arms and allowed him to carry her to the sofa.

Ford put her in charge of where the decorations were hung, while he and Danny labored like factory workers to produce strings of popcorn and cranberries. Ford had purchased red ribbon, which he tied onto the boughs.

Finally he opened the great box, revealing tiny kerosene lamps that hooked over the branches. Each clear glass bulb was filled with kerosene and a small scrap of red or green wool, making the lamps bright as any ornament.

"Why, they are lovely." Abby smiled at the effect.

"Wait until we light them," said Ford. "But that's for Christmas Eve. For now, though, we got one more thing. Danny, open that last box."

Danny carefully unwrapped the brown paper from the long, rectangular box.

"Ohhh," he sighed, lifting the porcelain doll from its resting place.

Swathed in silver and gold, the little angel had white feather wings.

"Mama, look." Danny ran the doll to her.

She accepted the tree-topper, gasping at the lovely creation. Abby fussed with the tiny skirt, trying to clear the squeezing pressure that stole her voice.

"It comes all the way from Italy," said Ford.

She could not speak past the lump in her throat and pinched her lips together against the tears that threatened to humiliate her.

"Don't you like it?" said Ford. "I tried to find one with brown hair, but the shopkeeper says they only come in blond, as if angels didn't come in all colors."

Abby cleared her throat. "It's the most beautiful thing I have ever seen." But she couldn't accept it. "It's too much, Mr. Statler." Their eyes met and she saw the happiness radiating from his face, where earlier there had been only sorrow. How could she not accept this gift, when it pleased him so much to offer it? "Thank you." She returned the doll to her son. "Let Mr. Statler have the honor of setting her in place."

Danny offered the angel to Ford, but instead of taking it, he swept her son up into the air. Danny gave a whoop and lifted the doll, setting it carefully in place at the very top of the tree.

"It's the prettiest tree ever," announced Danny.

Ford returned him to the floor, and Danny ran to his mother and then turned to admire their work.

Abby extended her arm and Danny gave her a hug. The only thing the tree lacked was a gift for her son. Somehow she planned to correct that, but how to do it in only two days?

Chapter Eight

Abby woke to the sound of ice hitting the windowpane. She opened her eyes to greet the gray dawn.

Only one day until Christmas.

She lay staring at the ceiling waiting for her arm to begin the familiar throbbing. When it didn't, she gave a tentative shrug and smiled. Her wound felt much better. The doctor told her the stitches could come out the day after Christmas, providing she didn't pull them out again.

She glanced at Ford, asleep on the couch beside her bed. How she admired him for not giving a whit what others thought or said.

In an effort not to disturb him, she quietly lifted the covers and slipped to the edge of the bed. The mattress creaked and he was on his feet before she could swing her legs to the carpet.

He held her elbow solicitously as she came to her feet.

She flapped one arm in frustration. "I've never met such a light sleeper. I didn't want to disturb you."

"That'd be impossible."

"I don't understand."

"I've been disturbed by you since I first laid eyes on you." The desire in his gaze left her no doubt as to his meaning.

Her face heated and she tried not to smile in delight. But she could not encourage his unspoken question. After all, he had made it crystal clear that he would not be staying, and she was worldly enough to know what kind of trouble she could get into before they parted ways. He might not care about his reputation, but she had to look out for herself and Danny.

"But you can't stay," she reminded him.

He didn't confirm her words at first, giving her time to wonder how different she would feel if he told her he had changed his mind.

"Can you?" She held her breath, waiting for his answer.

"No, angel," he said at last. Did she detect a note of regret in his tone or was that just wishful thinking? "Where you headed—chamber pot?"

"I wanted to have one of the maids fetch some yarn from my room." Though how she would pay for the errand, she had no notion. She had no funds and nothing to barter but a torn, blood-stained dress and worn black shoes.

"This *here* is your room."

"I have another above the milliner's shop. It's close to Faber's Restaurant, where I work."

"Cooking." Now she heard clear disapproval. It straightened her spine.

"What of it?"

"You're too smart to be shoveling hash. You got an education, I'd bet my bounty on it. Why you frying other folks' bacon?"

She sat back on the bed, and he did not move off but rather sat close enough for his thigh to press against hers. She must be feeling better, for all she could think about was running her fingers through his thick hair.

"I was hired as a companion for the trip to San Francisco."

"Fell a mite shy."

"I had difficulties with my employer and we parted ways."

"Way I hear it, you got caught with the woman's husband."

She gasped. "That is not true!"

"It's nothing to me."

The fact that he did not care a whit whether she had sullied herself further fueled her fury. "Her wretched husband made a pass at me, which I rejected with such vehemence, it drew my employer's attention."

"And she sacked you."

Abby lowered her head. "Yes."

"Easier to blame you than fire her husband, I suppose."

She lifted her gaze to meet his. "You believe me?"

He took her hand. "Sure do."

"Why?"

His fingers moved and he stroked her bare forearm with a feathery touch that left her heart beating like galloping horses.

"'Cause I've been thinking along the same lines. Can't fault a man for wanting to kiss you. But I do hold him accountable for doing it without your say-so." He paused then, his fingers making erotic little circles on her heated flesh.

Her heart skipped as she realized he was waiting for her consent.

She wanted to. The force with which she wanted to frightened her nearly as much as the reciprocal desire she saw in his gaze. But soon he'd be gone from here and she didn't fancy nursing a broken heart. "Only one day until Christmas."

His hopeful expression faded and he drew back.

"What you do want with that wool?"

"I need it to make Danny a pair of socks for Christmas."

He motioned to her shoulder. "How you fixin' to do that?"

"I thought to brace one needle against my side."

"I'll buy him a new pair."

"Mr. Statler, that will hardly do. I want the gift to come from me."

"Put your name on the card, then."

"No, thank you."

"You're a stubborn woman."

She smiled. "Just so."

He turned tail and left the room. In the stillness that followed she managed to complete her toilet unassisted. Though brushing her hair was painful, she managed to draw it into a loose braid before returning to bed. She rested until Danny crawled from his pallet and then she saw to him, as well. Breakfast arrived on a tray, shortly after her son relieved her of the comb and finished his ablutions unassisted. Abby drew the maid aside and spoke to her, handing off her old brown coat.

"Where's she taking that?" asked Danny.

"Oh, well, um, to be mended." Abby hoped Danny didn't see the lie. But she had little else to barter.

Ford returned before lunch with a bag filled with yarn and various knitting needles for Abby.

"These aren't mine," she said, fingering the bounty.

"They are now."

"Oh, I couldn't." She pushed the offering toward him.

He pushed it back. "Well, I don't know how to knit."

She lifted a thick blue wool, measuring its weight with her fingers and smiled. "Thank you, Ford."

He nodded. "I got another surprise for you."

"Oh, you've done too much already. I'll be forever in your debt."

His gaze heated as he stared, capturing her attention and causing her heart to skip a beat. "That so?"

Her throat felt suddenly dry. "Why, of course."

His smile was devilish, sending a curling shaft of heat through her body. Something had changed here. He no longer merely cared for her needs, but seemed anxious to please her. If she didn't know better, she'd say he was courting her.

Warning bells sounded deep within her. She'd been easily wooed once before and her impulsiveness had ended in disaster. The experience left her cautious. This man was equally unsuitable, not because she thought herself above him, oh no, but because of his chosen profession. He lived a dangerous life—a life on the edge and that was no place for a woman to raise a son. She needed a responsible man with a safe, predictable profession, like dry goods. But how would she ever find a man as exciting as this one?

No—she was a mother now, and mothers needed to be practical. Furthermore, she would not have her son trailing Ford Statler as if he were the Pied Piper.

But he already did. She bit her lip, as the truth of that settled in her bones like a January chill. Danny already set the moon by Ford and if she were honest, she'd admit that she was equally captivated by this solitary, contradictory man.

The groan of a man exerting himself reached her, followed by a thump. A knock came at the door, a moment later and Ford grinned.

"Who is that?" asked Abby.

Ford wiggled his eyebrows in answer and admitted two men who wheeled in an upright piano.

Ford turned to her son. "Danny, get the bench."

Danny darted into the hall and returned a moment later struggling to carry an unwieldy load that was nearly as big as he was. Abby rose to help him, but Ford stayed her with a light touch. Danny managed to put the bench down near the piano, beaming with pride. Ford patted him on the back.

"That a boy!"

"Goodness gracious," said Abby.

Ford had the men place the piano beside the tree and then returned for her, scooping her into his arms as if she were his bride.

"I'm quite capable of walking," she admonished.

His grin was devilish. "Any excuse."

He set her on the sofa and then tipped the movers. Danny held the door and waved as they departed.

"Merry Christmas," he called.

Ford rested a hand on the piano, and Abby rose to stand beside him.

"How did you know I played?" she asked.

"You do?"

"Why yes, but…Mr. Statler, do you play?" He couldn't. The idea of a man such as he practicing the piano seemed as impossible as a wolf learning to waltz.

In answer, he opened the lid and placed his fingers confidently upon the keys. A moment later the resonant music of "Silent Night" filled the room.

Her wolf was waltzing.

Chapter Nine

Ford had a fine singing voice and excellent command of the piano. Without sheet music, he played carol after carol. She had nearly gotten over her shock of this discovery when he began a rousing rendition of "Angels We Have Heard on High." The smoldering look he cast her throughout gave her gooseflesh.

The last strands of the finale faded in the air. Abby clasped her hands across her heart.

"You are wonderful, Mr. Statler. Wherever did you learn to play?"

"My ma taught me."

Danny, sitting beside him on the bench, lowered his head. She had tried to teach her son, but Danny did not think music the kind of activity a boy should pursue.

For the first time Abby wondered if Ford might be a good influence upon her son.

"Last one before you're off to bed, Danny-boy."

He used her nickname for him. She inhaled to object and found that she could not. The two sat, happy as clams. Danny whined a bit at the topic of bed, but she could see he was tired.

"You pick the last song," said Ford.

"'O Christmas Tree,'" Danny said at once.

"Naturally."

The two sang well together. All too soon the song was done.

"Now you wash up and get into bed. You can listen to your ma and me sing you to sleep." He gave Danny a little shove to send him on his way, before turning to her.

Abby set aside her knitting to oversee Danny's washing.

"He can do it," said Ford in a low voice.

Abby hesitated, watching her son head to the washstand and carefully pour the water. He really could. She just helped from force of habit. Or was it her refusal to see that her child was growing up?

"Call when you're in bed," she said to Danny, and sat back on the sofa to listen to Ford play "Good King Wenceslas." A few minutes later she tucked Danny in, lifting the blanket to his chin and smoothing the covers. It was the first time she'd felt well enough to do so since before the accident. She smiled at the return of their normal routine. She'd be well again in no time.

The smile faded from her lips. Was it only a few days ago that she had been so anxious to be rid of Ford? Now the mere thought of their upcoming separation made her chest ache.

Stop it, you ninny. He has his own life and no place for a woman and small boy. She pictured them huddling behind a rock, waiting for Ford to kill a bank robber, and groaned.

"You all right, Mama?"

She kissed her son and smiled. "Good as gold. Off to sleep now. Close your eyes."

He did, and she rose without difficulty, turning back to Ford. He patted the place beside him on the bench that Danny had just vacated. The innocent expression seemed forced, and she eyed him suspiciously.

"You said you can walk, so walk on over here."

She did, though thought better of it as she neared him.

"You know 'O Holy Night'?"

"Of course."

"Let's hear it, then." He played an introduction as she settled on the narrow bench.

It was quite impossible for their thighs not to touch. She felt the heat of him straight through her gown and wrapper.

She cleared her throat, trying to ignore the scent of after-shave and leather that clung to him. But despite her best efforts to concentrate, he thoroughly distracted her and she missed the start and he had to repeat the introduction. This time she began to sing on cue. By the second verse he had his eyes closed. Not pinched closed, so she did not think her voice offended. Others had told her she had a clear soprano, and she had been welcomed to sing at any family gathering. She found herself growing anxious as she continued, hoping to please him and worried why she should care so much what he thought of her.

The song ended, and she sat nervous as a new mother.

He smiled, letting his hands slip from the keys and onto his strong thighs. His long fingers lay a mere hair's breadth from her leg. "You sing like an angel, too."

For a moment they just shared a smile. His expression changed, and she had that feeling he wanted to kiss her again.

Fearing that would reveal her unwanted attraction to him, she cleared her throat and spoke.

"Do you know 'Deck the Halls'?"

His expression of gladness vanished like a fleeing dove. He stiffened, clenching his fists upon his thighs.

He broke eye contact, his expression grim. "I do. It was my daughter's favorite."

She was glad he looked away, for it kept him from seeing her gape as she tried to grasp what he told her. He had a daughter?

Ice water flooded her as she realized he said it *was* his

daughter's favorite. He'd lost her. But perhaps her mother just took her away, an estrangement. She clung to that hope as his bleak visage gave fuel to her fears.

"Did she—" She couldn't form the words.

"Dead," he said.

Her intake of breath was sharp. A stabbing pain pierced her heart at the thought of such a horror. She had come as close to losing a child as she ever wanted to, just days ago. Her fear had dissipated at finding Danny unharmed. But what if he had died? What would become of her then?

Glancing at Ford to find him staring fixedly at her, she saw the answer. There he sat, a man with a vengeful heart and no care at all if he lived or died. She understood perfectly now, and her heart went out to him.

She couldn't think on it for more than an instant before the tears streamed down her face. He had lost his daughter. She could not bear to ask him how.

"How did you survive it?" she whispered.

"I didn't. Not really. There's little left, now that they're gone."

"You lost your wife *and* child?"

"Their names were Rebecca and Ellie. Ellie was only four. I was told my wife refused to give the train robber her mother's locket so he crushed her skull with the butt of his rifle. My daughter tried to take his pistol and he shot her in the throat. It's my fault, 'cause I put them on that train alone. I should have been there to protect my own."

The silence in the room settled over her like a shroud. Could he hear her heart breaking for him?

"That's why you chase criminals."

He nodded.

"Did you find him?"

He didn't ask who, but instead he gave the slightest inclination of his head. "Four years back, in Dodge City, already fitted for a pine box. He cheated the wrong man at cards and the gambler cheated me of my revenge."

"But you didn't stop."

"I never found any reason to."

Suddenly she wanted to be that reason. She understood it all now, why he chased these outlaws and why he kept everyone at arm's length—except her. She sat right beside him and he was baring his soul to her.

She knew he didn't often speak of this.

"When will it be enough?"

"I just got nothing else but my anger. It's all that keeps me from—"

He broke eye contact, sliding his hand to the keys and playing a minor chord.

She placed her hand over his, stilling his fingers. "Are you trying to die, as well?"

The thought had crossed his mind on more than one occasion, but he had never had anyone dare to ask him such a thing.

"Mostly I just try and stop these men from killing innocent folk and wait for the day it goes wrong. When it does, I wouldn't be missed."

She grasped his hand, holding tight. "I'd miss you."

The sorrow, so much a part of him, seemed to ebb from his glistening eyes. His hand came around her back, cradling her. Desire flared deep in her belly as he held her in his arms, in his gaze.

"Would you, Abby?"

She nodded.

He tipped his head and leaned forward. She knew he meant to kiss her, and this time she did not try to stop him but lifted her chin in welcome.

His mouth descended, hard and possessive. His kisses were desperate as if he were starving for her. Never in her life had she experienced anything like the consuming fire he roused within her. She went liquid in his arms, like melting wax.

His fingers wove into her hair, and he held her captive for his seduction. She whimpered as the ache to touch him grew stronger than her restraint. He tensed, drawing back.

"Have I hurt you?"

She grasped him behind the neck with one hand, like some wanton hussy. She knew her desperation for his touch reflected in her eyes, but she was past shame, past doubt. How could she have ever thought herself in love before this? What she'd felt for Henry had been a mere girlhood crush. And with his leaving, all he'd hurt was her vanity. Her heart remained intact, waiting for this man.

And such a man—this dangerous, haunted man—he touched her heart and soul. How she wanted him. If she did not take care, she would fall in love with him. With a sigh of surrender, she realized she already had.

He had loved his wife. She knew she could not replace such a love, but did he have room in his heart for two more loves?

He drew back.

"Don't stop," she whispered.

It was all the urging he needed. With a feral growl, he clasped her up in his arms and pulled her tight.

Abby pressed herself against him, molding her soft breasts to him, robbing him of reason.

Her tongue stroked his bottom lip and then laved his teeth as if seeking admittance. He'd never felt this desperate wanting. He kissed her again, his tongue mating with her in a primitive dance of desire.

His angel, his savior. This woman who drew him from despair and brought joy back to his somber world. She and Danny were the light that he had thought forever extinguished. Dead and buried.

Buried.

The image of Rebecca rose in his mind, and he stiffened. He had not kissed a woman since he had laid his wife in the earth. How could he forget her? How could he lust after another woman?

But it wasn't lust, and that truth frightened him witless.

"What's the matter?" Her sweet voice brought him back to his senses. "Ford, look at me."

He did. Her hair lay in disarray and her mouth was swollen from his kisses. He had done that to her and he wanted to do more.

Guilt washed through him.

"I know you loved your wife, Ford, and I would not want to replace her. But I have strong feelings for you. I thought you should know."

His hands slipped from her waist. How could he give her what she deserved? How could he betray his wife and love this woman, this woman who he took so quickly into his heart?

He stood and staggered backward as the truth hit him like the bullet he always expected would end his miserable existence.

He already loved her. Just like that, he had set Rebecca aside and taken this woman in her place. He nearly had taken her right in the room beside her sleeping child.

What kind of man had he become?

"Ford? What is it, you look pale as death."

He glanced about as if expecting to see Rebecca's image standing in the room. For whether Abby could see her or not, she did stand between them.

"I'm sorry, Abby."

She rose, taking a step toward him, but he backed away, reaching the door.

"Ford, wait."

He was out in the hall and down the stairs in a blink. A moment later he was standing on the road. Snow fell from the heavens, melting on the hot tears that stained his cheeks.

Chapter Ten

Abby waited beside Danny's tree for Ford to reappear, but he did not. She tried to press down the worry. It had been too soon for him; she realized that.

He still mourned his wife, still felt guilty for not being there to protect his family when they needed him most and perhaps even felt guilty for kissing her.

She should have kept her feelings to herself, not blurted them out like a schoolgirl. He needed time to get used to her.

Her fingers moved automatically, knitting and purling. As the night wore on, she completed Danny's socks, but did not stop, taking up the task of making Ford a pair, as well. It gave her hope that he would come back.

Her wound tugged as she moved, but she ignored it. The pain was good company, for it suited her mood.

She did not rest or stop until she finished the task and then she rose stiffly and set the new socks on the branches of Danny's tree. Tomorrow was Christmas day, the day Ford said they would part ways.

But he wouldn't go without saying goodbye. Surely he wouldn't. The ache in the pit of her stomach continued to gnaw, as if a beaver tried to cut her in half.

She glanced toward his saddlebags and coat. He couldn't go far without them. Abby settled on the couch where Ford usually slept, and waited.

As the night stole on, Abby kept a vigil telling herself she would not rest until she explained. A chill crept across the floor as the coal burned low in the stove.

Abby drew his blanket about her shoulders and waited. Gradually her head fell back upon the couch.

The door clicked open as Ford crept, like a thief, into the room. He'd spent the better part of the evening haunting the saloons. But he found no answers in the whiskey and no diversion in cards. His mind came back again and again to the same sad thought.

He wasn't strong enough to go through it again.

Abby was a good woman and Danny a fine boy. But losing his wife and child had nearly killed him.

She wouldn't understand it, especially if she knew that he did love her. She had never lost a child, a wife—a life—and he prayed she never would know that hollow place left when your world burns to ashes.

He found her asleep on the sofa still sitting up, his blanket wrapped tightly about her shoulders. She was a fine woman and he was a stray dog to steal into her life and sneak off in the night.

She'd never understand and she'd never forgive him. Perhaps her anger would soften the hurt.

He checked on Danny, to find him sleeping peacefully on his pallet. Dreaming of sugar plums, Ford hoped.

Next he walked to the tree. The scent of pine hung all about him. Tomorrow was Christmas day. A day for families. How he longed to make them his. But he was not the man for her. He was gun-shy and broken by his past—not good for anything but killing.

Ford gathered his belongings and then returned to look at her once more. She brought him back to life or she had tried.

He drew his pocket watch from his vest pocket and glanced at the dial—2:00 a.m.

"Merry Christmas, angel." His kiss was gentle, and she did not wake.

Was he doing the right thing or just running?

Abby jolted awake in the early-morning gloom, unable to find what had awakened her. She glanced at Danny and found him sleeping peacefully by her bedside. The room seemed too quiet.

And then she knew what was missing—the steady breathing of Ford. She stretched and cringed at the pain of her healing arm.

Even in the gray dawn she could see that Ford's saddlebags were gone.

"No," she whispered, as if that plea would make him suddenly appear, seated at her side. But perhaps he had just gone out and would return. He wouldn't miss their Christmas morning together—would he?

His promise returned now to haunt her. *You'll agree to my nursing and I'll agree to be gone by Christmas day.*

She was well now, or nearly so, and he had gone without a word. Her heart broke like an icicle dropping on frozen ground. Tears trickled from her eyes, for she did not have the courage to deceive herself any longer. He had taken the trouble of sneaking in here while she slept and escaped without rousing her. That did not speak of a man who could not bear to be out of her sight, but rather one who had gotten in over his head.

Danny shifted in his pallet. She pushed back her heartache and set to work lighting all the kerosene lamps that decked the tree. The cheery glow pushed back the gray morning gloom. She had only just sat down upon the piano bench to admire Danny's tree, when he gave a sigh and then a groan. She was waiting with a hug when Danny remembered it was Christmas and sprang from his pallet. If she held him a little too tightly and for a moment too long, he did not notice it. Nor did he see the tears, because of his hurry to see his tree.

"Mama, look! New socks." He grasped the offering from the tree and spun back to her. "These are from you!"

She didn't deny it and accepted another hug, gladly.

"There's a pair for Ford, too." Danny rounded the bed and skidded to a halt.

Her smile faltered.

"Where is he?"

"I'm not sure."

Danny looked about the quiet room. "Maybe he's getting us breakfast."

"That's it, certainly." When had she become such a consummate liar?

"I hope he brings hot chocolate."

Abby wondered if he had paid for the day, for she planned to stay in this hotel until she was asked to go. She would not spoil Danny's Christmas for anything in the world.

"I have something for you, Mama." Danny burrowed into his bedding and returned clutching something. He held out a small pink satin pouch, clumsily sewn and drawn together with a bit of ribbon. "It's a satchel. I dried the rose petals that fell off the roses in the lobby. Ford helped me sew the pouch, see?" Danny released the ribbon and the dried petals spilled out on the rumbled sheets. "Uh-oh."

The faint fragrance of roses scented the air.

"Ford says you put it in your drawer and it makes your clothes smell nice."

Together they scooped up the crumbling pieces. When the petals were once more sheathed in satin, she hugged Danny.

"It is the most special gift ever." She kissed his brow.

He tolerated it, no doubt in honor of the day. Then he wiggled away and sat beneath his tree to don his new socks. They came up over his knees, and he modeled them by performing an impromptu dance.

A soft knock sounded at the door. Danny slipped and skidded across the wood floor in his hurry to reach the door.

"Ford?" He threw open the lock before there was any answer.

There stood a chamber maid holding a heavy tray. Not much of a Christmas morning for her, either, thought Abby, watching the woman struggle with her load. As she entered, Abby noted a second woman carrying boxes.

She recognized the maid as the one who had taken her coat and breathed a sigh of relief.

"Mr. Statler ordered breakfast for you," said the first maid. She laid the tray upon the side table near the tree. Abby noted there were only two teacups.

"Mama, presents!"

The second woman, carrying boxes wrapped in brown paper and string, laid the packages beneath the tree. The maid grinned at Danny and pointed to the smaller square boxes. "Those ones have your name on them, little man."

Abby frowned in confusion. "Aren't they all for him?"

The woman cocked her head. A moment later understanding dawned. "Oh, no, ma'am. That other matter—I couldn't find a buyer. I'm sorry, ma'am."

"Then where did there come from?"

"From Santa!" Danny clutched up a box. "Can I open it, Mama, can I?"

Abby had a suspicion that Santa was not responsible, but she could not deny Danny his gift. "Certainly."

The three women watched as Danny tore into the paper.

Abby leaned toward the maid. "Mr. Statler?" she asked.

"He paid for the room through the week before leaving, ma'am. Said you're to have board, as well."

He was really gone. Abby held her chin up, willing herself not to curl into a ball. "That was kind of him."

"Is there anything else, ma'am?"

Abby shook her head, and the two departed.

How was it possible that she had again fallen in love with a man who abandoned her? But this man had not taken advantage, though she'd given him permission. He had behaved as a gentleman and he'd told her from the start that he would not be staying past Christmas.

Her wish was to go after him, shameful as that was. But he had made his decision and she must honor it.

A niggling voice within pricked at her. Wasn't it possible that he did have feelings for her and they frightened him? He proved he was not the kind of man to trifle with a woman's emotions, but his kiss spoke of such passion. All about her were signs of his esteem, or were they just kindnesses? Doubt nipped at her, making Abby uncertain as to what she should do.

"Look, Mama!" Danny held up a handful of jacks and a red rubber ball. He tried the ball out before setting it aside to reach for the next box. He cried out in joy as he unearthed a leather pouch full of marbles including two impressive shooters. "Look, Mama!"

He poured the bounty into her lap.

"How wonderful."

"There's one more!"

"Well, open it!"

He did, removing a shinny brass cylinder. "It's a kaleidoscope!" He held it to his eye and pointed the other end toward the window. "Ohh!"

His legs folded beneath him and he came to perfect stillness for several moments. Abby collected the marbles from her lap and placed them carefully in Danny's new calfskin pouch.

Abby again felt grateful to the man who made all this

possible. He was their Christmas angel, and despite her heartbreak, she felt lucky to have crossed his path.

Danny sprang to his feet and brought the kaleidoscope to her. "Look, Mama!"

She did. Colors fractured into beautiful array, like a patchwork quilt in motion. She gasped. "How lovely."

She lowered the scope to her lap and Danny scrambled back to his tree. "You forgot to open yours."

He held out the large rectangular box. She had not the heart to open it. Only the joy in Danny's face could have made her. She would not spoil his pleasure with her pain.

Abby returned his kaleidoscope and accepted the box. Danny, impatient at her fumbling, helped her remove the paper and string, before tearing the lid off the box.

Inside lay an emerald-green wool dress with cream-colored lace trim. She gasped and lifted the dress only to reveal a red velvet coat beneath. She laid the dress across her lap and admired the coat, fingering the fine fabric and the shiny black buttons.

Danny petted the coat as if it were a puppy. "It's so soft."

She had no business wearing such a fancy dress or coat, but she loved them. As she lifted it to her cheek, the envelope tumbled to her lap. Abby lifted it. The envelope bulged, as if stuffed with fabric.

Breaking the seal, she lifted the flap. Twenty-dollar notes fluttered from within, littering the floor.

Danny delved his hands into the pile. "Ma! He gave you money."

Abby instructed Danny to count the money, giving her a chance to read Ford's letter.

Dear angel,
I hope you like the coat. I guess it is the least I can do, since
I shot a hole through the other one. This color will make

you easier to spot. Please accept the rest of the bounty money. Without Danny I never would have lived to collect it. Use it as you see fit, maybe it will buy you both a fresh start.

I am truly sorry if I have hurt you. Please understand, I just can't lose another person in my life.

With warmest affection,

Ford M. Statler

Abby lowered the letter. He had once told her he killed for money. But ruthless men did not give away a fortune, not even to a woman they fancied. She scanned the second paragraph once more: "…can't lose another person."

Her eyes narrowed as the pain melted into anger. She had taken Ford for many things, most of them wrongly. But one thing she had not taken him for was a coward.

Danny finished his arithmetic and lifted his gaze to her. "It's $738."

Every last dime of the bounty, she was certain. Abby stood, feeling suddenly sure of what must be done.

"Get dressed, Danny."

Chapter Eleven

Abby's new coat glowed like a beacon in the gray morning light. She felt like one of Santa's elves as she made her way down to the telegraph office. Her stride had purpose, and more than one gentleman stepped aside, doffing his hat as she passed.

She felt like her old self again, that confident girl she had been before Henry's leaving had humiliated her and brought her low. She had nothing to fight for when he had gone, but now she did.

She loved this man. Of that she had no doubt. His departure had made her realize just how much, and she was prepared to fight to win him back.

The bell on the door of the telegraph office jingled merrily as they entered. Abby stepped up to the clerk and laid a page of paper on the counter.

"I want this telegram to go to the sheriff of Ouray, Denver and Golden."

Not knowing what direction Ford had taken, she sent her message along all possible routes.

The thin young man's smile lifted the ends of his busy mustache. "Certainly, ma'am."

He drew the page to him and read. His smile faded and he

glanced up several times. She wasn't certain if he was judging her conviction or her sanity, but his gaze grew increasingly worried.

"Ma'am?"

"Yes?"

"You certain you want to send this?"

"Unquestionably."

He rubbed the back of his neck. "All righty then." He turned to the telegraph and began tapping. The clickly-click of metal on metal marked that her message was speeding along the wires overhead.

Abby squeezed her fists, praying for a miracle.

Ford rode through the bustle of Golden on his way to the sheriff, still wondering how he had ever let his guard down enough to let Abby and Danny slip into his heart.

He'd warned himself not to get attached, but that was plain hooey. The moment he'd seen Abby lying in the snow he was lost, and Danny had grown on him like a pea vine in a pumpkin patch. There was no defense against either one.

It surprised him mightily to learn he was capable of love when all this time he'd assumed that part of him had died with his family.

Well, there was no denying it. The best he could do was see them taken care of and leave while he still could.

One more of Abby's kisses and he would have done, well, what any man in his right mind would have done. Then he'd have to make an honorable proposal, and that would be taking a chance he just couldn't take. The chance that they'd die on him, as well.

His horse stopped at the hitching post of the Jefferson County Sheriff's Office without any help from him.

"Damn." He was so distracted he'd likely walk right into a lake, if they weren't all frozen up.

He needed a job, a tough one, something to take his mind off her.

He was sorry he couldn't see Danny's face when he opened that kaleidoscope. Did Abby like the coat? He pictured her walking right down the middle of the sidewalk. How she'd look. His head hung to his chest. Would she ever forgive him?

Ford dismounted and crossed to the door, kicking the snow from his boots, before making use of the boot scraper to remove the mud.

Inside, he found Dennis Hoyt sitting behind his desk next to the woodstove, writing in a large ledger. Ford wouldn't say they were friends, but rather acquaintances who had crossed paths on many occasions.

"Be with you in a minute," said Hoyt without glancing up.

"Not much of a welcome for a man on Christmas day."

Hoyt smiled, meeting Ford's gaze. He tossed the pen aside and slapped the ledger closed.

"Well, what a coincidence." He crossed to Ford and offered his hand. "Coffee?"

Ford nodded. "I'd be obliged."

"What brings you in? You don't have a body tied to your horse, do you?"

"Not today. I'm looking for work. Like to see your 'Wanteds.'"

"Way I hear it you bagged Donahue. Figured your purse might be causing you to limp."

Ford remained silent, giving nothing away. At last, Hoyt returned to his desk and opened the bottom drawer, flipping through pages.

"I got one here that might interest you."

"What'd he do?"

"Oh, I'm not rightly sure, but it must have been something terrible." Hoyt's jovial expression did not match his words, causing Ford to scowl. There was something all together off about the sheriff today. He looked positively gleeful.

"You all right, there?" asked Ford as he reached for the paper the sheriff extended to him.

"Oh, fine. You're the one I'm worried about."

Ford righted the page and glanced down, scanning the wanted poster.

Wanted Alive
$738 REWARD
for information on the
whereabouts of the bounty hunter
Ford Statler
sought in connections to
crimes of the heart
Contact:
Abby March,
Gilford Hotel, Durango, CO

Ford glanced up, fisting the page.

"What the hell is this?"

Hoyt was laughing now. "Don't rightly know. But I'm laying good odds that you do. Leave some unfinished business up there in Durango, son?"

Ford glanced at the page again: "Crimes of the heart." He sank into the hardwood chair in front of the sheriff's desk. Hadn't he left her enough money to make a fresh start? Instead she'd used it to track him down like a criminal—$738, the exact amount he'd left. It was a damned foolish thing to do. Someone would call her bluff, and she and Danny would be left with nothing.

"If you took advantage of a lady, Ford, you best turn that horse around, before I shoot you myself."

Ford felt more lost than he had in years. He had not one notion as to what to do.

The sheriff poured a cup of coffee and placed it before Ford. "You want to tell me about it, son?"

He did. He told him about his angel: how he'd shot her and then seen her through the trouble he'd caused; how he'd fallen in love with her and her son.

"But I never took advantage. I swear."

Hoyt assessed him with his lawman's stare—cold and cynical. "I believe you. But the lady thinks you've got business. Why is that?"

Ford lowered his head and explained how he sneaked out like a thief in the night. His words shamed him, and he felt his face heat with his humiliation.

"She sounds like a good woman."

"She is that."

"So why are you here instead of there?"

Ford told the sheriff about his Rebecca and how he mourned his wife and child. How it felt wrong to love another woman when his was dead.

"They didn't bury you. You're stuck here with the living. Best you can hope for is to find a good woman to look after you. I know your Rebecca wouldn't want to see you like this."

Ford took offense, lowering his chin and speaking through clenched teeth. "Like what?"

"Like a man trying to end his days early. I know the chances you take. It's no better than suicide."

Why was it he could face a bullet easier than the thought of losing Abby like he did Rebecca?

"I don't ever want to fall in love like that again. It hurts too much to lose them."

Hoyt rose and rounded the desk, sliding the coffee aside to sit on the edge, just beside Ford.

"Like to see the man that can stop himself from falling in love. Besides, it's too late already. You love her, don't you?"

Ford did not trust his voice and so he simply nodded.

"Thought as much. You're being gun-shy is understandable, but it's brought you to the same spot."

Ford lifted his head and met the man's steely gaze. "What do you mean?"

The lawman laid a comforting hand on Ford's shoulder. "Losing her—you already have, son."

Ford stiffened as the truth of that settled in. If he kept on, Abby was dead to him as surely as if she were gone from this world.

The sheriff's hand slid away. "If God sent you another woman to love, then you sure are riding in the wrong direction."

Ford rose slowly to his feet as if rising from the dead. He thought of his Becky and knew that if God had let him spend just one more day with his wife and little girl, he'd have taken it and damn the consequences. Yet he'd left Abby behind. He glanced around the office. What the hell was he doing here?

Hoyt nodded his approval at Ford's consternation.

"So, you going to ride back up those mountains or am I going to hog-tie you and collect my first bounty?"

Chapter Twelve

Abby vacated the room the day after Christmas. The room was paid for until the end of the week, but somehow she no longer wanted to be in the place when Ford was not.

Her attempts to play Christmas carols with Danny had fallen flat. Not that she had lost her command of the instrument, but the joy was forced. Danny quickly discovered that Ford had gone without so much as a by-your-leave. She had held him through the tears.

They had both taken one on the chin and Abby saw no reason not to face facts. She did make one small concession, however. The room included board, and so she and Danny walked to the hotel each evening after she finished her work and settled in the dining room for their meal.

Tonight the popovers were disappearing down Danny's throat at a rate that alarmed her. If his appetite continued to grow as fast as he did, she'd soon need a second job, just to feed him.

"Elbows off the table, Danny."

Her son straightened, still gripping a buttery muffin in his hand.

He smiled, swinging his legs back and forth as he ate. Each

swing showed a flash of royal blue where his knickers ended and his new stockings began.

She wondered if Ford had seen her poster yet? Her heart ached each time she thought of him. How had she fallen so hard and so fast?

Well, the man was a godsend and no mistake. She should be grateful for the gifts he had given them, most of all the gift of his affection.

She wondered who would collect the bounty, which now rested in the Bank of Durango for safekeeping.

Likely it was foolish to waste such a fortune, but somehow all she wanted in this world was to tell Ford that she still wanted him, even if she could never earn a place in his heart.

The matter rested with him, and she must do what was necessary to keep body and soul together.

"Ma?"

Danny had caught her wool-gathering.

She smiled and lifted her eyebrows in a silent question.

"Do you think we'll ever see him again?"

She wanted to say who, but didn't have the heart.

"I hope so."

"Why did he leave?"

"He has a life to return to Danny." And we are not a part of it. He stared at his plate.

"It wasn't anything you did, Danny. He told us he would have to go eventually."

Danny nodded. "I miss him."

"Yes." She gripped his forearm and squeezed. "Yes, I do, too."

"It was kinda like having a pa. I mean, it was like I thought it would be."

Her son would break her heart, there was no doubt about it. She pressed her lips together to keep them from trembling. But she could do nothing about the tears welling in her eyes.

Now Danny looked frightened. He hated to see her cry.

"I'm so sorry, Danny. A boy *should* have a pa." She'd never intended to hurt her son. Yet, she'd seen the possible danger of such attachments. It was the reason she had been averse to the arrangement at the outset. But Ford had won her over, at last, and so her attempt to protect her son had failed miserably. Danny could not keep from wanting Ford to stay, any better than she could.

The waitress cleared their plates and brought Danny a slice of mince pie. She dawdled over her coffee and then rose, leaving two bits for a tip.

She shrugged into her new red velvet coat. Her arm barely twinged at the movement. Abby placed a hand on Danny's shoulder and out they went into the night. They strolled along the wooden walkways past the hotel and then the hardware store, turning up the alley after the milliner's shop.

Mrs. Shasta, her landlady, ran the business and, with all the women now arriving in Durango, she had more work than she could handle. Abby had offered to take in sewing, and Mrs. Shasta had agreed. The wages were far better than working as a cook, so with luck and some hard work, she'd soon be able to quit taking in laundry.

Abby glanced down at Danny, thinking that her new job came not a moment too soon, as she noted the flash of skin that showed between his stockings and his knickers. He'd be in long pants before she knew it.

They rounded the building and made for the back stairs when Abby saw movement out of the corner of her eye.

She stiffened as a large man stepped out of the shadows.

"Hello, angel."

"Ford?" She breathed his name like a prayer and took a step forward to embrace him. Realizing, belatedly that she had not the right, she came to an awkward halt. His return did not mean he'd come back to her. Likely he was here to give her a dressing down about her little stunt with the Wanted poster. Danny, however, showed no such restraint.

"Ford!" He leaped into the air, slamming into Ford with enough force to drive him back a step as he wrapped Danny in a tremendous hug.

Abby was not a jealous woman, especially where her son was concerned, but she did envy him in that moment.

Ford set Danny down, but her son hopped and bounced at his side like a puppy that could not quite reach the face that needed licking.

"You came back!"

Ford stilled him with a gentle hand upon the boy's shoulder. He squatted before him, looking Danny in the eye. "Did you like the kaleidoscope?"

"Oh, yes. I *love* it."

"Can I see it?"

Danny ran up the back stairs two at a time.

Ford turned to Abby and she gulped back her dread.

"I got your message." His voice revealed nothing. At that moment she thought he would be a wonderful poker player, for she could read no hint of his emotions in his expression.

"Did you?" She fumbled with her reticule, suddenly unable to meet his gaze.

"Damn foolish thing to do. You could have lost that money to any man who showed up and pointed west. You could have lost it all."

"I had lost something more important."

He stepped closer, hovering so near that she could feel his warm breath on her face. He smelled of horses and leather, and all she wanted to do was bury her face in the hard muscles of his chest and inhale.

"What's that?"

"My heart."

"So the poster said, 'Crimes of the heart.' But, Abby, I never promised I'd stay past Christmas."

"You came to tell me that?"

"No." He touched her chin, lifting it with two fingers, forcing her gaze to his. "I came to tell you I'm a damned fool. I just got scared."

Her eyes rounded in wonder. "But you're not afraid now."

"I'm shaking in my boots. I'm so scared something will happen to you or Danny, I can barely swallow. I just didn't want to lose you, too. Took a friend to point out that if I didn't turn back, I already had."

She smiled. "I love you, Ford."

"That's what I figured. I feel the same. So what are we going to do about it?"

"You make it sound like some kind of problem."

His arm circled her waist and he forced her up against the hard evidence of his wanting.

"Oh," she gasped. "I see."

He lowered his lips to the shell of her ear, his whisper harsh with his desire. "You see my problem."

"I do."

He laughed. "Not before I hear you say those words before a preacher, you don't."

She stilled. "Are you proposing?"

"I am."

Danny's voice came from two floors up. "*Ma!* Where's the key to the back door?"

The piano played the wedding march, and Danny lifted his elbow for Abby to grasp. Together they walked down the aisle to meet Ford and their new life as a family.

Ford stood as solemnly as the minister, dressed in a black suit with his hat in his hands. His hair still needed a trim, but the barber had obviously applied some oil, for the waves were gone and it shone darkly in the morning light. She much preferred the unruly chestnut locks, but thought he had never looked more striking.

He kept his gaze locked to hers as she made her way to his side. Danny stopped at the appointed spot and seemed relieved when Ford took her elbow, allowing him to move to her opposite side.

The ceremony was mercifully short. Ford spoke his vows in a clear, deep voice that held no note of uncertainty. To her embarrassment, her voice shook with emotion, and she cried as she accepted him as her husband.

The minister had barely pronounced them man and wife, when Ford drew her toward him for a scorching kiss that left her quite breathless.

He swept her up the aisle and waited by her side for the waves of well-wishers to disperse. A bridal luncheon followed at the hotel for the wedding party. Ford, she noticed, had no better appetite than she. At last Mrs. Shasta announced that she was leaving with Danny.

Her son kissed her cheek and then proceeded to shake Ford's hand.

"Good luck," said Danny.

That brought laughter to most.

"I don't think I'll need any more luck," Ford managed, past his grin. "I'm already the luckiest man on earth."

Abby's heart gave a little flutter. She kissed Danny's cheek and set him aside. "We'll see you tomorrow."

Danny nodded and followed Mrs. Shasta out of the restaurant.

No sooner had the door closed behind them than Ford was

on his feet. He extended his hand and waited. "Come on, angel, time for me to take us both to heaven."

And that is exactly what he did.

* * * * *

ONE MAGIC EVE

Pam Crooks

Dear Reader,

When I was asked to write this story for you based on a recipe that held a special place in my life at Christmas, I immediately thought of my Italian grandmother's rosettes.

I can still vividly recall her dining-room table being full of the flower-shaped cookies. After the thin batter was fried and cooled, the cookies remained very fragile. In fact, they were so light, they seemed to melt in my mouth whenever I had one. Which, of course, gave me the perfect excuse to have a second. Or a third.

My grandmother would dust the cookies with powdered sugar or dip their tops in a thin, tinted frosting to make them even more festive. Oh, how we loved them!

Many years later my mother surprised us by resurrecting the recipe, finding the iron and making the treasured treat. She boxed them up and gave them to us on Christmas. Her gift was our favorite, and a tradition we intend to keep alive for our own children.

Rosettes are known by a variety of names in countries throughout the world and decorated in ways similar, but each one remains the same. Positively yummy!

I'm happy to share the recipe. I hope you take time to try them, and you'll agree.

Merry Christmas!

Pam

ROSETTE COOKIES

Ingredients:

2 tsp sugar
2 eggs, slightly beaten
1 cup milk
1 cup sifted flour
1/4 tsp salt
1 tbsp lemon extract

Add sugar to eggs, then add milk. Sift flour with salt. Stir into egg mixture and beat until smooth (about consistency of heavy cream). Add flavoring. Using rosette iron(s), fry and cool as directed.

When cool, or before serving, sprinkle with powdered sugar, or cinnamon-sugar combination. In place of lemon extract, flavor with vanilla, brandy, anise or rum extract. May dip tops in tinted icing.

Makes approximately 45–50 rosettes.

For my Sicilian grandmother, who always made me feel extra special for being her very first grandchild.

Chapter One

December 23, 1886
Montana Territory

"She's the Bird Lady, Beau. She ain't gonna know nothin' about doctorin' a pup."

Sonja Kaplan's pencil stilled over the page of her inventory record book as the boy's voice drifted in through the pigeon loft's small window.

Beau? Chet Lattimer's son?

"How do you know?" a younger voice—Beau's—hissed back.

"'Cuz I'm older 'n smarter than you, and I know a bird ain't nothin' like a pup."

"So what? She's expert at trainin' pigeons, isn't she? Maybe she'll know somethin' about pups, too."

"Aw, Beau, that's just plain stupid." Disgust roughened the other boy's tone. "But bein's I brought you all the way out here so's you can ask her, then you go right on ahead. Just pay me my penny first."

Sonja frowned. These boys had ridden out to see her? Rarely

did folks stop by to visit. Almost never. Were they by themselves? And what's this about a penny?

She set her record book and pencil down on the ledge holding the rows of nest boxes, then pulled her knitted shawl closer around her shoulders. She left her rifle propped against the ledge, pushed open the narrow door and quietly stepped outside.

It didn't take long to find the pair, huddled against the opposite side of the loft. Clearly, they'd had no idea she'd been inside, eavesdropping upon their scheme. And they had no idea she was outside, standing behind them now.

Strangely reluctant to confront them.

She well knew her reputation in their small frontier community. That she was very much an outcast because of her work—covertly training homing pigeons for the United States Army. They didn't understand. No one did, except for the grateful soldiers, and because of the townspeople's ignorance, their suspicions grew into malicious gossip and—

Well, it didn't matter. Not really.

But she guessed her less-than-respectable reputation had something to do with these young boys sneaking onto her small parcel of land and hiding against the loft, out of sight from her cabin just across the yard. It was why they didn't come forward and knock on her door like any visitor should.

Were they afraid of her?

Or of what they'd done, coming out here to see her, against the certainty of their parents' disapproval?

And since no rig waited in the drive, only a lone pony in the shadow of the pines nearby, it was evident they'd come alone.

She recognized Herbie Grinnell, the nine-year-old son of one of Chet Lattimer's ranch hands. Herbie's mother watched over Beau during the day since Beau, several years younger, didn't have a mother of his own anymore. Herbie helped keep him occupied, Sonja supposed, with mischievous escapades like this one.

Except Beau had seemed genuinely anxious to talk to her. Only then did she notice the furry bundle he struggled to keep in his arms while rooting in his trousers pocket for the penny Herbie demanded.

The bundle growled and squirmed, loosening the small blanket Beau kept around him. Sonja glimpsed a stain of bright crimson on the covering from an injury the animal sustained, the reason Beau had ridden out to see her. She made a sound of sympathy.

Both boys whirled, and their faces paled.

"It's her!" Herbie choked, but not before he snatched the penny from Beau and fisted his hand around it. "The Bird Lady!"

Sonja wasn't sure what they'd expected to find—a woman covered in feathers perhaps?—but she took a careful step forward.

"And you're Herbie Grinnell, aren't you?" She smiled to assure them she was quite normal.

"You know who I am?" he asked, looking alarmed. "You ain't gonna tell my ma I came out here, are you? She won't like it, bein's what folks say 'bout you and all." He took a wary stride backward, then another. "Please don't tell her, else I'll be in a heap of trouble."

Sonja's smile wavered, but she managed to keep it in place. "I have no reason to say anything, Herbie. Your secret is safe with me. I promise."

The chances of Sonja speaking with Esther Grinnell were slim, besides. A coincidental meeting in town, perhaps, and most likely not even then. The woman, she'd learned, was a notorious gossip.

"C'mon, Beau. Let's get out of here."

"No." Defiant, Beau shook his head and stayed right where he was. "Not till I know she can help."

"Suit yourself, then." Herbie kept moving backward, closer

to the pony in the pines. "But I'm not stayin'." Suddenly he turned and broke into a full run.

"Wait!" Startled, Sonja called after him.

"Herbie, stop!" Beau called, too.

But the boy kept running, without a backward glance to the friend he'd left behind. He vaulted onto the pony's back, dug in his heels and galloped off.

Sonja waffled between exasperation for his cowardliness to stinging hurt that one so young thought of her the way he did.

Just like everyone else.

But there was no help for it. She couldn't bring him back if she wanted to.

Which she didn't. Not when little Beau worried her more.

She turned her attention back to him, still crouched beside the loft and staring dumbfounded after Herbie. Her heart squeezed. What was he thinking, being abandoned like this?

"Beau," she said gently.

He turned wide eyes on her. Eyes thickly lashed and a rich, deep brown like rich chocolate. He wore a child-size version of a Stetson, which still seemed a mite too big for his head. The brim slipped down over his forehead. He pushed it up again to see her better.

"You know my name, too?" he asked.

She knelt beside him, entranced by those eyes, so much like Chet's. "Of course I do." It became imperative that he didn't shun her like Herbie did, that he would be assured she'd be his friend and wasn't the strumpet everyone else around these parts thought she was. "Your papa told me about you."

His face lit up. "You know my pa?"

She hesitated. "Yes."

But not as well as she'd like.

Something curled in Sonja's belly and nudged aside the loneliness she often felt living by herself with only the pigeons to keep her company. Something warm and arousing whenever she thought of Chet Lattimer, and was there anything more foolish?

His spread butted her land. He provided her with the straw she needed for the birds, and occasionally cut the firewood she needed for herself, but she had little more dealings with him than that.

Yet from the moment they'd met, she had a swift and disconcerting attraction to him that he didn't seem to notice. And she didn't dare reveal.

"He told me your full name was Beauregard Charlemagne, but you refused to be called anything but Beau," she said softly. The child listened, his expression rapt, as if he'd forgotten the injured pup in his arms. As if he was hungry to hear all Sonja had to say about his father. "He told me you were six years old, and you're one of the best cowboys he's ever known."

Well, she was stretching the truth a bit on that, but she figured the little boy needed to hear it, considering he'd only arrived in Montana Territory a few weeks ago. With no warning to the man who'd fathered him.

"Really?" Beau's sweet face beamed with pleasure.

"Really," she said, that pleasure wrapping ribbons around her heart.

Chet Lattimer was a handsome, rugged, blood-stirringly virile man. And aloof as could be. She suspected the feelings he had for his son, whatever they might be, were kept locked inside until he could come to terms with them.

The thought saddened her. This little boy clearly craved what Chet wasn't ready to give. As far as Sonja knew, Chet Lattimer had never been married. Beau had no mother, only Esther Grinnell, who looked after him during the day.

But for now he had her, she realized. Sonja. The Bird Lady he believed could help the injured pup. Beau had paid his penny and braved an illicit ride out to see her. His trust and hope in her could not be dismissed. She would do nothing to disappoint him.

Besides, Christmas was only two days away, and she couldn't help thinking Beau Lattimer was an unexpected gift.

Chet pulled up in front of the Grinnells' cabin with his thoughts riding on different roads. He didn't dismount but glanced up into the sky instead, the dirty gray clouds forming thick and heavy. He could smell snow in the air, which meant he'd have to haul extra hay out to the cattle. Break up the ice in the tanks, too, so they'd have water. A few of his cows could calve early, and he'd need to bring them in to the home range where he could keep an eye on them if they did.

And then there was Beau to take care of. The son he never knew he had until he showed up on Chet's doorstep, clutching the hand of a man claiming to know the boy's mother before she died. Chet had been stunned to recall the one evening he'd spent with her, a flirtatious actress from a troupe traveling through town seven years earlier and whom he hadn't seen since. The gruff troupe owner produced a worn page from a Bible showing him as Beau's father, as well as a letter from the woman pleading that he take their son in for raising. The man was gone before Chet could fathom the turn his life has taken.

It'd taken a big turn, for sure. And he'd yet to decide if it was a good one.

Fatherhood didn't fit into his plans, not when he had his ranch to run and troublesome Indians to fend off. He had no time to raise a child, had pitifully little knowledge of how, besides. And with Christmas coming, what was he expected to do?

He sighed. He needed a mother for the boy, no doubt about it. But unfortunately, females were few in this part of the country. Those that had settled in had already been claimed.

Except for Sonja Kaplan.

His thoughts locked on her and stayed put, which they tended to do when he least expected it. Sonja was a beautiful woman, fair-haired with eyes a soft shade of blue that could drag a man in and hold him captive before he even realized he'd been caught.

Trouble was, she was a strange one. Her obsession with those damn birds…he couldn't figure it. Most women preferred to do something different with their time and talent—raise a family, sew, cook, tend a garden—and the way folks talked about her….

Well, Chet refused to let himself get drawn in by malicious gossip. Truth was, though, she was alone out there in that cabin of hers with those pigeons. Understandable he'd be thinking of her like he was.

He was concerned about her, that's all.

Concerned.

"Oh, Mr. Lattimer!" Looking surprised, Esther Grinnell stopped short coming out her front door. Her husband, Don, had worked for Chet for years. Both of them, honest and trustworthy. "I didn't know you were out here."

Chet's thoughts scattered. The woman would think it odd to see him in her yard just sitting in the saddle, ruminating like he'd been.

"Sorry I'm late picking up Beau, Esther. Not enough hours in the day lately."

He made a move to dismount, though his son was nowhere in sight. Usually the boy came running out to meet him.

She held up a work-roughened hand to stop him. A large woman, she wore her gray hair in a severe bun, and her smiles were few and far between. But she was clean, upright and dependable. Main thing was, she took good care of Beau. Chet knew the extra money he paid her was appreciated.

"Don't bother gettin' down, Mr. Lattimer," she said. The tight set to her mouth showed displeasure. "He ain't here."

Chet tossed her a hard look. "What do you mean he's not here?"

"I'll let Herbie explain." She disappeared inside the cabin, but stepped right out again, dragging her son by his shirt sleeve. "Go on, boy. Tell him."

Herbie's downcast expression spelled guilt about something he was loath to admit. And that something included Beau. Unease crawled through Chet.

"I'm listening," he said sharply.

"We rode out to the Bird Lady's place this afternoon," Herbie mumbled.

Chet blinked. A five-mile ride, one that took them off Lattimer land. Herbie knew better. *Beau* knew better.

"That's right," Esther said, grim. "To see that hussy, Sonja Kaplan."

"Why? What business did you have with her, Herbie?" Chet asked, disregarding the woman's jaded opinion of Sonja.

"We was just ridin' out by the Yellowstone River 'cuz we didn't have nothin' else to do, but then Beau saw a wild pup with his leg caught in the rocks. He was yippin' and bleedin' bad, the pup was, so we got him out. It was Beau's idea to ask the Bird Lady to doctor him, Mr. Lattimer. Not mine. No, sir."

Chet's mind worked to put together the pieces. "So what'd you do? Leave him there?"

The boy hung his head. "Yes, sir."

"With the pup?"

"Yes, sir."

Chet breathed an oath. "Why?"

"Guess I got scared."

He narrowed an eye, tried hard not to show his annoyance with the boy.

"She do anything to make you that way?" he demanded, his gut telling him Sonja would've done nothing of the sort.

"No, sir. But well, Ma says she's strange, you know, bein' around those pigeons all the time."

Chet glanced up at the sky and those gray, darkening clouds. Nightfall would come early because of them. He thought of how narrow-minded Herbie Grinnell was, too, and how his mother's gossip affected the boy's thinking.

"I told Beau we had to go," Herbie said. "Honest, I did! But he wouldn't listen."

"Didn't mean you should've left him behind, did it?" Chet countered, letting his disapproval show.

"That's not all, Mr. Lattimer." Esther gave her son a firm nudge on the shoulder. "Go on. Finish the story, Herbie."

Herbie dug in his pocket, pulled out a shiny penny and held it out to Chet.

"Ma don't want me to have this," he muttered, looking guilty again.

"Tell him why," Esther prodded.

"Beau paid me to take him out to the Bird Lady's. Guess I don't deserve it for runnin' off and not bringin' him home like I should, bein's it's Christmas and all."

Chet gathered up the reins. He ignored the boy's outstretched hand and hoped Beau hadn't tried to make it home on his own. He'd get lost for sure, alone in the cold and dark, and Chet tried not to think of the consequences.

"Reckon Christmas doesn't have a thing to do with it, Herbie," he said, then turned his mount and rode hard toward Sonja's place.

Chapter Two

With Beau standing beside her at a worktable in the barn, Sonja carefully wrapped the furry leg with a long strip of white cotton. The gash, though not deep, was jagged and unsightly, and worry creased Beau's brow.

"You sure he's not gonna die?" he asked in an anguished tone, his concentration fixed on holding the pup still during her ministrations.

"I'm quite sure of it." Once the bleeding had stopped, she cleaned the wound and applied healing salve; all that remained was securing the bandage. Working quickly around the wiggling limb, she finally managed it. "There. See how strong he is? You can barely hold him. He'll be fine in a day or two."

"Honest?" Beau seemed amazed.

"Honest." She smiled.

His worry faded by degrees. "I knew you'd know what to do."

She couldn't fathom how he would, but she treasured the words, even as she wondered why he hadn't turned to Chet for help. When before had a child been so trusting in her?

His smile turned shy. "Thanks, Miss Sonja."

She'd been quick to discourage him from calling her the Bird

Lady and suggested he use her first name instead of anything more formal. She resisted reaching out to touch his cheek in affection. "You're welcome."

"Can I take him home now?"

Sonja lifted a wooden crate onto the table. The railroad used containers like this one to transport her pigeons out to Montana Territory, and the crate would be a good size for the pup to rest in. "I'm afraid not. His leg will hurt him too much. He'll have to stay here so I can watch over him and make sure he gets well."

His crestfallen expression tugged at her. "How long?"

"Tonight for sure." She set the cage next to the weary animal, lying quietly on the bloodstained blanket. She contemplated the orange-red fur, the black legs, the pointed black ears. The pup was not a pup, at least not in a dog sense. She chose her words carefully. "Beau, you have to understand he's not a dog like you thought. He's a red fox, and you can't keep him as a pet."

Beau's surprised glance dropped to the pup, then lifted to her with dismay. "I can't?"

"No." This time she did touch him, gently on his cool cheek, to soften the disappointment from all she must tell him. "He's not meant to live with people like us, even though I know you'd try hard to take good care of him. He was born to live in the wild with all the other foxes."

Sonja didn't explain the pup wouldn't be weaned yet from his mother, and that she and her mate could be looking for him at this very moment. Their threat to the safety of her pigeons had Sonja enduring waves of unease.

Yet she could do no less than watch over this injured creature for a little while, until she was assured he could survive on his own.

For Beau's sake. And the innocent trust he'd placed in her.

"Pa's not gonna like it I caught a fox, then," he mumbled.

She frowned. Would he really be as angry as Beau feared?

"He'll know you meant well and just made an honest mistake," she said, hoping to assure him.

He shrugged, looking miserable. "I'm always makin' mistakes."

"I'm sure that's not true."

"Pa's smart, and he knows everything."

"Hmm." She supposed he did, or at least, nearly so. Chet was well regarded in the community and had been one of the first ranchers to settle in the Territory. "But your father isn't six, either."

Looking troubled, Beau absently stroked the orange-red fur. He would have large hands when he grew up, she noted. Lean fingers, too. Strong like Chet's.

"He's gonna be mad that I'm here," Beau said.

She thought of Herbie Grinnell, long home by now. "Yes, well, that isn't entirely your fault, is it? Would you like to help me get the pup into the cage?"

The task helped distract Beau, if only for a bit. Once the pup was comfortable inside, she secured the lid.

"Are you going to leave him out here?" Beau asked.

"I am." She pulled her shawl closer against the afternoon's deepening chill. "It's quiet and safe. See his eyes closing? He wants to sleep. I'll come out later and feed him. How about that?"

"All right." He hunched his small shoulders and shuffled his feet in the dirt. "Then I guess it's time for me to go home."

Sonja could see his reluctance. Did he think she'd let him go without her?

But what remained of the daylight would be gone before she could get them both bundled up and ready for the ride back to the Lattimer ranch. And she had no desire to make the journey in the dark, not with the threat of troublesome Indians in the area.

"You'll do no such thing. Your father is probably on his way over here to get you right now. If he's not, he soon will be." She reached out her hand, and he slipped his own into hers without hesitation. Again that trust he had in her, and it was more endearing than ever.

Her thought took a different turn, that of seeing Chet again. It'd only be because of Beau, she told herself firmly, but she couldn't help the silly skittering of her pulse, nonetheless.

"Are you hungry?" she asked, walking with the boy out of the barn.

"Yeah. Mrs. Grinnell says I'm always hungry, like I got an empty leg or something."

Sonja laughed. It was then she remembered it was almost Christmas, and oh, how she'd loved this time of year when she was his age. "Well then. I'll just have to see what I can make for you, won't I?"

But before her mind could bring alive the beloved memories her mother had instilled in her from her native Sweden, Beau halted in his tracks.

"Miss Sonja, look! There's an Indian!" he choked and tugged on her hand. "Run, before he sees us!"

Her heart jumped to her throat; her gaze jerked in the direction he pointed, her front yard, her eyes expecting to see the demonic savage who'd killed in cold blood the man she almost married. A warrior brave who kept his face smeared with black war paint and who rode a coal-black pony and brought terror into the lives of innocent people throughout Montana Territory and beyond.

Black Thunder.

But it wasn't him. Oh, thank God, it wasn't.

Sonja pressed a hand to her breast in relief, her gaze clinging to the brightly colored, striped blanket of her friend Three Feathers—Black Thunder's half brother. Three Feathers suffered great shame from the crimes Black Thunder committed in the white man's world, which brought much disgrace to their people.

Three Feathers held a line with two trout on it, and Sonja knew then why he'd come.

"It's all right, Beau. He's brought us a gift." She slid her arm around his narrow shoulders and pulled him against her in comfort. "Come with me. I'd like you to meet him."

"Evening, Mr. Lattimer," the young soldier called out.

Chet slowed his horse at the buckboard wagon's approach. He'd seen the man in town a time or two and knew he was stationed at nearby Fort Keough, north of the river a spell. Recalled him as a friendly sort.

Which was something Chet didn't need or want right now.

Friendly.

He touched a finger to the brim of his Stetson to return the greeting. "Evening."

The wagon halted. Common courtesy forced Chet to do the same, though the impatience to keep moving simmered inside him.

"You headed out to Sonja's place?" the soldier asked.

Sonja. Not Miss Kaplan.

"I am," he said, frowning. "How'd you know?"

He grinned. "Because you're almost there. Been there a time or two myself."

...to see that hussy, Sonja Kaplan.

Esther Grinnell's words shot back into his memory. The soldier's familiarity with her rankled, gave credence to the gossip Esther relished besides—and did little to salvage Sonja's tarnished reputation.

"Have you?" Chet said, his tone cool.

"Yes, sir." From beneath his fur cap, he slanted Chet a knowing glance. "She's sure easy on the eyes, isn't she?"

An instant image of her formed in Chet's mind. Hair the color of warm honey. A smile that could make him forget to breathe. And skin so creamy and smooth, a man would be hard-pressed to keep from touching her to discover every silken inch....

Chet scowled. What the hell was he thinking? He'd never touched Sonja Kaplan in his life. Didn't intend to, either. And he wouldn't be riding all the way out to see her if it wasn't for Beau, which only went to show the more time he wasted talking to the soldier was time spent away from getting there.

Resolute, Chet gathered up his reins.

"My son went out to see her today," he said to quash any ideas the lusty fellow might have about Chet's intentions. "I need to bring him home, that's all." He hesitated. The worry that Beau might have tried to head back alone had been persistent since he left the Grinnells. "You didn't happen to see him, did you? A six-year-old, wearing a Stetson and blue dungarees?"

"Out here?" The soldier appeared surprised. "No, sir. Haven't seen a soul."

Chet nodded, taking some reassurance; though, just because the soldier hadn't seen him didn't mean Beau wasn't lost somewhere else. "Good."

"Wouldn't be safe for a young'un, not with Indians around, showing up when folks least expect it."

His lips thinned. He'd heard stories to chill his blood. Sonja's had been one of the worst, being this close to home. It'd been a damn shame her intended had been killed by that renegade band of warriors. Wasn't fair she'd had to endure it. And it scared the hell out of Chet that his son might be in danger, no matter how remote the chances.

"No. It wouldn't," he said.

The soldier regarded him with a look that was more astute than Chet would've liked.

"She's a good woman, Mr. Lattimer. We're lucky to have her."

He supposed time would tell on that. Most likely, gossips like Esther wouldn't agree. He gave the soldier a curt nod and spurred his horse forward.

"Tell her Private Fetterman said hello, would you?" he called after Chet. "Reckon she'll remember who I am."

Chet set his teeth and kept riding. He had no plans to tell Sonja anything. It was no business of his who her friends were, male or otherwise. Why they knew her. Or how.

An honorable line of thinking that went up like smoke when he entered the lane leading up to her cabin and spied an Indian brave climbing onto his horse, tethered in her yard. The bright stripes on his blanket splashed color into the deepening dusk.

Recognition hit Chet hard.

Three Feathers. Black Thunder's half brother.

Alarm stabbed through Chet, swift as a warrior's arrow. For a moment he sat frozen, the fear cutting through him that Three Feathers had attacked Sonja and Beau, and they were lying dead inside her cabin. A raw debilitating fear that Chet had arrived too late to save them from their suffering.

But Three Feathers appeared in no hurry to leave, and his vicious brother was nowhere to be seen. The brave uttered no blood-curdling cries, had no war paint smeared on his dark cheeks.

He appeared at ease, riding off on his pony.

Peaceful.

As if he was just a friend, paying a call to a woman living alone, and what the *hell* business would she have with him if he was?

Chet didn't know, but by God he intended to find out. If she was sweetening up soldiers in the United States Army, then befriending an Indian brave with ties to the enemy… If she was betraying her country in any way, and if Beau was there, witness to it all…

His mind spinning with ugly suspicions, Chet rode up to the cabin, leaped off his horse and burst through her front door.

Chapter Three

He didn't expect to see them at the kitchen table with their hands busy and their heads together, talking quietly while they worked.

Which they stopped doing at his abrupt arrival.

Seeing him, Beau jumped.

Sonja cried out. Whatever it was she'd been making flew from her fingers and scattered over the tabletop.

Straw, he realized. Pieces of straw.

"Pa!"

"Chet, oh!"

He ignored them both. The fragrant smell of bread baking assailed his senses. A couple of filleted fish lay on paper, ready for frying. Next to them, a bowl heaped with chopped potatoes.

Normal, like any woman's kitchen would be.

He closed the door. His suspicions about her wavered.

Maybe she hadn't betrayed anyone, after all.

Maybe he should apologize for barging into her home without knocking.

But he didn't. Not yet.

She had a nice home. Smaller than his own, neat and clean.

Her furniture, what pieces she owned, gleamed in the lantern light.

A fire crackled at the hearth, too. The warmth drew him inward, closer to the kitchen table. To them. Reminded him how cold it was outside. That snow was coming. Reminded him, too, of all he had to do to get ready for it.

"I suspect you've come for Beau," Sonja said stiffly.

She didn't act as if she had anything to hide. But she looked miffed with him. Maybe a little hurt, too.

She was entitled, he knew. Considering.

"Yes." His voice sounded gruff, even to his own ears. "He shouldn't have come out here."

"Herbie and I—" Beau began to explain.

"I know." Chet cut him short. "He told me."

"They found a pup—" Sonja tried to defend him.

Chet swung a hard gaze toward her. "I know that, too."

Her lips clamped shut. He sensed she had more to say, but she didn't. Not in front of Beau.

"Let's go, son," Chet said.

He had more to say, too. The scolding Beau deserved for his disobedience. But Chet would do so later. A long-ride-home's worth of later.

"But—" The boy looked dismayed.

"Now." He kept his tone firm.

"Aw, Pa."

"He's hungry, Chet." Sonja rose from her chair. "Won't you at least stay for supper? The bread will be done soon, and I'll fry up the trout and potatoes—"

"No."

The word was out before Chet could stop it, before he could think through how appealing a woman's hot-cooked meal would be in his empty stomach. That the cold ride home would be better endured after being fed and warmed in her kitchen.

"Three Feathers caught the fish, Pa!" Beau said. "Just for us."

Chet's brow shot up. "Us?"

Again his suspicions reared. What relationship did the Indian have with her? What had his son witnessed?

"Yeah, and he said I should have some tonight. Honest!"

"He did, did he?"

"Can we stay? Can we?"

Chet steeled himself against the boy's pleas. "It's late. We have to leave."

"Aw, Pa."

"You heard me, Beau. I'll not say it again."

Beau turned to Sonja, his brown eyes wide and appealing, his expression all but begging her to do something to change Chet's mind.

She reached out and smoothed the boy's hair. Her smile appeared forced. "You have to mind your father, Beau. He knows what's best for you."

Reluctantly he rose from his chair. "All right."

She turned to Chet, her smile gone. "At least let me send something home with you," she said firmly. "Some hard-boiled eggs and corn muffins." Her chin lifted to a defiant angle. "Or will you deny him those, too?"

The challenge stung. Her eyes—no longer softly blue, but darkened and accusing—held his without wavering. He stood his ground with her, not moving, not speaking, but probing the depths of that stormy gaze.

He found no guilt in them. No shame. If Sonja Kaplan had illicit dealings with Three Feathers in some way, Chet could find no sign of it.

Instead he read her rebellion, reminding him her challenge to give Beau something to eat still hung in the air between them.

"Fine," he said at last. "The eggs and corn muffins will be…fine."

In moments she had them wrapped in a towel for taking. Fighting tears, Beau found his coat and Stetson, but it was Sonja who buttoned him up, clear to his neck.

"Will you remember to feed my pup?" he asked in a plaintive voice.

"Of course I will. Did you think I would forget?" She pulled his collar up, covering his ears, her own voice not quite steady.

"Thanks, Miss Sonja." Suddenly Beau flung his arms around her neck. "I liked being with you today. You're my bestest friend now."

Her eyes closed, and she held him for a long moment. "You're my best friend, too. I'll see you soon, all right?"

"I guess."

But the boy didn't seem convinced. Head hanging, he pulled out of her arms and shuffled toward Chet.

Something tightened, deep in his chest. He didn't know what to make of this attachment his son had formed for this woman, but Chet was all too aware it was an attachment Beau had never shown toward *him.*

Troubled by it, Chet lifted Beau into the saddle, climbed up behind him, and headed back to the cold emptiness of his own home.

Sonja leaned her head back against the door and listened to the sound of hoofbeats fade away.

For a long time she didn't move. The ache in her heart left her numb and hurting from a sense of loss that had her hovering on the verge of tears.

This ache—it was different from what she'd experienced when her parents had died, leaving her alone in the world and forcing her to fend for herself at a young age. And it was different from losing Robert, too, the man she'd almost married before Black Thunder ruthlessly killed him last winter.

No, the ache came from a hurt far more tangible, a deep need to be loved for the woman she was. Not for the one gossiping neighbors had created, who wove rumors around her because they didn't understand. But a living, breathing woman longing for a husband and children to fill the emptiness in her life.

The family she'd lost, not once but twice.

Beau Lattimer understood. In his short time with her, he'd sensed her need to love. Her capacity for it. He'd responded to her need quickly, with innocence and trust.

Because he needed to be loved, too.

And that made her hurt all the more. He was such a sweet child—perhaps Chet was blind to the affection his son craved. Most likely Chet was too stubborn to acknowledge he needed some affection, too.

Was he too busy struggling with the responsibilities of unexpected fatherhood that he'd blinded himself to the joys that came from being one?

Sonja moaned in frustration. Chet Lattimer had everything most men worked years for—land, cattle, success. A son. All he lacked was someone to share them with. A woman on his arm and at his side.

Why couldn't it be her? Lonely Sonja Kaplan. She was willing and available. She could love his son as her own.

She could love him, too.

Maybe she already did.

Is that why she was thinking about him like this? Because she'd fallen in love with him? She'd always admired his place in the community, the respect he'd earned amongst the townspeople. Had she been so easily swayed by his masculinity, the strengths that seemed so much a part of him? Had she thought too often of how his arms would feel around her? His kisses hot and hungry on her mouth? Had she dreamed too vividly what it would be like to be wanted forever by Chet Lattimer?

Her lip curled. But no. He wouldn't want her. The Bird Lady. He'd want someone different, a woman regarded with more esteem, who possessed the same honor in the community he did.

Besides, he'd ask questions she could give no answers for. The reason for her devotion to the pigeons—her secret work for the United States Army. She could say nothing until Black Thunder was captured for his crimes, and who knew when that would be?

Sonja straightened and resolutely stepped away from the door. She had to forget about Chet and Beau. She had to give up thinking about being part of their lives. She had to keep going on with her own.

She couldn't be foolish. Or sad. Or lonely.

She had to be strong and independent.

Her attention fell on the straw figures scattered on her kitchen table. Swedish Christmas ornaments, cherished from her childhood. Beau had been intrigued by them—stars, pinecones, angels—and their intricate designs. It'd been sheer impulse to show him how to make one.

Pensive, Sonja lifted the star he'd been working on when his father arrived. Beau had wanted to tie narrow strips of red ribbon on each point himself to hold the ends of the straw together. His efforts had been charmingly crude, and Sonja promised him he could take it home when they finished.

Neither happened.

The hapless-looking ornament reminded Sonja of herself— half-decorated. She, too, needed some ribbon in her life to brighten her days. A man, to make her complete.

Someone like Chet.

Feeling the dismal weight of her disappointment, the loneliness that seemed worse than before, she gathered up the straw ornaments and tried to put him and his son from her mind.

Chapter Four

December 24

"Esther will have Christmas dinner on the table by noon," Don Grinnell said. "You're welcome to bring Beau over and help us eat it."

Chet stabbed his long-pronged pitchfork into the hay, hefted a good-size pile and tossed it over the edge of the wagon. A small group of cattle moseyed over to have a taste. He glanced at his foreman.

"Thanks for the offer," he said.

Don watched him with a grin. "Is that a yes or a no?"

Chet rested his arm on the fork handle and frowned.

"Never been one to take the time to celebrate Christmas," he admitted. "Always had too much work to do."

"Yep."

Being on Chet's payroll as long as he'd been would confirm Chet wasn't telling the man something he didn't already know. Every year Don invited him for Christmas dinner, and every year Chet declined.

"But you're gonna have to change that," Don said. "You got Beau to think of now."

Chet grunted. Don didn't need to remind him. It'd been on his mind these past few days how to make the time special for his son. The boy deserved a little fussing over. It'd be his first Christmas without his mother, and Chet figured he'd be missing her a bunch.

Not that Beau talked about her much. She'd been sick a long time. Might be they hadn't celebrated, either.

Which didn't make it right, Chet knew, his frown deepening. A kid was a kid, no matter what. As his father, Chet had a duty to start building some happy memories for him. If he didn't, who would?

Trouble was, Chet had no idea how. He didn't have a gift ready, didn't have a special meal planned, didn't have any decorations hung. What did a six-year-old expect, anyway? What would one want?

And here it was, Christmas Eve, and Chet was plumb out of time.

He glanced up into the sky, to the snow-swollen clouds spread out as far as he could see. He could talk to Esther about it, he supposed. She had a passel of kids, Herbie being one of the oldest. Surely she'd have an idea or two to share with him.

And then there was Sonja.

She'd been on his mind, too.

A lot.

And not about Christmas, either.

He'd behaved like an ass with her last night. By the time the realization soaked into his stubborn, thick-headed skull, it was too late. The damage had been done. Enough hurt feelings to last them all a good long while.

Chet grimaced. It'd serve him right if she never spoke a civil word to him again. Serve him right if Beau didn't, either. The ride home had been somber, to say the least. Chet had never seen the boy looking so sad, and his gut twisted that it was his fault for making him that way.

He was a sorry excuse for a father. No doubt about it.

"Well now, look over there," Don murmured.

Chet roused himself from his grim thoughts. Realized his foreman had stopped forking hay and had climbed into the wagon seat, the reins in his hands, ready to move further down the range.

Chet straightened, his gaze sharpening in the direction Don pointed, and found movement on the horizon. A pony and rider trotting along at a good pace, just the two of them, with no one else around.

As if they knew just where they wanted to go.

And that rider was a six-year-old boy who'd decided to defy his father and ride back out to be with the woman who'd come to mean something to him.

Sonja checked the identification band on the pigeon's right leg, compared it to the number stamped in ink on the fourth feather of the right wing, and then the sixth feather of the left. All of them matched. Which meant all her birds were accounted for.

Once she recorded the identification number in her inventory book, the Monthly Loft Inventory report would be complete. She'd already finished her classification report, which contained flight records and percentages of birds who could deliver their messages within a reasonable amount of time. She was pleased to see they arrived at their destinations seventy-five percent of the time and higher.

A fine testament to the training she'd given them.

Her records were absolutely essential to know which homing pigeons she must use when the Army needed them most.

Like now. To track down Black Thunder.

Because her birds could fly faster than a horse could run, the military posts used the pigeons to communicate with one another about the renegade's whereabouts and to keep civilians safe from his band's marauding.

The Army appreciated her work, even if her neighbors didn't. But then, the soldiers understood the secrets she must keep.

Her neighbors merely gossiped about them.

Sonja closed her book and set it aside. She blamed her peevish mood on a restless night made worse by awakening only to remember that tonight would be Christmas Eve and that she would spend it alone.

Again.

She dreaded the prospect more than she'd ever dreaded it before. Was it because of Beau and seeing his joy yesterday from her prized straw ornaments? Was it because he had no mother to spoil him? Was it because she had no husband or child of her own, and what was Christmas if she didn't have anyone to share it with?

Yes. All those things.

She bit her lip and fought despair. Wallowed in it for a good long while, right there in the pigeon loft, until a seed of a notion formed and took root, then flowered inside her.

So what if she was alone? That didn't mean she couldn't *find* someone to celebrate Christmas with, did it? And that someone would be Chet and Beau, of course, who had no woman in their lives to make the holiday special for them.

Sonya could make it special—by using her mother's beloved traditions, brought with her all the way from Sweden before Sonja had been born. Sonja had grown to love them as much as she did.

Her mind filled with a rush of memories. She could make cookies—her favorite rosettes, the delicate fried cookies lightly sweetened with powdered sugar. She could tell Beau the story about Tomte, the Christmas gnome who had a long white beard and who wore red robes and who rode a goat named Julbok. She could light candles and tell him the blessed story of the Christ Child, too.

Surely Chet wasn't angry anymore and would appreciate her efforts. He'd see her as someone different from the mysterious Bird Lady everyone scorned, and then maybe she could invite him over for Christmas dinner. He would bring Beau, of course, and they could stay as long as they'd like.

The whole day, if they wanted.

With the excitement building inside her, the anticipation of being able to see Chet and Beau again, of having a new beginning with them, she left the pigeon loft and secured the door behind her. She'd start frying the cookies first, then—

She stopped short, seeing the man standing at her door, his hands clasped behind him. Evidently he'd knocked and was waiting for her to answer, not knowing she wasn't inside the cabin, but instead in the loft.

General Nelson Miles rarely came to see her. Only once, in fact, and that was to bring her the news of Robert's death.

His presence would mean something happened, something grave, and an instant fear for Chet and Beau shot through her. Had they run into trouble last night while they were riding home in the dark?

Trouble with Black Thunder?

Sonja tried not to be afraid. She gathered her composure. Squared her shoulders. Managed a smile and strode forward.

"General Miles. How nice to see you."

He turned at her voice. "Miss Kaplan. There you are."

He carried an air of authority about him fitting for his rank. Double rows of brass buttons adorned the front of his dark-blue uniform, and he kept a holster in plain view. Yet despite the power he wielded, Sonja found him gracious and kind, an impression at odds with his ruthless prowess in military matters.

"Have you come alone?" she asked, considering it odd he had none of his men with him as escort.

"I've only made a run into town to do some shopping." His expression twinkled. "Mrs. Miles would never forgive me if I didn't have a gift waiting for her under the tree tomorrow morning."

"As well she shouldn't." Sonja's mouth softened. Some of her apprehension lifted at his light-hearted tone. Perhaps the purpose for his visit wasn't serious, after all.

"I'm on my way back to Fort Keough now. Forgive me for stopping by when you weren't expecting me."

She inclined her head. "Of course. As long as it isn't bad news that compelled you to do so."

"It isn't. At least, I hope it won't be."

"Would you like to come in?" She hid her relief. "We can talk where it's warm. And the coffee should still be hot on the stove."

"I won't stay long." He gestured that she should go ahead of him. "I'm sure you have much to do to get ready for the holiday. A busy time for everyone."

Sonja grasped the wooden handle, but before she could turn it and go inside, a horse snuffled from somewhere just beyond her range of vision. She froze, reason telling her it wasn't General Miles's mount, tethered in the front and in plain view, but another's beyond the cabin, in the direction of the pigeon loft. From the growing sound of hoofbeats, the horse was coming closer at a steady lope.

Sonja's fears kicked in—Black Thunder, always Black Thunder—and the general went for his revolver, his fears forming as quickly as hers.

The pony appeared, looming into view from around the corner, but drawing up short in the yard.

General Miles chuckled. "Well, I'll be damned."

Sonja stared at the boy sitting in the saddle, looking far too young to be in one, and by himself, especially.

He grinned and pushed up the brim of his hat. "Hello, Miss Sonja."

"Beau! What are you doing here?"

"I come to see you."

His expression revealed his triumph that he'd managed it. Instinct told her it was a decision he'd made on his own.

She pressed her fingers to her lips in alarm. "Alone?"

"Yes, ma'am." But a bit of that triumph faded, as if he guessed what she'd ask next.

She moved away from the door toward him. "Does your father know?"

She reached up to help him down. On the ground again, he stuffed his hands into his pockets. His glance dropped.

"No, ma'am."

"Oh, Beau," she breathed, troubled.

Sonja didn't relish another encounter with Chet like they'd had last night. He'd be angry all over again. Disappointed, too, and—Sonja had to admit—rightly so.

"But I'll tell him, Miss Sonja. Honest I will! When I get back home."

"Reckon it's too late for that, son."

At the low voice behind them, Sonja whirled, a squeak of surprise slipping from her throat. Beau paled. Even General Miles appeared startled.

And all three of them watched Chet get down from his horse and walk toward them.

Chapter Five

But it was Sonja's gaze he met and held.

"Hello, Chet," she said.

He heard the slight quaver in her voice. Saw the worry, the apprehension in her features from what he might say. Or do.

Who did she think he was? A monster for a father?

After last night, well, hell, maybe she did.

But he didn't want to be. And wasn't. He'd show her he wasn't.

He pulled his gaze away and squatted in front of Beau. Chet half expected him to bury his face in Sonja's skirts. He had a powerful ally in her, for sure. Might be he'd try to use her to hide from the repercussions of what he'd done. Seek her protection from whatever he expected Chet to do.

He didn't. He met Chet's glance square. Owned up to what he'd done. His stance revealed he braced himself for the consequences.

Chet admired him for it.

"Hello, Pa," Beau said.

"Hello, Beau." He kept his voice low, easy. "Quite a ride you took by yourself."

"Yes, sir." He shuffled. "How'd you know I was here?"

"I followed you, that's how."

"Oh."

"Took some courage to do what you did. Took some smart thinking to remember how to come out here, too. Five miles is a long way for a boy your age. But you didn't take a wrong turn. Not a one."

Beau didn't seem to know what was coming. Just nodded carefully.

"I'm proud of you for that, at least. You could've gotten yourself good and lost," Chet said.

"Aren't you mad at me?" Beau eyed him warily, as if he couldn't believe it.

"I've been doing some figuring on it. But Miss Sonja has a guest, and right now he's more important. We'll talk about this later." Chet's voice turned firm. He didn't want Beau believing his actions would have no outcome.

Beau's gaze jumped to the other man, as if just now getting a good look at him. His glance touched on the brass buttons, and his expression turned to awe.

"Beau, why don't you go to the barn and see the pup?" Sonja suggested. "His leg is much better today."

"Can I?" His attention quickly swayed, his gaze swung toward her with a leap of excitement.

"Of course. But leave him in the cage until your father and I can help you with him."

"Thanks, Miss Sonja!" Boots clomping in the dirt, he took off at a full run toward the barn.

Chet rose, and Sonja's gaze followed him up. Those eyes of hers...blue and deep. Soft looking. He sensed her pleasure at what he'd done. Her approval. The promise of something more....

Chet couldn't let himself drown in the sweet pools. He was

on the brink, for sure, but this officer from the United States Army, standing patient and silent, had a purpose in being with her.

Chet had to know what it was. The truth of why the military kept company with the mysterious Sonja Kaplan. He had to learn, once and for all, if the gossip believed by people like Esther Grinnell had any merit.

"Let me introduce you, Chet," Sonja said.

The words held a quiet kind of pride. Had she known what he was thinking? The conclusions he'd drawn from seeing a military man who'd been ready to walk into the privacy of her home. Just the two of them. Alone.

"I'd like that," he said roughly.

He refused to break the pull of her gaze, wanted his own to tell her it was important to him to know. That he wanted to trust her, but couldn't. Not yet.

Most likely she suspected he was no better than the rest. Weak and too easily led by the opinions of others. Chet had tried to keep her business out of his own, but it wasn't easy, not when Beau held her in high regard. She was a beautiful woman, surviving on her own, with no one to warm her bed at night.

And wasn't that a hell of a shame?

When he had no one in his, either.

But the officer made the first move by stepping forward and extending his hand. "I'm General Nelson Miles."

"Chet Lattimer." He hid his surprise and took the hand in a firm grasp. "An honor, sir."

He'd heard of the man. Who around these parts hadn't? The general had built an illustrious career in campaigns against vengeful Indian tribes all over the plains. His gallantry was legendary.

"My apologies if my son intruded upon your intentions," Chet said.

"He didn't. Beau, isn't it? A fine-looking boy."

Chet frowned. "With a mind of his own, I'm afraid."

The general chuckled. "I've been a father twice over. Think of it as independence that will serve him well when he's full grown."

Liking the man for his perspective, Chet grinned. "I'll do that."

"I've invited General Miles in for coffee, Chet," Sonja said. "Come in and join us, won't you?"

"I'll not be staying, after all, Miss Kaplan," the officer said before Chet could respond. "Now that you've got callers, I don't want to intrude."

"Oh, but you're not," she said quickly.

"My son and I are the ones who are intruding," Chet added, well aware the general had arrived first.

"Not at all." His decision sounded firm. "I was on my way to Fort Keough before stopping here to see Miss Kaplan and really must be on my way. What I have to say won't take long, and it's something you need to hear besides, Chet. In fact, spread the word as best you can."

His grave expression had Chet's attention. "I'm listening."

"Black Thunder is somewhere in the area," he said without preamble. "His penchant to spill the white man's blood has me sick with fear for the safety of the innocent citizens around these parts."

Sonja shivered, her skin paling.

"I'm troubled he may want to retaliate against you for your work." The general looked grim. "And here you are, living by yourself."

Chet's blood turned cold at the danger Sonja was in, that the vicious Indian brave would single her out for revenge.

"Her work for you?" Chet didn't care if he was too bold for asking. "What kind of work?"

The officer's glance touched on Sonja. Her lashes lowered,

and she angled her face away, clearly reluctant to have the information revealed.

What did she have to hide?

"Miss Kaplan trains pigeons so we may use them to glean covert intelligence on the enemy," General Miles said. "Black Thunder, you realize, is only one enemy amongst many. However, at the moment he's the most immediate."

Chet's world tilted. The rumors, the speculating he'd done himself—never once had he thought the strange devotion to her birds was for the benefit of the Army. A necessity they depended on for the safekeeping of the citizenry—and themselves.

"Her skill is unmatched. The service she's given to her country is invaluable." General Miles's pride in her was obvious, yet his concern overshadowed it. "However, her skill is not without its risks. I must urge you both to use extreme caution until Black Thunder is stopped once and for all." He frowned. "I wish I had more information for you, but I don't." Stepping back, he touched a finger to his fur cap and gave a wry smile. "Now, I must take my leave before Mrs. Miles starts to fret. Merry Christmas to you."

"Merry Christmas," Chet and Sonja murmured automatically.

The general mounted up and left, the irony of his greeting lingering in his wake.

"Well." Sonja pivoted away then. "I'd best see to Beau in the barn."

Chet grasped her elbow, stopping her in midstride. "Not so fast."

Her gaze flew upward and clashed with his. "Whatever you're thinking, don't."

"I'm thinking you deserve an apology."

Her brow arched, giving her a haughty look.

"You do?" she said coolly. "From whom?"

"From me. From everyone."

"Why? Because I'm not what everyone thought I was?" Her chin kicked higher.

…that hussy, Sonja Kaplan.

He scowled at Esther's words marching through his memory. "Yes, damn it."

She tugged against his hold, but he refused to release her. "Nothing has changed, Chet. I'm the same person I was before you learned the truth about what I do. I'm still the Bird Lady."

"You've been ridiculed by the very people you're trying to protect."

"It doesn't matter what others say or think about me. My conscience is clear."

"Mine isn't."

"Please." The fight seemed to drain from her. "This is silly. I can't stop what people say, and I'm not going to try."

But Chet wasn't ready to give up just yet. "Folks made assumptions based on what they saw." Why did he feel this need to make excuses for them? And himself, right along with them? "And—"

"Oh?" Again that brow came up. "What did they see? Besides a loft full of pigeons?"

"Soldiers." Chet hated how petty he sounded.

"Ah. Soldiers."

"Sonja." He searched for the words to make it all right and settled for what he knew, deep in his gut. "It wasn't fair to you. When folks find out—if they ever hear—well, damn it, *then* they'll understand."

"Yes. I suppose they would."

But she didn't look as if she believed it.

He remembered he still held her elbow, and that she only wore a knitted shawl against the morning's chill. Snow would begin to fall soon, and the longer he stood here with her, the better the chances he and Beau would get caught in it before they got home.

But he didn't want to leave. Not yet.

He wanted to warm her. Comfort her. Take her into his arms and fold her against him. Maybe give her a good, long kiss to soothe the hurt she'd been feeling these past weeks and months. The loneliness she would've endured being an outcast in the community through no fault of her own.

And then there was Black Thunder.

Chet didn't know how he could leave her to defend herself against the warrior if he attacked. Given the danger she was in, how could anyone?

"Let me go, please," she said quietly, as if she could read the questions warring in his head. "I have to check on Beau."

Knowing they both should, he released her. Reluctantly. She turned and strode toward the barn, not waiting to see if he followed.

He did, though he had one more question that needed an answer, one more suspicion to be laid to rest.

How Black Thunder's half brother, Three Feathers, fit into her life.

Chapter Six

"You didn't tell me the pup was a red fox," Chet said in quiet surprise.

He leaned a hip against the worktable with his arms crossed over his chest. His sheepskin coat broadened his shoulders, added bulk to a body already tall and contoured with muscle. His presence dominated the confines of her small barn. Sonja could hardly think with him standing next to her like this, the three of them huddled around the fox's cage.

He kept his voice low, she knew, for Beau's sake. Free from re-crimination. She could tell by the furrow of his dark brows he had the same concerns she did about letting the boy keep the animal.

"I thought Beau would've mentioned it," she said.

"He didn't." His somber glance touched on his son, captivated by the pup peering out at him through the wire screen. "He hasn't said much of anything to me, I'm afraid."

Sonja didn't press the issue. She could only hope Chet's relationship with his son would begin to thrive from here on out. Beau needed love; Chet showed signs of giving it. And once he was able to acknowledge how much Beau meant to him, wouldn't he want a woman to love, too?

Sonja didn't know what to think. She certainly was afraid to hope. And she scolded herself for being foolish enough to already have. More than she should.

"Reckon you're not kin to having a fox around your birds," Chet murmured. "Even a pup as young as this one."

"I'm not," she admitted. Beau appeared oblivious to their conversation, being too busy making little-boy cooing noises at the fox.

"Trouble waiting to happen, for sure."

She found herself drawn to their cautious camaraderie. Besides the soldiers assigned to work with the birds, she rarely spoke of them to civilians. Now that Chet knew of their purpose, well, now she could.

She had General Miles to thank for that. Her secret no longer secret. Clearly he'd been worried about the threat Black Thunder posed to her and felt Chet could be trusted.

Sonja felt he could, too. A womanly intuition which insisted Chet Lattimer was an upright and honorable man. Loyal to his country and those determined to defend it. Hadn't he inspired respect throughout the Territory because of those very things?

"You've done a good job doctoring the pup," Chet said. "I know you did it for Beau, despite the risks."

Her glance shifted to him. Heat smoldered in his dark eyes, sending her pulse into a skittish rhythm. Warming her blood.

But she sensed something else, deep in that warmth.

A question, uncertainty she couldn't quite define.

Or was she being too sensitive?

"How could I have refused him?" she said, flustered, her voice not as steady as it should have been. "He'd taken a few risks of his own to come out here."

"Look, Miss Sonja! He wants to play with me!" Beau exclaimed.

Sonja dragged her glance from Chet and settled it over his

son. The fox did indeed appear restless, pawing at the screen and making growling noises in his throat.

"Can we take him out? Can we?" Beau asked.

"Beau." Chet's low voice tempered the boy's enthusiasm. "He's not used to being in a cage. He wants out, all right, but it's not a good idea. He's not meant to be played with, like a dog."

Sonja leaned toward Beau and touched his cheek gently. "Remember when I told you last night he'll want to live with other foxes when he feels better?" She kept her smile bright. "He's missing them, so it's time to let him go back home."

"Now?" His disappointment tugged at her heartstrings.

"It'll be snowing soon, son." Chet glanced out the barn's window, as if checking to see if flakes had already begun to fall. "Best to set him free before it starts."

Sonja stilled. She hadn't figured on snow. Her mind leaped to the plans she'd made only a short time ago, the rosettes she wanted to fry as a treat for Chet and Beau. The Christmas stories waiting to be told. Even the straw ornament Beau needed to finish….

Disappointment rolled through her. Of course Chet would want to get them both home before the weather changed. It'd make sense for him to set the fox free on the way there, too, and now she wouldn't have time to make them rosettes, after all.

"I guess," Beau mumbled, crestfallen. But in the next moment his expression lit up. "Can Miss Sonja come with us, then, Pa?"

The question startled her. Scattered her thoughts from frying cookies to the prospect of riding with them to the river, just the three of them.

And what a delight that would be.

"I'd like that, son," Chet said, his tone a husky rumble. "But we'd better ask her first."

He leveled her with another intense gaze. Probing and dark.

And there that feeling came again. Chet Lattimer holding back, clinging to an uncertainty he'd yet to voice.

Was it the gossip? Did he still think it was true?

Maybe.

The possibility stung. What would she have to do? Strip her heart and soul naked so he could see the person she truly was? That she wasn't a hussy, wasn't mysterious, wasn't doing anything illicit?

That she was simply Sonja Kaplan, who just happened to train pigeons for the Army for reasons that were very, very important?

Evidently General Miles's explanation wasn't enough. Maybe it would never be enough. But today was the day before Christmas, and she wanted to spend as little of it alone as she could.

"I'd love to come with you," she said. "Thank you for asking."

Beau whooped and swung his arms; he threw his whole body into an exuberant jump. "Hooray! Miss Sonja's going on a horse ride with us!"

A corner of Chet's mouth lifted. "Seems to me you're looking mighty happy to let the pup go home now."

"Yeah, because Miss Sonja makes me feel happy." He pushed his hat up higher above his eyes.

"She does, does she?"

"Yeah." And he whooped again.

Trying not to laugh, but touched beyond words, Sonja took a step to leave. "I'll get my coat."

"Not so fast, Sonja."

She halted at the quiet command. Chet unfolded his long body and straightened from the worktable.

"Beau, you left your pony stand-hitched in the yard," he said. "Bring him on up to the barn. We'll leave as soon as Miss Sonja is ready."

"Sure, Pa." He took off at a run out the door.

Chet turned toward her. Blocked her path so she couldn't step away. "I don't want you to stay here alone."

"Here?" Taken aback, she stared at him. "In my home?"

"It's not safe."

Though General Miles's warning played in her mind, her brow arched with barely concealed exasperation. "Then, where would you have me go?"

"I'll help you find someplace. I have friends who'll take you in."

Like Esther Grinnell? Who gossiped about her and thought her strange and nothing but a hussy?

"Your friends, but not mine," she said stiffly. "You expect me to show up at their door unannounced. On Christmas Eve, no less." This time she did show her exasperation.

"There's a boardinghouse in town, then."

"No."

His lips thinned. "Black Thunder won't go looking for you there."

"You're very kind to be concerned for my welfare, but I'm not leaving."

He scowled. "Has nothing to do with being kind."

"I have my pigeons to think of."

"Get one of the general's soldiers to take care of them. Just until Black Thunder is gone."

She blinked. "You're joking, of course."

"I'm completely serious, Sonja."

And she could tell he was. The hard set to his jaw showed him to be resolved in his purpose of keeping her out of harm's way.

A man like Chet Lattimer could do no less for a woman who lived alone under the threat of danger. But if his conscience compelled him to protect her, well, hers steadfastly refused to let him.

"I can't leave. And I won't." She drew herself up as tall as she could to look him square in the eye. "But thank you for your concern."

"Didn't Robert's death teach you anything?" he growled.

She stood stock still. How dare he confront her with the brutality of her intended's death? How could he possibly think it meant nothing?

"That was his name, wasn't it? Robert Walker? The man you would've married if Black Thunder and his band hadn't killed him first." Chet pressed on, ruthless to drive his point home. "You, more than anyone, should know you could be next."

"I've lived with the possibility for months. I'm armed. I can defend myself."

"You can defend yourself." His scowl revealed his opinion of that.

"I'm not afraid."

"Well, damn it, you should be."

"Chet." Her hand fisted to keep from touching him. How long had it been since she'd had a man worry over her? Since Papa, and that'd been so long ago. "Really, I don't want to leave. My work is important. I can't simply walk away from it."

His eyes darkened, giving warning to the tempest brewing within him. "I don't know what the hell Robert was thinking, saddling you with those pigeons. He should've known the risks."

"He did, I assure you."

"Funny way, then, for a man to show his love for the woman he planned to marry."

She stiffened. "I resent that."

"Too bad you do."

Chet Lattimer wasn't a man to back down from his beliefs. Or expressing them. His stark honesty revealed he held yet another misconception about her, and she was determined that he, especially, must know the truth.

"I don't think he knew me long enough to love me, Chet. If he did, he certainly never showed it."

For a moment Chet didn't move. As if he needed a little time to absorb what she'd told him. "Then he was a damned fool."

She glanced away. Chet said the words as if they were wrenched from him, and her breath caught. The woman fortunate enough to be loved by him would know she was, every day of her life.

"I never knew Robert until I stepped off the train that brought me out here," she said quietly. She stared out the barn's lone window, seeing only the past. "I was a mail-order bride. Except we never made it to the bride part." She'd been robbed of a proper courtship and the bliss of falling in love. At the time, it hadn't seemed important, but after she'd met Chet, the longing returned, with a vengeance. "He was twenty years older than me and retired from the Army as a soldier. He continued training pigeons for them, but his health wasn't good. He needed someone in his life. We both did."

Sonja had hoped to banish the loneliness in hers forever, never dreaming Robert would be killed so soon, before their vows could be spoken.

"Why him, Sonja?" Chet asked. "A man so much older. A stranger."

"Because he was a pigeoneer, and I had always been fascinated by the homing instincts of the birds. My father worked for Reuters, a telegram company based out of London, so I grew up knowing the importance of imparting vital information throughout the world. It was the one thing Robert and I had in common."

"He hoped you'd take over his work?"

"Yes." The pigeons gave purpose to her days. What would she have done without them? "Maybe we would've learned to love each other eventually. Who knows?"

He stepped closer, as if he intended to take her into his arms.

"How could he not have fallen in love with you?" Chet demanded roughly.

Her pulse fluttered at the possibility of being held by Chet, maybe even kissed, too. Her mind was quick to imagine the feel of sliding her arms beneath his thick sheepskin coat. She'd press her body to his, burrow into his warmth. His male heat. She'd lift her mouth…

He'd make her feel protected, deliciously feminine, and the way his brows furrowed, his dark eyes smoldering with their hidden fires, she could tell he was thinking those things, too.

But the barn door hinges squeaked. Boot soles clomped on the packed dirt floor.

"Hey, Miss Sonja!" Beau exclaimed. "Don't you have your coat on *yet?*"

Chapter Seven

Snowflakes the size of quarter dollars floated lazily from the sky, as if all those fat gray clouds just couldn't hold them in anymore. Chet was glad there wasn't any wind to kick them around. If there was, they'd be in for a blizzard, for sure.

But the snow fell peaceably for the time being. Even made for something pretty to look at while they rode toward the river, considering the flakes hadn't yet begun to collect on the ground. Once the temperature started to drop in a few hours' time, though, bringing in nightfall, they would.

He'd lived through his share of winters in Montana Territory. This part of the country would look completely different by morning.

But for now, he'd enjoy the ride and forget about the chores he left undone on the ranch. Don was a hard worker; he'd get done what he could without Chet. What he didn't, well, they'd both get to tomorrow.

This ride with Sonja and Beau, Chet was enjoying it, all right. He found some satisfaction in being with them, in no real hurry, but with a sense of purpose that would have Beau remembering.

And Sonja, hell, she was the best part of the whole thing. His glance took her in, riding straight-backed beside him, Beau slightly ahead. She was a beautiful woman, dressed in a black wool coat with a velvet collar and knitted scarf, her bonnet tied warmly under her chin.

Beautiful.

He'd appreciated her honesty in telling him about Robert. For some reason, it'd been important to know about the man, his place in her life. Whether she loved him or not.

A relief she hadn't.

Chet knew it was selfish to think that way and none of his business, besides, but he couldn't deny the relief. The feeling had been strong, freeing, and he'd almost helped himself to a long, soul-stirring kiss from those full lips of hers.

Probably a good thing Beau came in when he did, Chet admitted. From the way Sonja had tilted her head back, from the way she'd been looking at him, her mouth parted, as if she was waiting, wanting him to kiss her....

Hell, no telling what would've happened.

She belonged with a man who could kiss her senseless every day of her life. Every night, too. She deserved the family he could give her, the children she was meant to have.

Beau was proof she had a way with them. The boy was smitten, but good.

"He's not even thinking about Christmas," Sonja murmured. "Have you noticed?"

Chet hadn't noticed anything but her beside him, and his brain scrambled. "Who?"

Her brows puckered in delicate surprise. "Beau. Your son."

He dragged his glance toward the boy, a horse's length ahead, and endured a stab of guilt. Beau had been willing to lead them to the place where he'd found the little fox; in fact, he seemed proud that Chet trusted him to get them there. But Sonja was right. He acted as if nothing else but the pup was on his mind.

"Not once has he talked about Santa coming," she said. "He's never mentioned a toy he's been hoping for. No gift at all."

Chet recalled his intent to speak to Esther. That was before Beau took off for Sonja's, though, and now Chet wouldn't have a chance.

"He's six," Sonja said. "He should be talking about those things. A lot."

Chet heaved a long, troubled sigh. His incompetence as a father was at fault. "I know."

"Has he never had a proper Christmas before?"

He squinted into the sky. "I've never asked."

"Oh, Chet."

He braced himself against the concern in her voice.

"Damned if I know what to do about it, either," he admitted. "But I'll figure out something."

"When?" She eyed him doubtfully. "Before Christmas? Or after?"

She was scaring him, for sure. "I'll ride into town after we see to the pup. If I hurry, I can—"

But they both knew he couldn't. Not anymore. The stores in town would close early, if they hadn't already. Folks would want to go home to their families, attend services at church. And with the snow coming down heavier than before...

"I can make Christmas special for him, Chet."

Sonja's quiet voice jolted his growing panic.

"You can?" He grabbed on to the words, like a drowning man clinging to a pole. "How?"

She lifted a slender shoulder. "Many ways."

He blew out a breath, an easing of his guilty panic. "Yeah?"

She nodded, looking strangely somber. "But then it would mean you'd be spending Christmas Eve with me."

He couldn't figure why she looked so serious. "Is that a problem?"

Her eyes turned a troubled shade of blue. "I'm the Bird Lady, remember? Or the local hussy, depending on your point of view."

He stared.

"Your friends will talk about us," she said, as if she had to get it all off her chest. "Esther. Everyone. I don't care about myself. I…I'm used to the gossip. But you, well, folks respect you, and I don't want to be the cause—"

Chet gritted his teeth, leaned over and grasped her saddle horn. His tug brought her horse bumping into his. She had to know he meant what he was about to tell her, and if he could drag her out of the saddle and into his arms to prove it, he would.

"I don't care what people say, y'hear me?" he grated. "In fact, spending Christmas Eve with you will be one of the best things I've had the pleasure of doing in a hell of a long time. And you know what? Beau and I will spend Christmas Day with you, too. How about that?"

"You will?" Her eyes filled. She pressed her fingers to her lips.

"Damn right we will."

"Oh." She swallowed. Managed a tremulous smile. "I'd like that."

He had no idea his decision would affect her like this. If only he had thought of it sooner, and now that he had, now that she wouldn't be alone, he realized Black Thunder wouldn't be able to retaliate against her. At least, not without a good fight.

"Hey, Pa. We're here," Beau said.

Chet glanced up to see his son halted in front of an outcropping of rock. Nearby, the icy Yellowstone River snaked a wide swath through buttes covered in ponderosa pines. Peaceful silence filled the air around them.

He released Sonja's saddle horn. Tossed her a look that promised more of their conversation later, and her lashes lowered.

Thickening snowfall left him glad their ride hadn't taken long. He shifted his attention to his son. "Good job, Beau. You knew right where to go."

"I sure did, Pa." He twisted in his saddle, finding Sonja. "The pup's gonna be happy he's home, isn't he, Miss Sonja?"

"Yes, he will. I think his mother's been watching for him," she said. "Now they'll be a family again."

"Yeah." Beau's expression turned serious beneath his Stetson's brim. "Bet he's glad he has a ma watching for him, huh?"

Sonja hesitated, exchanging a glance with Chet. "He knows she'll take care of him for as long as he needs her to."

"Yeah."

The boy's wistfulness affected Chet, the same as it did Sonja. Until now, Beau didn't let on he missed his old life, the woman who raised him, her family and friends. Might be he was more unhappy than Chet realized.

Might be Chet had been too busy to notice.

Or maybe it was because it was Christmas, and Chet hadn't given him anything to look forward to.

Damn.

He'd make it up to the boy. With Sonja's help, they both would.

Suddenly impatient to set the fox free and see the vow through, Chet dismounted. He'd tied the cage to the back of his saddle, and the scratching sounds coming from inside the box indicated the pup sensed his home territory.

"Give me a hand, will you, Beau?" Chet pulled off his gloves to loosen the rope. "You'll need to tell him goodbye before we let him loose."

Beau jumped off his pony. Chet set the cage down on the ground and waited for Sonja to join them.

"Can I hold him one last time, Pa?" Beau asked.

The frenzied pawing concerned Chet. "Better not, son. He might bite, he's so excited to be home."

"I'd say his wiggling is a sign his leg's not bothering him much anymore," Sonja said. "He's got you to thank for that."

Beau appeared bewildered. "But you doctored him, Miss Sonja."

"You were the one who brought him to me. I wouldn't have known he was hurt otherwise."

"That's right. A kindly thing you did for him." Chet squeezed Beau's thin shoulder in approval. "I'm proud of you."

Chet declined to explain how handling injured animals in the wild could get him injured, too, at least without someone older to help, but he'd save that for another day. Right now the boy's pleasure in their compliments was more important.

"Thanks, Pa," he said, turning shy. "I was scared you was gonna be mad 'cuz I thought he was a dog instead of a fox."

"Easy mistake to make. I would've thought the same if I were you."

"You would?" His eyes widened. "But you *never* make mistakes, Pa."

His declaration startled Chet, left him humbled by the boy's impression of him. An erroneous one, for sure, and intimidating, to boot. How would he be able to live up to that kind of thinking?

"All three of us will be making a mistake if we stay out here much longer," Sonja said. She tapped the brim of Beau's hat. Snow fell onto his coat. "See? The snow is getting heavier."

The way the flakes swirled now and again, the wind was picking up, too. Chet put a hand on the cage's latch.

"She's right. Tell him goodbye, son," he urged.

"'Bye, pup." Beau peered through the screen and waggled his fingers. "Go find your ma now, y'hear?" He drew back. Chet looked for sadness in his features and found none. Could be he was convinced setting the animal free was best, after all. "Okay, Pa. You can let him go now."

The moment the cage opened, the fox bolted in a run for freedom. He leaped up the rocks with amazing agility and disappeared somewhere on the other side.

"Guess he was in a real hurry, huh?" Beau said, staring after him.

"Seems so." Chet straightened, bringing the empty cage up with him.

Beau pushed back his hat and peered up. "Do we have to ride home now? Can we stay with Miss Sonja a little longer?"

Chet glanced at Sonja for help in answering the question. Did she still want to spend Christmas Eve with them?

But she hadn't been listening, not with her attention snagged on something in the rocks. With Black Thunder close in Chet's mind, instant alarm shot through him.

"Chet, look." She pointed.

He did. In a hurry. He saw no one. Nothing out of the ordinary.

"A tree," she exclaimed.

He raked his gaze over the outcropping, roughened with brush in places and not much else.

But there *was* one scrawny-looking pine.

"It's perfect." Smiling, she turned toward him.

His brows furrowed. "For what?"

"Christmas! Can we cut it down? Oh, Chet. Would you mind?"

The cold rosied up her cheeks. Brightened her soft-blue eyes, too. Yet it was the excitement sparkling in her voice that moved him most. How could he refuse her?

How could any man?

"Whatever you want, Sonja," he said, and realized it was true. If he could, he'd give her anything she asked for.

Her gloved hand reached out and splayed against his chest. "Thank you."

Chet found himself more aware of her touching him than the gratitude she expressed. Aware of what it'd be like to have her step closer, slide both her hands up around his neck, press herself into his embrace. What if neither of them were wearing their heavy coats, but instead something thinner, much thinner, maybe nothing at all, and he could feel the fullness of her breasts against him? The slender span of her waist? He could bury his nose in the softness of her hair, too, inhale deeply of the clean scent without her bonnet to keep him from it.

"What're you gonna do with the tree, Miss Sonja?" Beau asked.

Chet's imaginings crashed to a halt. He'd forgotten about his son standing there. Her hand fell away, and she turned toward the boy.

"Why, I'm going to decorate it, sweetie," she said, bending to fasten the top button of his coat against the cold. "Would you like to come home with me and help?"

His eyes rounded. "You're gonna decorate it for Christmas? With candles and everything?"

"I am. And ornaments and ribbons, and lots of other things, too."

Beau sucked in an excited breath and tilted his head back to see Chet. "Can we go home with her, Pa?"

Chet grinned at his exuberance. He was feeling some of his own over the whole thing. "Reckon she's going to need a hand getting her tree gussied up. We'd better give her one."

"Yippee!"

Chet headed toward his horse. The snow turned the ground white and gave shape to each boot step. "Won't take long for me to cut it down. I don't want you wandering off, son. Understand?"

"I won't. I'll just climb up on the rocks and watch you." Beau bounded off toward the outcropping.

Chet retied the empty cage to the back of the cantle, flipped open his saddle bag and pulled out a small ax. He strode toward Sonja and slid a watchful eye toward Beau, clamoring up the rough hill.

"Hey, Miss Sonja!" He plucked a long stick from near the brush and tapped the snow off the bark. "This looks like the one Three Feathers uses!"

"To catch fish?" she asked.

"Yeah." He made stabbing motions, as if he was spearing a trout in the water.

"It sure does." Sonja laughed at his demonstrations.

Suspicion about the Indian brave hurtled back into Chet's memory. Three Feathers's relationship with Sonja. His relationship with his half brother, Black Thunder. The gut feeling that Three Feathers couldn't be loyal to one without betraying the other.

He halted beside her and scowled. "Keep Beau away from him."

Sonja's merriment faltered. "From Three Feathers?"

"Yes. Until I tell you otherwise. I have some figuring to do on him yet." He halted beside her, both of them next to the scrubby pine. He leaned in and grasped the trunk, gave it a shake to knock off the snow.

"Chet." A glimmer of hurt threaded his name. "Three Feathers is my friend. He would never do anything to hurt Beau."

"Your opinion. I'll make one of my own." Voice low to keep his playful son from hearing, Chet knelt and bettered his grip on the ax. "When I do, you'll be the first to know."

"Is that supposed to make me feel better?" she said, dropping to her knees beside him, blue eyes flashing.

He'd fired her up for a good argument. He didn't like that he did, but under the circumstances, it couldn't be helped.

"Just keeping things clear between us, Sonja." He whacked the blade against the base of the tree again and again.

"What isn't clear to me, Chet Lattimer, is what you're thinking. Am I not to be trusted with the company of your son? Or maybe you're thinking all the rumors about me are true. Maybe you *want* them to be true, because you're no better than the gossips who spread them."

The trunk split and cracked. Chet caught the tree with one hand and glared at her.

She glared back.

Her stubbornness rankled.

"You're wrong." He stood, teeth clenched. He'd been called a lot of things in his life, but as far as he knew, a flap-jawed gossipmonger hadn't been one of them.

"I don't think so." Clearly miffed, she stood, too, then swung from him and worked her way down to level ground.

Dragging the pine with him, he followed. "Black Thunder killed your intended. How can you be sure you're safe with his brother?"

"*Half* brother."

"Blood is thicker than water." He halted next to his horse, grabbed his rope and whipped the end around the base of the tree.

"I thought you were different from the rest of the folks around here." She sniffed. "How stupid of me."

Her words hit a raw spot. He didn't want to be like the others. He wasn't, not by a long shot, and he opened his mouth to defend himself, but Beau called to them.

"Hey, Pa! Miss Sonja! Look at me!"

They turned toward him. Beau had meandered to the far side of the rocky bluff and stood on a narrow ledge above the banks of the Yellowstone River.

"I can see fish down there," he said.

He jabbed his stick, imitating the thrust Three Feathers would have used with far more skill. Before Chet could tell him to stop and get down, Beau's booted foot slipped, his arms flailed and he tumbled over the edge with a startled cry.

Then disappeared from sight.
Water splashed.
And Chet died a thousand deaths.

Chapter Eight

Sonja screamed Beau's name. Chet dropped the pine tree and bolted into a full run toward the riverbank. His heart pounded wildly. His lips moved in a frantic prayer that the Almighty would save the boy. Chet had never considered himself a religious man, but if ever he needed a miracle, now was the time.

His boot soles slipped on the snow-slick grass and rocks leading down to the river's edge. A thin layer of ice covered the water, but Chet plowed through it, heedless of the wet cold seeping in through the tops of his boots.

He saw Beau's hat first, bobbing with the sluggish current and too far out to reach. Gripped by gut-wrenching fear, he kept moving, his gaze clinging to the river's broken surface, to the sloshing water that would show his son struggling.

Suddenly Beau popped up with a gasp, his arms floundering to bring himself upright. Chet scooped him up before he could go under again.

"Pa!" Beau erupted into a fit of coughing.

"I've got you, son. You're all right now."

He hoped his assurance would be true. He headed back toward shore, holding Beau as close as he could. He stumbled out of the water, and Sonja was there, her arms reaching to get the boy warm as soon as they could.

"We have to get his coat off," Chet muttered.

He left Sonja to unbutton the sodden garment while his fingers undid his own. He helped her drag the coat off Beau's shivering body, one side and then the other. He parted his coat, tucked his son within the sheepskin and sucked in a breath at the sensation of the cold, wet body pressed against his chest.

"Does anything hurt, Beau?" he demanded. "Your head, maybe? Your arm, your leg?"

"N-no, Pa," he stuttered. "I'm jus' c-cold."

"We have to get his boots off or else his toes will freeze." Sonja removed the first with one brisk pull. Water streamed out. The second followed with more of the same. She peeled off each wet sock, too, then removed her gloves and pushed a small foot inside each.

"Am I g-going to freeze to d-death, Miss Sonja?" he asked through his chattering teeth.

"You absolutely will not," she said, removing her knitted scarf next. "Your father and I will get you warm again in no time. Lift your head, sweetie." Working quickly, she wrapped the scarf turban-style around his dripping hair and tied the ends beneath his chin. "There. You're feeling better already, aren't you?"

"Y-yeah."

"Let's get out of here," Chet growled.

Her arm on his stayed him. "Your boots, Chet—they have water inside. You should take them off and—"

"Later."

"But your feet could freeze."

"Later, I said."

The discomfort, the risk didn't matter, he realized, striding toward his horse, Sonja hurrying beside him. Nothing mattered but Beau and getting him home, dry and safe, as soon as possible. His survival depended on it.

She held the bridle on Chet's mount while he reached up to grasp the saddle horn.

"It'll be faster to go to my place," she said quietly.

He paused. A quick calculation of their bearings proved her correct. The ranch house was a fair ride away. And in the swirling snow, growing deeper by the minute, it'd take even longer to get there....

Chet shifted his glance to her. In those blue, blue eyes, he read what she was thinking, that if he agreed, if he took Beau to her home, they wouldn't leave until tomorrow. They'd spend the night together, the three of them, like a family, and his breath hitched at the prospect.

"It's Christmas Eve, Chet," she murmured softly.

He didn't want to spend it alone. Clearly, she didn't, either. Beau deserved to be with her, and she deserved to be with him. With both of them.

Still he hesitated. She was unmarried, just as he was. "Once folks got wind of us—"

"I don't care what they think," she said.

"No," he murmured.

He believed her in that. She was accustomed to being the subject of people's conversations, but he didn't want her hurt any more than she'd already been.

A fat snowflake drifted onto her eyelashes, and he gently brushed it away with his thumb. He thought of what it'd be like to be a family with her, if only for one night. The three of them. Together. Instinct told him the experience would be something they'd all remember.

And, yeah, it was Christmas Eve.

"So what are we waiting for?" he asked.

She appeared relieved. Hesitantly pleased. "We have to hurry."

She fussed over Beau one last time, assuring herself he was warm as could be before she collected the reins of his pony, then climbed onto her horse. Chet lifted a foot into the stirrup, swung into the saddle one-handed and settled in.

Beau drew up his knees and snuggled into him. Chet shifted his hold, and the boy's eyes closed. A touch of color had returned to his lips. He appeared relaxed in Chet's lap, trusting, as if he knew that from here on out, his ordeal was over, that he'd be taken care of by two people who'd do everything they could to keep him safe.

A curious softening stole through Chet. This little boy, his flesh and blood….

It'd been a quirk of fate that had landed him in Chet's life. Chet hadn't been ready for it, wasn't even sure he wanted it, but Sonja had helped him realize that with the boy came an unexpected gift.

Fatherhood.

His fall into the river had Chet experiencing a good scare. Most likely, it wouldn't be his last. The fall had him realizing how easy it could be to lose Beau forever. Being there, saving him, was like being given a second chance.

To love him.

If Chet celebrated nothing else this Christmas, he'd for sure celebrate that.

Beau's coat hung over the back of a chair to dry in the heat of the fire Chet kept stoked high. On the hearth, his small boots stood next to Chet's bigger ones. Next to them, two pair of socks were lined in a neat row. Beau's dungarees, shirt and knitted underwear filled a line Chet had strung in the corner.

By morning they'd be ready to wear, as if they'd never gotten a good dunking in the river.

Sonja shuddered yet again from the experience, a tragedy

certain to happen if Chet hadn't been there to prevent it. She thought of all that could've gone wrong if Beau had been alone, if the water had been deeper, the ice thicker—

If, if, if.

She stopped and reminded herself none of those things happened. And they wouldn't.

Beau was safe, warm and dry.

They all were.

And was there a better Christmas gift than that?

After their harried ride to her cabin, she'd gotten Beau out of his wet clothes and Chet out of his wet socks and boots. Then she'd plied them with plenty of hot chicken soup and strong coffee. Sonja was determined to put the terrible scare out of their minds and concentrate instead on taking care of them.

And how she enjoyed that. Fussing and mothering. As if it was something she was meant to do.

Having both handsome Lattimers with her vanquished the loneliness in her heart and the emptiness in her home. The sound of Chet's low voice filled the rooms with his presence, Beau's excited chatter filled them with life.

Like now, while she made the fried rosettes.

"Mrs. Grinnell never makes cookies like this," he said, kneeling on a chair beside her.

She'd found a flannel blouse for him to wear as a nightshirt, and he looked endearing with the sleeves rolled over and over at his wrists. He wore a pair of her wool socks, too, pulled up past his knobby knees.

"This is a different kind of cookie." She dipped the metal flower-shaped mold into hot oil and waited a few moments. "They're not baked in an oven like most all the others."

Once the iron was hot enough, she soaked up the dripping oil, then lowered the mold into a bowl of batter. Beau watched, as intrigued with this rosette as he'd been with the first. She returned the iron to the hot oil, fried the batter until crisp, then carefully slid the golden cookie onto paper to cool.

"There. That's the last of them," she said.

Beau grinned like a little wolf at the rows spread on her tabletop. "Can I eat one now?"

"You may." She set the iron aside, reached for the sifter and dusted them with powdered sugar. "But first you have to make a wish."

His eyes closed tight. "I wish I could eat *all* of Miss Sonja's rosettes!"

"No, no. Not like that." Laughing, Sonja shook her head.

Those sweet chocolate eyes opened again. "But it's what I want."

"Let me explain how to make the wish." She set one of the fragile cookies in front of him. "When I was a little girl, my mother used to tell me a special story she learned when she lived in Sweden."

"Where's Sweden?" he asked.

"It's a small country, far away. Across the ocean."

"Oh."

"The story says if you make a wish, and if you can break a rosette into three pieces when you tap it with your finger, your wish will come true."

His jaw dropped. "It will?"

"Want to try?"

"Yeah."

"All right. Make another wish. A real one this time. And don't tell me what it is."

"But I want you to know."

She regarded him with grave seriousness. "You might jinx it."

"All right," he said with equal gravity.

"Are you ready?"

"Yeah." Furrows formed between his dark brows, and his eyes closed tight again.

He fell silent so long Sonja couldn't help wondering what absorbed him. She glanced over at Chet, hunkered in front of the fire, one arm relaxed on his knee. His amusement indicated he'd been listening, and seeing him like that, relaxed and amused, sent her belly into a funny flip.

It suited him. He was a man whose days were filled with hard work, little rest and endless worries. A life heavy with responsibility.

Of which Beau had unexpectedly become a big part.

She doubted Chet relaxed much. Maybe never, and she was glad more than ever he was here, snowed in on Christmas Eve with her and his son.

"I'm done, Miss Sonja," Beau said. "I made my wish."

Sonja's glance returned to him. She smiled at his sweet innocence. "Very good. Are you ready to break the rosette?"

He nodded, his concentration rapt on what he was about to do. He steadied his stance. His small finger hovered over the cookie. He drew in a breath, let it out again. Then made his move.

The fragile rosette broke into three nearly equal-size pieces.

He gasped.

Sonja exclaimed, as surprised as he. In all her life, she had never done it.

Their eyes met, and they both emitted a hearty cheer. Even Chet chuckled at the accomplishment.

"Yippee! I'm gonna get my wish!" With his face-splitting grin, Beau looked as proud as a strutting peacock. "*Now* can I eat the cookie?"

"Of course, you can! In fact, have two." He'd earned them certainly, and she slid a second in front of him. "Would you like some milk, too?"

He took a big crunchy bite.

"Yes, please," he mumbled around the mouthful, powdered sugar on his lips.

Sonja's heart swelled. If she hadn't already fallen in love with this little boy, she was right on the brink.

She handed him a filled glass, but on the way back to the ice box, she paused.

The lure of the Swedish legend still held her, as vivid now as it'd been when she was a child. She pondered the golden rosettes all but covering her kitchen table.

She had a wish of her own to make.

Carefully she held one of the fragile treats in her palm. Her eyes closed. Her thoughts wrapped around what she wanted most and held on tight.

Handsome, rugged Chet Lattimer. To have him love her forever so she would never be lonely again. To be a family with him and Beau, like they were tonight, on this special Christmas Eve.

Her eyes opened, part of her realizing how silly she was to play a child's game, but there lingered in her the hope of one. She held her breath yet again and carefully struck the delicate center. The cookie broke—into three perfect parts.

Sonja stared.

"Seems luck is everywhere around here tonight," Chet murmured.

His low voice somewhere behind her gave her a start, so intent she'd been on what she'd done, and she jerked in surprise. The featherlight rosette pieces tumbled from her hand. And shattered.

She gaped at the crumbs scattered at her feet.

"Damn." Chet stared, too. "Does this mean you won't get your wish?"

She bit her lip. "I don't know."

He stood so close he filled her range of vision and overwhelmed her senses. Made her forget about fanciful legends, hopes and dreams and even Beau at the table behind them.

He made her think of Chet, the man. Virile and powerful and strong.

The scent of wood smoke clung to his skin and clothes. His tan shirt fell open at the throat, and wisps of dark hair teased her imagination of what he'd look like not wearing a shirt at all.

And she had no right to wonder such things, as if he belonged to her. Which he didn't and probably wouldn't. Ever.

"I've never seen Beau this happy," Chet said, his voice husky. Intimate. "You have a way with him."

His nearness flowed over her. She had to struggle to stay with the conversation, to keep from leaning into him. Touch him with her whole body.

"Little boys, pigeons, injured foxes." He trailed a knuckle down her cheek, her jaw, in a long, lazy caress. "And me."

Nerve endings sprang to life from that sultry caress. A sudden yearning to have him stroke her all over with both of his strong hands. Every single inch of her skin.

"You?" she said, breathless, afraid to hope, to interpret more from his words than he intended.

"Yes, me." A corner of his mouth lifted. Did he know the effect he had on her? Was it so obvious? "I could get used to this." He made an expressive gesture, indicating their surroundings. "Being here with you. Having you take care of me. Us, I mean. Even if it wasn't Christmas."

She couldn't think, couldn't manage a sophisticated response. Would he say those things if they weren't true? Dare she believe him?

A shadow of a beard roughened his jaw, giving him the look of a man who was a little wild, a little primitive, and the way his provocative gaze moved leisurely to her mouth…

An ache to feel his lips formed in her belly. A yearning so deep, so compelling, a tiny, forlorn sigh slipped from her throat.

"Oh, Chet, if only—"

Mortified she'd said too much, that she laid her heart open before him, she halted.

Pathetic Sonja Kaplan. Lonely and hungry for love. Would he think her as needy as she sounded?

"What, Sonja?" he murmured. "If only what?"

She could barely say the words. The courage for honesty eluded her. Yet if she told him she'd fallen in love with him, that she wanted to take care of him and his son for the rest of her life, would he even want to hear it?

She'd probably send him running to someone else. A woman more respectable. Someone of whom the gossips approved.

Still, the way his heavy-lashed eyes clung to her, darkly intense, as if he really wanted to know....

"Hey, Miss Sonja?"

Beau's voice fractured the moment. Dashed her thoughts. Reminded her of where she was, in her kitchen, standing close to Chet with her cookie still on the floor and the milk jug in her hand.

They both turned toward Beau. He extended his empty glass and grinned.

"Can I have some more milk?"

Chapter Nine

Chet had to admit the scrawny pine didn't look half bad standing there, in front of her window.

Sonja had worked wonders with the thing, adding bits of ribbon and fringe to its bare branches. Her Swedish straw ornaments looked nice, too, and Beau was proud to have his star hung clear at the top. Sonja had put Chet to work stringing popcorn and berries while Beau helped her make paper cornucopias, then fill them with nuts and rock candy. All the while, the two chattered like a pair of magpies, Sonja patient as a saint to the boy's questions and storytelling.

Best, though, were the candles. She'd clipped little candle-holders to the tips of the branches, then made a ceremony of lighting each one. Even went so far as to douse the kerosene lamps, allowing only the glow from those tiny flickering flames to illuminate the darkened room.

The candles added a fine touch to the rest of her decorations, for sure. And Beau was impressed.

Chet held back while they stood near the pine, their arms around one another, singing their hearts full of "Silent Night" and "O, Come all Ye Faithful." Damned if he could remember the words to the songs, but listening to their voices helped make up for his lack.

Besides, it gave him a chance to watch them. Enjoy them. Soak up the memory of this night. Of all Sonja had done for Beau and him to make Christmas special.

Meaningful.

Chet would never forget. More important, Beau wouldn't, either. Nor would Sonja, he suspected. And what was he to do about it?

The worry weighed on him. He didn't know how he was going to pull Beau away and leave her when Christmas was over. Thinking of the emptiness of their own home back at the ranch left a cold spot deep inside him.

A spot Sonja knew how to warm.

After tomorrow she'd be alone. Again. She was used to it, of course, but that didn't change things. Black Thunder was still out there. A threat to her life. Her work.

Chet's jaw tightened. Her refusal to leave her pigeons had become a real problem. Might be Chet had no right to expect her to give them up for safety's sake, but damned if he could think of a viable solution.

Except to keep her with him. Protect her himself until Black Thunder was out of Montana Territory for good. A solution that took root and felt right the more he thought about it.

And he'd been thinking of it a lot.

Trouble was, Sonja wouldn't agree. She had something on her mind that she hesitated to reveal, but it was there—in her eyes and in the way she held herself back from him.

If only he could break through her reservations. If only she could trust him so she'd know he had her best interests in mind and nothing more.

Or was there? Did he want more than he should? More than she could give?

And there came those two little words again. *If only.* The same two words she'd said to him earlier before Beau interrupted and kept her from explaining.

Their singing ended, and she turned toward him, her mouth parted in a soft smile, the elation from the season evident in her expression. Candles glowed behind her and wreathed her in a golden shimmer. Firelight glinted on her hair, still swept up onto her head, and the strands sparkled.

He had a sudden longing to undo their pins just to see that hair tumble into a silken mass over her shoulders and back. He'd plunge his hands into the thickness and slide the satiny strands through each one of his fingers.

Then, he'd kiss her. More than once. Again and again. From the way she had him feeling, and thinking, he wouldn't be able to stop himself if he tried.

But then, maybe she wouldn't want him to stop. Maybe, just maybe, she'd *like* it if he kissed her over and over.

And wouldn't that make it harder than ever to leave her?

As if she read his lusty thoughts in the candles' glow, her lashes lowered, and she tugged her shawl closer. She seemed determined not to look at him and concentrated on Beau instead. Her fingers gently smoothed the hair from the boy's forehead.

"It's getting late, sweetie," she said. "Would you like to sleep in front of the fire tonight?"

"Yeah." He swung his gaze toward Chet. "Where're you gonna sleep, Pa?"

An instant image of sharing Sonja's bed formed in his mind. Heated his blood. Took all his willpower to quash it, too.

"I'll be close by, son," he said.

Sonja had yet to look Chet in the eye. "I'll get you a quilt and pillow, Beau."

With a soft rustle of her skirts, she disappeared into the darkness of her room; in a moment, a lamp glowed through the doorway.

Beau tugged on Chet's hand, a demand for his attention.

"Us boys have to talk, Pa," he said in a loud whisper.

Clearly, he didn't want Sonja to hear. Chet crouched down, bringing himself to Beau's level. "About what?"

Little furrows formed between his brows. "I think we have to marry Miss Sonja."

"Do you?" Chet's mouth curved.

But Beau was serious. He nodded. "Else she won't have nobody when we leave tomorrow."

Chet's amusement died. The boy's concern was unexpected and showed a sensitivity that went beyond his years. "I've been thinking about that, too."

Beau shot a quick glance toward her bedroom. The sound of a drawer opening drifted toward them. He appealed to Chet again.

"She said I can't tell her my wish else I'll jinx it, but I can tell you, can't I, Pa?"

Chet frowned. He never claimed to know the rules of the rosette's legend, but clearly, his son had a need to speak of the secret he'd been compelled to keep to himself. Chet could see no harm since it meant so much to him.

"You can tell me most anything, Beau. Reckon it won't hurt in this case."

He seemed relieved. "I wished that she would have us for her family forever and ever."

A wish that had far less to do with wanting something for himself, a child on Christmas Eve. Chet needed a moment to push the emotion from his throat. "You did, did you?"

"Yeah, 'cuz she needs us to take care of her."

Chet figured it was more the other way around, considering the fussing she'd done over them, making sure they were both warm, dry and well fed. Which didn't even begin to touch on the meaning she'd put into Christmas.

Sonja had a natural ability to be a better mother to his son than Chet had been a father. The knowledge stung. And for the man lucky enough to be her husband someday, claiming he'd be proud to have her as his wife would be one hell of an understatement.

Little wonder Beau had a streak of protectiveness for her.

His perspective of the matter moved Chet, and if he'd ever been more humbled in his life to have the privilege of being able to call Beau "son"…

Chet swallowed hard.

Damn.

A privilege of the finest caliber.

Beau watched him with his dark eyes seeming to peer into Chet's soul, waiting for the answer Chet hadn't yet given.

Chet nodded then and smiled in male camaraderie. "She needs us, all right. We'll have to see what we can do about convincing her, won't we?"

Beau's expression showed sweeping relief. Had he thought Chet would refuse him?

Chet's arms opened. Beau took a hesitant step forward.

"I love you, Beau," he said roughly, needing to assure him.

Now seemed the time to say it, Chet's first, and from the wide grin on the boy's face, Beau had been waiting to hear it. Too long, Chet knew, but from here on out, he'd hear Chet tell him more often. Beau flung his arms around Chet's neck; Chet held him tight.

Sonja's footsteps halted.

"Oh," she said in gentle surprise. A smile curved her lips. "Looks like I interrupted something important."

"Nah." Beau stepped out of Chet's arms. "We was just talkin', that's all."

"I see." She strode forward again, holding bedding. "Well, I'm very glad you were, then."

She spread the quilt on the floor a safe distance from the fire, and Beau snuggled into its folds. She knelt beside him and pulled the edges up to his chin.

"This was the bestest Christmas Eve I ever had, Miss Sonja," he said.

"That makes me happy, Beau."

"Do you think the pup found his ma yet?"

"I do. She was waiting for him, remember?"

"Yeah. Maybe they're celebrating Christmas Eve, too."

Sonja kept a straight face. Chet marveled at it. "Maybe they are."

"No, Miss Sonja." Beau let out a guffaw. "Foxes don't know nothin' about Christmas."

She tweaked his nose. "You were teasing me, weren't you?"

"Yeah. Do Indians have Christmas like we do?"

"Depends if they've been taught about God from the missionaries or not."

Beau yawned. "Does Three Feathers know about it?"

"He certainly does. Now, enough questions. You've had quite a day, and look at you. You can barely keep your eyes open." She bent and pressed a kiss to his forehead. "Good night, Beau. Merry Christmas."

"Merry Christmas, Miss Sonja." He rolled onto his side, and his lids drifted closed. "Merry Christmas, Pa."

"Merry Christmas, son," Chet said, knowing it'd been one already for him.

He helped Sonja to her feet, and for a moment they stood together, looking down at his sleeping son.

"He's an angel," she said in a hushed voice.

Chet grunted. "A good kid."

She turned toward him, angling her body away from Beau. "We have nothing for him for Christmas. What are we going to do?"

He rather liked her use of the word *we*. But including herself in his responsibility didn't seem right. He took her elbow and moved her away, closer to the candlelit pine tree, so Beau wouldn't overhear.

"Sonja, having nothing for him can't be helped. Under the circumstances—"

"But the circumstances don't matter," she said and clucked her tongue in dismay. "He's a little boy, Chet. He *needs* a gift for Christmas morning."

Flickering firelight shimmered over her face and hair, an intriguing dance of moving shadows on her skin. If he could, Chet would stand here all night, just watching her face, losing himself in the beauty of it.

"You've given him plenty already," he managed to say.

Her eyes rolled. "A few cookies, a couple of songs. That's nothing."

"Sonja." Chet frowned. "It's more than that. You know it is."

She nibbled on her lip. "I have a few peppermint sticks to put in his stocking. He'd like some shiny pennies, too, wouldn't he?"

"I'll take care of it."

"But that's not much. He needs a *real* gift from Santa. A toy to play with." She sighed, her brows puckering. "If only I had more time, I could make him something."

Her worry moved Chet. This woman, beautiful and vibrant and feminine, filled with compassion, capable of great love—she'd gotten under his skin and into his heart.

As if she belonged there.

In his life.

Forever.

He wanted her. The realization rocked him, left him panicky from the certainty he would lose her.

When it was all over. When the candles were burned down,

the rosettes eaten, the pine tree stripped and hauled outside, barren as before. When Black Thunder was no longer a threat.

He would lose her.

Unless he did something to keep her.

Like take her into his arms and kiss her with a passion he'd never felt for another woman before. Convince her she meant something to him, a *hell* of a lot of something, so much that maybe he'd fallen in love with her.

He swallowed. Yeah, that was it.

He'd fallen in love with her.

Chet didn't know how it happened, or when, but it had, and what a fine gift that proved to be.

Loving Sonja.

He reached for her, the need to take her into his arms running strong within him, but before he could, before she knew his intention, movement in the window stopped him cold.

The sharp, angular planes of a man's face, dark and somber, appeared in the firelit glass.

Startled, Sonja gasped.

Chet scowled in recognition.

Three Feathers.

Chapter Ten

Sonja stiffened at the suspicion that leaped into Chet's expression.

"What does *he* want?" he asked in a rough tone.

"He's my friend, Chet," she said firmly. "No matter what you think of him, I hope you treat him as one."

She took a step toward the door. Chet stopped her.

"How is he your friend, Sonja?" His quiet demand expected answers. Now. Before Three Feathers could be let inside. "Why do you trust him so much?"

She recalled their argument at the river that afternoon. Chet's distrust had been such that he refused to allow Beau in Three Feathers' company again. Sonja's feelings had been hurt, but she knew Chet's misgivings resulted from the gossip he'd heard about her.

He claimed he wanted to form his own opinion about the Indian brave. To do so he had to know the truth.

Sonja intended to give it to him. Every lurid detail.

"He saved my life, Chet," Sonja said. "That awful afternoon when Black Thunder killed Robert, he would've attacked me next. Three Feathers fought Black Thunder until he retreated with his band and left the Territory."

"Why did he fight his own brother?" he asked with thinly veiled skepticism.

"Because of the pigeons." Sonja dragged herself back from the horror. "He'd been working secretly with the Army to capture Black Thunder and stop the shame his brother brought to his people. Three Feathers knew the importance of the birds to help him do that."

Chet didn't move, didn't speak. But a muscle leaped in his cheek.

"By the time the Army arrived, Three Feathers was almost dead from his injuries. The soldiers took him to Fort Keough where he eventually recovered." Thinking of the rumors that surrounded the events of that day, she regarded Chet coolly. "I suspect you don't know they applauded him as a hero."

"No," he grated. "I didn't."

"Too bad no one else did, either."

Chet cleared his throat.

"You thought my friendship with him was…tainted, didn't you?" Sonja asked.

"I thought—"

"That I was conspiring with him. Against my country."

He blew out a breath. "Sonja, look. I'm sorry."

"It doesn't matter." She managed a smile through the hurt. She should've been used to it. Somehow she wasn't. Maybe she never would be. "He's still standing outside. May I let him in now?"

His gaze, darkly troubled in the candles' glow, clung to hers. "Damn it, yes."

She stepped around him and pulled open the door. A waft of cold air hit her, but the peace of the night struck her more. Snow fell thick, silent and lay deep on the ground.

Wrapped in his striped blanket, Three Feathers moved away from the window. "How."

"How." Sonja returned his greeting and strained to see him

in the faint light. Curiosity flared from why he was here, at this late hour. She held the door wider. "Please come in."

"No. I will not stay long."

His keen, black-eyed gaze locked on Chet, standing close behind her. Protective, still challenging. Both of them silent, assessing the other.

Sonja held her breath. Surely Three Feathers knew she'd come to no harm with Chet. And hadn't she explained the same to Chet?

"Beau's father," the Indian said finally, without animosity.

"Yes," she said. Some of her unease faded. "Chet Lattimer."

"I hear of him." He grunted, a small sound indicating his approval. "His people respect him."

A moment passed, Chet absorbing his response.

"As they respect you, including my son," he said then. "Thank you for the kindness you've shown him."

The brave nodded once, accepting the gratitude. He returned his gaze to her. She sensed the seriousness of what he was about to impart. "Black Thunder is dead."

Sonja sucked in a breath. "Are you sure?"

"I was with the soldiers who killed him."

The shock rolled through her. The relief. She shivered from both. Chet slid an arm around her waist and pulled her against him. Warming her. Steadying her.

"When?" he demanded.

"Today. After the snow comes." Three Feathers pointed toward the Yellowstone River. "Not far from here."

Chet muttered an oath. "We were out there."

Sonja pressed trembling fingers to her lips. "Yes. Setting the fox free."

Three Feathers peered into the cabin, at Beau sleeping behind them. He grunted again. "Not easy for boy to let him go."

"No," she murmured, still thinking of the ruthless warrior who would never attack again.

"Tonight, white man's Santa will come." Three Feathers' teeth showed in a small smile.

She frowned. "Hopefully."

He stepped back. "I will go. Beau must not wake."

Reluctant to let him leave without first giving him something hot to drink, or a rosette to enjoy, Sonja reached for him. "Three Feathers, wait."

But he was gone, as silently as he arrived.

She murmured in disappointment. Chet tugged on her elbow. "Come in, Sonja. It's cold."

He shut the door behind them, and she pulled her shawl closer. She hadn't realized how chilled she'd become until the warmth of her home reminded her.

Chet sighed heavily and raked a hand through his hair. "I've been an ass about this whole thing. I'm sorry. Really sorry."

She cocked her head. Oddly, the hurt was gone, assuaged by Black Thunder's death. Montana Territory would enjoy peace again, which was far more important than her tender sensibilities.

But Chet looked so repentant, she had to fight hard to keep from sliding her arms around his neck and peppering his face with forgiving kisses.

"It's over," she said quietly. "Now you know the truth."

"I wish I had known sooner. I could've helped spare the gossip against you."

"Perhaps I should have told someone sooner." She considered her pride, which had kept her from revealing her relationship with Three Feathers and her work for the Army. Her mouth softened. "That's what I do, after all. Communicate."

In the pine tree's flickering candle light, his dark eyes glittered. With yearning. With promise. With the need to do some strong communicating of his own.

And the first stirrings of hope stretched deep within her breast. With the obstacles gone between them, dare she reveal her love for him? Tell him she wanted a life together? Would he even want her, the Bird Lady, after Christmas was over?

A faint noise distracted the questions leaping inside her. A scratching sound that snagged her attention away from Chet and tugged it toward the window to see if Three Feathers had returned after all.

But nothing showed from the other side of the glass, only the black night of Christmas Eve.

Yet the sound came again, stronger this time.

Chet strode toward the door, opened it, his tall, lean body braced for what he might find. Sonja joined her gaze with his.

And saw nothing.

Until she heard an endearing little bark.

In unison, their glances dropped—to the puppy prancing at their feet, his furry tail wagging, his head tilted back, mouth open in blatant eagerness for their attention.

"Oh, Chet, look!" she exclaimed.

"I'll be damned."

He bent and scooped up the wiggling bundle in one hand, then leaned out the doorway to sweep his glance from one side to the other, a search of the darkness for the one who'd left the puppy behind. Sonja squeezed in the doorway, too, and added her wildly curious search to his.

But no one was there. Not Three Feathers. Not a horse. Not even footprints in the snow.

"I'll be damned," Chet said again, stepped back inside and closed the door.

Sonja stared, captivated at the sight of the furry black and white body snuggled against his chest.

"Wherever he came from, he's been cared for," Chet said, looking him over. "He's clean, well fed."

"But not long weaned from his mother, I think. Oh, my. Let me hold him, Chet." She lifted the small creature and cuddled him against her; her hand stroked the silky fur again and again. "Isn't he cute?"

Chet grinned. "Someone wanted you to have him."

"No." Never before had Sonja experienced the true magic of Christmas like this, in all its glory. "Someone wanted *Beau* to have him." Excitement coursed through her. "Don't you see, Chet? This little puppy is the gift we needed." She darted a quick glance toward the fire. Beau hadn't stirred, but he would if they kept talking like this. And what if the dog barked again? "We have to hide him."

She turned and headed toward her bedroom. Chet followed her in and closed the door.

Sonja opened a dresser drawer and one-handedly arranged the linens she kept stored there. Carefully she settled the puppy in his new makeshift bed with gentle admonishments to stay quiet until Beau awakened in the morning. The little dog seemed to understand; he lowered his chin onto his paws and sighed.

Content.

As if he knew he'd found his home.

Struck by the innocence of that sigh, its meaning, Sonja rose, knowing that at last her Christmas was complete.

Or was it?

Her glance found Chet, watching her from where he stood, in front of the closed door.

Beneath the thick fringe of his lashes, his dark eyes smoldered. She sensed something different about him, something vastly removed from Christmas, something she could define only as…an aching hunger.

He strolled toward her, his tread silent in his stocking feet. With the dresser on one side of her, the bed on the other, she had nowhere else to go.

She waited for him to come, an odd anticipation strumming through her veins. He halted, tall and mesmerizing and incredibly male.

He stood so close she could feel his heat. The need he'd yet to put into words.

"Thank you," he rumbled. "For everything you've done."

She needed all her willpower to keep from touching him. "I've done nothing you wouldn't have, if you'd known how."

His mouth curved. He drew his finger along the bridge of her nose. "That's just it, Sonja. I didn't know. You did." He traced the shape of her lips with his thumb. "You've given Beau a Christmas he'll never forget."

Her mouth came alive from his touch. The blood in her veins, too.

"Yet I have nothing for you," she said.

"Don't you?"

His low voice challenged her, seduced her, made her think of things she wanted but couldn't have. Like never being lonely again. And being loved forever by this man.

"What would you like, Chet?" she whispered. "What can I give you?"

"Only one thing."

She'd give it to him, she knew. Anything he asked for. No matter the price.

"A kiss," he said, voice husky. "That's what I want from you."

She hadn't kissed a man for so long. Not even Robert. And did Chet know what a gift to *her* it was, that he wanted one?

A simple gift. Tender. Easily given. Yet her heart pounded as she raised up on tiptoe and pressed her lips to his cheek.

Before she could step away, his arm slid to her back.

"Another," he growled, holding her against his hard-muscled body. "Again, Sonja."

Her world tilted, and her hands fisted into his shirt to hold herself steady. Her lashes drifted closed, and she kissed him once more, on the other cheek.

But something broke inside her, a crumbling of her defenses, a roaring of her needs, a fear that too soon her time with him would run out.

And she'd have no more chances. Except now. This Christmas Eve.

Somehow her mouth moved over his. Or maybe he'd claimed it all on his own, an unrestrained capture that spoke of his need to have her, to destroy the loneliness that haunted them both.

"I love you, Sonja," he murmured between kisses. "Do you know how much?"

Elation soared through her. She slid her arms higher, tighter, around his neck. "If it's an inkling of my love for you, then— oh, Chet, it's *so* much."

He groaned and carried her to the bed. With incredible tenderness, he laid her on the mattress and gazed down at her.

Then, with breaths mingling, their bodies giving, they celebrated Christmas with a joy that surpassed the ages.

Early Morning, December 25

With Sonja asleep and the tiny candles on the pine tree extinguished, Chet contemplated the gifts he'd been given.

A beautiful woman.

A little boy.

Love, at its finest.

Each had shown him the true meaning of miracles. With them he needed nothing else in his life.

His son slept, content and warm in front of the fire. Chet's gaze tarried over the black-and-white bundle snuggled close beside him. The puppy had taken charge of matters a little while ago and ushered in the morning's gift-giving earlier than planned by waking Beau with a few excited barks and licks to the face. The memory of the boy's delight before falling back asleep— the absolute purity of it—would stay with Chet forever.

But Beau didn't know he had another gift coming. The one that said Sonja would be a part of their lives from here on out. She'd agreed to be Chet's wife. They'd be a family as soon as they could get themselves to the church.

Turned out to be quite a Christmas, for sure.

Amazed by it, he padded to the kitchen table. He studied the rows of rosettes still covering the top.

He wasn't prone to foolish legends, but he couldn't resist picking one up. He held the thing in his palm, like he'd seen Sonja do. He figured most every wish he could ever want had already come true, but he recited them anyway.

Afterward he held one finger above it and struck the center.

The cookie broke in three parts.

But then, he'd known it would.

He smiled. It was that kind of Christmas.

* * * * *

Melita had been expecting a chaste quick kiss of the generic variety. But this kiss with Sully was the kind that sparked a dying flame to life. The kind of kiss you can't plan for. The kind of kiss memories are built on.

The memory of her murdered lover, Nemo, came to her then and she made a starved little noise in the back of her throat. She raised her arms and threaded her fingers through Sully's hair, pulled him closer. Felt his body settle, then melt into her.

In that instant her hunger for him grew, and his for her. She pressed herself to him with more urgency, and he responded in kind.

Melita came out of her kiss-induced memory of Nemo with a start. "Wait a minute." She pushed Sully away from her. "You bastard!"

She spit two nasty words at him in Greek, then wiped his kiss from her lips.

"I thought you deserved some solid proof that I'm still in one piece." He started for the door. "The clock's ticking, honey. Come on, let's get out of here."

"That's it? You sucker me into kissing you, and that's all you have to say?"

"I'm sorry. How's that?"

He didn't sound sorry in the least. "You're—"

"Getting out of this godforsaken prison cell. Stop whining and let's go."

"Not if I was being shot at sunrise. Go. You deserve whatever you get if you walk out that door."

He turned back. "Freedom is what I'm going to get."

"A second of freedom before the guards in the hall shoot you." She jammed her hands on her hips. "And to think I was worried about you."

"If you're staying behind, it's no skin off my ass."

"Wait! What about our deal?"

"You just said you're not coming. Make up your mind."

"Have you forgotten we need a boat?"

"How could I? You keep harping on it."

"I'm not going without a boat. And those guards out there aren't going to just let you walk out of here. You need me and we need a plan."

"I already have a plan. I'm getting out of here. That's the plan."

"I should have realized that you never intended to take me with you from the very beginning. You're a liar and a coward."

Of everything she had read, there was nothing in Sully Paxton's file that hinted he was a coward, but it was the one word that seemed to register in that one-track mind of his. The look he nailed her with a second later was pure venom.

He came at her so quickly she didn't have time to get out of his way. "You know I'm not a coward."

"Prove it. Give me until dawn. I need one more night to put everything in place before we leave the island."

"You're asking me to stay in this cell one more night...and trust you?"

"Yes."

He snorted. "Yesterday you knew they were planning to harm me, but instead of doing something about it you went to bed and never gave me a second thought. Suppose tonight you do the same. By tomorrow I might damn well be in my grave."

"Okay, I screwed up. I won't do it again." Melita sucked in a ragged breath. "I can't leave this minute. Dawn, Sully. Wait until dawn." When he looked as if he was about to say no, she pleaded, "Please wait for me."

"You're asking a lot. The door's open now. I would be a fool to hang around here and trust that you'll be back."

"What you can trust is that I want off this island as badly as you do, and you're my only hope."

"I must be crazy."

"Is that a yes?"

"Dammit!" He turned his back on her. Swore twice more.

"You won't be sorry."

He turned around. "I already am. How about we seal this new deal?"

He was staring at her lips. Suddenly Melita knew what he expected. "We already sealed it."

"One more. You enjoyed it. Admit it."

"I enjoyed it because I was kissing someone else."

He laughed. "That's a good one."

"It's true. It might have been your lips, but it wasn't you I was kissing."

"If that's your excuse for wanting to kiss me, then—"

"I was kissing Nemo."

"What's a nemo?"

Melita gave Sully a look that clearly told him that he was trespassing on sacred ground. She was about to enforce it with a warning when a voice in the hall jerked them both to attention.

She bolted away from the wall. "Get back in bed. Hurry. I'll be here before dawn."

She didn't reach the door before he snagged her arm, pulled her up against him and planted a kiss on her lips that took her completely by surprise.

When he released her, he said, "If you're confused about who just kissed you, the name's Sully. I'll be here waiting at dawn. Don't be late."

Romantic
SUSPENSE

Sparked *by* Danger, Fueled *by* Passion.

Onyxx agent Sully Paxton's only chance of
survival lies in the hands of his enemy's daughter
Melita Krizova. He doesn't know he's a pawn in the
beautiful island girl's own plan for escape. Can
they survive their ruses and their fiery attraction?

Look for the next installment in the
Spy Games miniseries,

Sleeping with Danger

by Wendy Rosnau

Available November 2007 wherever you buy books.

At forty, Maureen Hart suddenly finds herself juggling men. Man #1: her six-year-old grandson, left with her while his mother goes off to compete for a million dollars on reality TV. Maureen is delighted, but to Man #2— her fiancé—the little boy represents an intrusion on their time. Then Man #3, the boy's paternal grandfather, offers to take the child off her hands… and maybe even sweep Maureen off her feet….

Look for

I'M YOUR MAN

by

SUSAN CROSBY

Available November wherever you buy books.

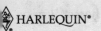
® HARLEQUIN®

EVERLASTING LOVE™
Every great love has a story to tell™

Charlie fell in love with Rose Kaufman
before he even met her, through stories her
husband, Joe, used to tell. When Joe is killed
in the trenches, Charlie helps Rose through
her grief and they make a new life together.
But for Charlie, a question remains—can
love be as true the second time around?
Only one woman can answer that....

Look for

*The Soldier and
the Rose*

by
Linda Barrett

Available November wherever you buy books.

REQUEST YOUR FREE BOOKS!

Harlequin® Historical
Historical Romantic Adventure!

2 FREE NOVELS PLUS 2 **FREE GIFTS!**

YES! Please send me 2 FREE Harlequin® Historical novels and my 2 FREE gifts. After receiving them, if I don't wish to receive any more books, I can return the shipping statement marked "cancel." If I don't cancel, I will receive 6 brand-new novels every month and be billed just $4.69 per book in the U.S., or $5.24 per book in Canada, plus 25¢ shipping and handling per book and applicable taxes, if any*. That's a savings of close to 15% off the cover price! I understand that accepting the 2 free books and gifts places me under no obligation to buy anything. I can always return a shipment and cancel at any time. Even if I never buy another book from Harlequin, the two free books and gifts are mine to keep forever.

246 HDN EEWW   349 HDN EEW9

Name	(PLEASE PRINT)	
Address		Apt. #
City	State/Prov.	Zip/Postal Code

Signature (if under 18, a parent or guardian must sign)

Mail to the **Harlequin Reader Service®**:
IN U.S.A.: P.O. Box 1867, Buffalo, NY 14240-1867
IN CANADA: P.O. Box 609, Fort Erie, Ontario L2A 5X3

Not valid to current Harlequin Historical subscribers.

Want to try two free books from another line?
Call 1-800-873-8635 or visit www.morefreebooks.com.

* Terms and prices subject to change without notice. NY residents add applicable sales tax. Canadian residents will be charged applicable provincial taxes and GST. This offer is limited to one order per household. All orders subject to approval. Credit or debit balances in a customer's account(s) may be offset by any other outstanding balance owed by or to the customer. Please allow 4 to 6 weeks for delivery.

Your Privacy: Harlequin is committed to protecting your privacy. Our Privacy Policy is available online at www.eHarlequin.com or upon request from the Reader Service. From time to time we make our lists of customers available to reputable firms who may have a product or service of interest to you. If you would prefer we not share your name and address, please check here. ☐

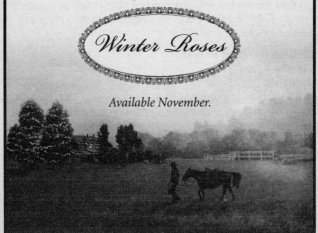

COMING NEXT MONTH FROM

HARLEQUIN®
HISTORICAL

- **CHRISTMAS WEDDING BELLES**
  by **Nicola Cornick, Margaret McPhee and Miranda Jarrett**
  (Regency)
  Enjoy all the fun of the Regency festive season as three Society
  brides tame their dashingly handsome rakes!

- **BODINE'S BOUNTY**
  by **Charlene Sands**
  (Western)
  He's a hard-bitten bounty hunter with no time for love. But when
  Bodine meets the woman he's sworn to guard, she might just
  change his life....

- **WICKED PLEASURES**
  by **Helen Dickson**
  (Victorian)
  Betrothed against her will, Adeline had been resigned to a loveless
  marriage. Can Christmas work its magic and lead to pleasures
  Adeline thought impossible?

- **BEDDED BY HER LORD**
  by **Denise Lynn**
  (Medieval)
  Guy of Hartford has returned from the dead—to claim his wife!
  Now Elizabeth must welcome an almost-stranger back into her
  life...and her bed!

HHCNM1007